Lawnmower Blues

Lawnmower Blues

Rex Anderson

Five Star • Waterville, Maine

First Edition
First Printing: September 2005

Published in 2005 in conjunction with Tekno Books and Ed Gorman.

Set in 11 pt. Plantin by Ramona Watson.

Printed in the United States on permanent paper.

Library of Congress Cataloging-in-Publication Data

Anderson, Rex.
Lawnmower blues / by Rex Anderson.—1st ed.
p. cm.
ISBN 1-59414-320-X (hc : alk. paper)
1. Private investigators—Texas—Houston—Fiction.
2. Inventors—Crimes against—Fiction. 3. Inheritance and succession—Fiction. 4. Houston (Tex.)—Fiction. I. Title.
PS3551.N379L39 2005
813′.54—dc22 2005013390

This book is dedicated to the memory of my aunt, Nell Tucker, Poet, Artist, Writer—one of the great Ladies of the world.

ONE

Don't Throw Away That Envelope!

The voice was gravelly. The message was short: "Tony, this is Maggie Hawk. Remember me? Give me a call."

I stared at the answering machine. Maggie Hawk?

The Maggie Hawk who was my favorite bartender until about a month ago, when she had most of the luck in the Western Hemisphere?

Yeah!

Just then, the cat came stalking out of the bedroom, tail stuck high, wondering as he always did these days just why any self-respecting goodies provider should be home in the middle of the afternoon when he ought to be out chasing down something good to eat.

"That was Maggie Hawk!" I said.

He wasn't nearly as impressed as I was. Showing me his butt, with an S-flip of his tail for emphasis, he did a right turn and went into the kitchen.

Grinning bigger than I had in days, I played Maggie's message again and wrote her name and telephone number on the back of a handy piece of scratch paper—one of my AAPT INVESTIGATIONS business cards.

Maggie Hawk!

The last time I saw her, she was on TV.

In Houston, the one thing that's guaranteed to get you

on the tube is money, especially when it's sudden money. And Maggie's money had been about as sudden as you can get—she won one of those magazine company sweepstakes like the one Ed McMahon kept pushing.

Ten million bucks! Five hundred thousand dollars a year for twenty years.

Maybe not as much of a deal as winning a big lottery jackpot. But not bad.

Especially not bad for a fifty-something woman whose whole life, according to the gushy little over-blonde, over-hair-sprayed trainee TV news anchorperson who interviewed her, had been taken up with serving booze and taking care of her disabled mother.

I was stunned when I recognized my old buddy, Maggie, on the TV news. It made me run right to the trash can and pull out that big brown envelope and start pasting stickers under Ed's smiling face.

Damn! I could have used a sweepstakes or two, myself. I could pay off the IRS and a lot of others, and could maybe finally afford to be in the damned private eye business—or afford to get out of it, which I'd like even better.

But if I couldn't win one, I was glad Maggie had. She was terrific. I liked her a lot. She came across as being rough as hell, but she was good to talk with when things were slow at the bar. Good? Actually, "good" doesn't quite say it.

The bar where Maggie used to work was on West Alabama Street. It was kind of a dump, really. But comfortable. A small neighborhood bar. Not glitzy enough for the Yups to bother with. There was plenty of real booze on the shelves behind the counter, but it was the kind of place where you'd feel pretentious about drinking anything but beer. Just a quiet, comfortable hangout.

Maggie fit in well with the place, looking used and tired and tough—like history's first female coal miner, maybe—but actually being very pleasant as long as you were pleasant with her.

I happened onto the place about six months ago, shortly after my grandfather died and I discovered that, instead of inheriting a small but successful detective agency, I had ended up with a disaster that had appeared successful only because he had been propping it up for years with Grandma's family money that she'd left him. And that money, which everyone had assumed was still intact and in a sizeable amount, was practically gone. Grandpa had timed things perfectly. He went out just days before the checks would have started bouncing.

Anyway, I fired our dumb but picturesque receptionist and weaseled out of the lease on our plush office and started dodging the IRS—and practically everybody else. I thought pretty seriously—longingly, actually—about getting completely out of the private detective business. But while Houston was getting along better economically than a lot of places, all the available jobs for ex-private eyes with liberal arts degrees that I knew anything about tended to have hamburgers and french fries and minimum wage attached to them. So I began operating out of my answering machine, going after whatever was available: mostly the stuff I hated more than anything—suspicious spouse cases.

With my real life going like that, it was therapeutic for me to drop into the Alabama Tavern and act like I was a big shot. Maybe not exactly admirable, but therapeutic as hell during a time when I needed all the therapy I could get, and couldn't afford any that cost more than about a buck-seventy-five a bottle.

Early on, Maggie and I got to chatting. First doing the generic what-do-you-do?

"What do you do for a living?" she asked in her gravelly voice, giving me a moderately enthusiastic hello-new-customer smile.

"Private investigations," I said, trying to sound as if it was something I was proud of.

Maggie's reaction practically knocked my socks off: she looked impressed. "You're a private detective?"

I tried not to give away my shock. "Uh . . . right."

She raised an eyebrow, but she was still impressed. "Aren't you pretty young for that? I thought private detectives were somebody like Robert Mitchum."

I liked this. Nobody had talked nice to me for quite a while. "I'm thirty-two," I said. "And my grandfather brought me up in the business."

Then we got technical.

Maggie leaned on the counter. "What kind of things do you work on?"

I played to my audience. "Just about anything. Criminal. Security. Industrial. And some domestic reconnaissance, of course. You name it."

"If you don't mind me asking, how much do private detectives charge these days?"

I figured that her fascinated expression would dissolve right away if I told her the truth, which was "Whatever I can get," so I lied a little: "Well, it varies. Mostly depending on the agency's reputation. What we charge is pretty much in the top range—five hundred a day plus expenses." With an unkind thought about Grandpa's business practices, I added, "In advance."

Maggie was as shocked as I would have been if somebody had actually paid me that. "Five hundred? A day?"

"Sure. You get what you pay for, you know."

Then came the war stories. I told great war stories. It helped me a lot after a day of sweet-talking the bill collectors and getting hassled by people who were pissed off at me instead of the person they'd wanted information about, to go to the bar and tell war stories to Maggie.

She ate them up. Like most people, of course, she was mostly interested in the crime stuff. And I obliged. I didn't tell her that I had had little to do with the criminal investigations because Grandpa always did those himself. In point of fact, while he was alive, I did darned little except diddle around with the security jobs we got, and collect my fat paychecks.

Nursing cheap beers in the Alabama Tavern, I told Maggie the war stories I'd heard Grandpa tell, but with some heavy glossing on the details of which personal pronoun belonged to whom. His business sense aside, my grandfather had been a really good private detective and was involved in some famous murder cases and other crimes, so I had some great stories. Sure, my conscience bothered me every once in a while, but it seemed harmless. Maggie and I both were getting good out of it: she was fascinated and kept pumping me for more; I'd walk out of the bar feeling as if I could face tomorrow's hassles.

I needed this harmless little game we had going more than ever a couple of months ago when my Big Break went all to hell.

What happened was that I had talked my way into a fantastic security deal with Houston's Video King. It put me in what Grandpa would have called hog heaven because it was going to get me—and Aapt Investigations—out of wife- or husband-watching, which I totally hated, and into the big-time security business. Exclusively into the security business, with no private-eye activity at all. And last, but definitely not least, into the black.

The specific job was protecting the Video King's twenty-six huge Stockpile Video stores from theft, both external and internal, and from the industrial espionage the VK was certain his arch-rival, Video Barn, was trying to perpetrate against him, and getting ready to move up with him as he expanded across the state and then nationwide.

It was The Big Break! So big that I didn't bother to dun the VK for payment of my invoices as I went along, and asked only for a little equipment money a couple of times. And borrowed money from my ex-wife to keep going. Big enough that she lent it to me without acting like an ex-wife and only charged me about triple the legal interest rate.

Then the Big Break went straight to hell. I stumbled onto the fact that somebody had embezzled more than a half million dollars of the VK's money over the last couple of years.

And stumbled right onto my face when the embezzler turned out to be Angela Wells, his secretary, with whom he turned out to be having what he was convinced was the Love Affair of the Millennium. What made things really rough was that when he was about thirty seconds into confronting her about the missing money, she broke down and tearfully told him she was pregnant and, if he was going to be so mean, she'd just have to go to his wife about it—and it was his wife's money that got him started in business.

That turned things completely around. The VK was the undisputed poster child of the American Association of Aging Boys and, here he was, bottoming out in mid-life crisis, and he finds out he's going to be a father at last.

Strike embezzlement.

Strike Angela's distraught remark about going to his wife.

Strike me. And my invoices.

One day, I was the Security King. The next day, my accounts receivable was in the toilet, and I was barred from the premises and sweating to pay my rent. So once again, I had to start doing the crap-work: deceived-spouse cases.

I don't exactly know what I would have done there for a while if I couldn't have gone to the bar and played fantasy-world with Maggie.

When she hit the big-time and won the sweepstakes, I missed her a lot.

And now I stood there grinning at my answering machine. It was *that* good to hear from her.

Apparently, she had figured out that it was lonely at the top, and wanted to do some chatting.

Fine with me. Therapy is definitely where and when you find it. Speaking of therapy, I could get some of my own by confessing to Maggie—finally—that all those big detective stories I used to tell her were bull.

I wanted to call her back immediately, but these days, business was definitely business.

I started to punch the buttons to play back the next message on the answering machine, but the cat reappeared and plopped himself down in the kitchen doorway and squalled.

Fine.

Reminding myself for the five-hundredth time that, seven or eight years ago, I had driven the pathetic black kitten that had turned up freezing and starving on the front step of Grandpa's office to the SPCA three separate times, but hadn't had the heart—or the good sense—to stop and take him inside, I went to see what problem we had this time.

It was a real problem. In Spooky's terms, anyway. There was only about a half-handful of dry food in his dry food dish. And this cat who had been so pathetically, purringly happy to get some crumbles out of my hamburger on that cold day seven or eight years ago, would now die before he'd eat the last stuff in any food dish. This morning's canned food still sat there untouched, of course.

Oh, boy. The zoologists have it all wrong. For years they've been saying cats are just animals. I know from experience that that's bunk. They're not animals at all. I've had it proved to me time and again that what they really are is tiny rock superstars in fur coats.

I was well-trained. I got the Cat Chow box out of the cabinet and shook it a bit for some sound effects and then poured the dish full, while Spooky wound himself ecstatically around my ankles.

Then he sniffed at the dish, crunched one little star-shaped morsel, and marched out of the kitchen, having demonstrated once again that he ran the household.

Yeah, well, the household . . . If it was going to keep sputtering along, I had to tend to business. Back to the answering machine, to check the next call.

If it turned out to be a teary lady—or gentleman—wanting to know if, and/or with whom her/his wife/husband was messing around, I'd . . .

Yeah. I'd smile sweetly and call back and make an appointment to go listen to all the heartbreaking circumstances that had led up to the devastating situation. Then I'd pack a six-pack and a sandwich and an industrial-sized can of Off and my trusty Minolta, and go sit in my car and fight mosquitos and stare at motels and hope the teary lady/gentleman didn't get pissed-off at me and stop payment on her/his check when I gave the bad news.

But the second message wasn't from a teary person. It was from a person who sounded way sweeter and sexier than I was used to: "Hi. I'm so sorry I missed you."

Oh, boy! For a second, I tried to think who this could be.

Then: "We're all so worried about the coming Year 2000 and those terrible Y2K problems. If you'll call me at 1-800-Y2K-HELP, I can take care of those computer worries. I can make your computer safe for just nineteen ninety-five. That number again . . ."

My dreams dashed, except that it was kind of nice that someone actually thought I had the money to buy something, I hit Stop, and went to the next message.

This one wasn't from a teary person, either. Just a semi-pissed-off one, to whom I had been married, not once, but twice.

Sarah.

"Tony, where's my check? When I lent you that money, you . . ."

"Hang in there, Sarah," I said, and cut off the machine.

This was definitely therapy-time. Picking up the telephone, I dialed Maggie's number.

Gravel: "Hello."

"Maggie, this is Tony Aapt. Glad you called. Congratulations! You were already gone from the bar when I heard you won the sweepstakes, so I didn't get a chance to tell you then."

"Thanks, Tony. How's everything with you?"

I glanced around my apartment: Gulf Coast shab—and the spoiled black cat-from-hell sitting in my favorite beat-up old chair, washing his face. Obviously everything was going just great with me. "Going just great, Maggie."

"Keeping busy?"

Out of habit, I stuck to our basic scenario. "Sure. Practically over my head."

I didn't expect what she said then, or how she sounded when she said it: positively disappointed. "Well, I was afraid so. But I thought I'd give you a call, anyway."

My pulse suddenly popped up to about four hundred a minute. Maybe she had something more on her mind than old home week! Maybe she had a job for me!

Damn! Confession would have been nice. But there was something about making a buck or two that appealed to me a lot more right now.

Maybe she needed some security stuff. Or maybe she needed a bodyguard. That'd be great! I could stop shaving and wear some Sylvester Stallone drag and think mean—and make some badly needed money doing it. Whatever, one thing I liked a lot: I'd never heard her mention a husband, so it shouldn't involve motel-watching. If worse came to worse, maybe I could sell her a cat.

I did nonchalant. "Oh? What did you have in mind?"

"Maybe you could come over and talk to me, Tony. My address is 2811 Audley."

I scribbled the address under her name and telephone number on the business card while playing cool, as if I had to take time out to check my overloaded appointment book. But I didn't take too much time. "Sure, Maggie. When did you have in mind?"

"What are you doing right now?" she asked. And showed that she knew a little about cool herself, using a voice that sounded just as gravelly, but much more confident than the one she used to use at the bar when she was asking if you were ready for another Lite. "Unless you're all booked-up, of course. Maybe you're all booked-up, and I'd better call somebody else."

I decided that enough cool was enough. I didn't really have to call Sarah back immediately—or this year, if I had any sense. And I could wait until tomorrow to go by the apartment manager's office and try to sweet-talk her into taking a post-dated check—again. "As a matter of fact," I said, "I do have a little free time. I could be there in about fifteen minutes."

"Be here in about fifteen minutes," she said.

TWO

I Wondered If Spenser Sat around and Daydreamed about Getting Antique Murder Cases

I thought it might get me in good with Maggie if I went as Ed McMahon, but I didn't have a jacket that was plaid enough and loud enough. So I settled on medium-Yup, putting on a blazer and smoothing down my hair and wearing a tie I gave my grandfather when I was about ten years old that had recently, and wholly unaccountably, come back into style. Then I checked Maggie's address and stuck the business card on which I had written it into my wallet.

In the car, I made the ultimate sacrifice and ran the air conditioner, trying not to think about the gas that good old Hizzie's antique engine was sucking. I needed this job. Spooky and Sarah and my apartment manager needed this job. I could sweat on the way home, but not on the way to Maggie's. If she had some kind of job for me, the important thing was for her to keep on thinking I was Mr. Success.

2811 Audley was in the middle of a block of upscale townhouses. Inner-, but not too inner-city. Four or five blocks from River Oaks. Nice neighborhood.

This group of townhouses had been built about four years ago. I drove by from time to time as they were going up behind an impressive sign that said, "Audley Square—Elegant Townhomes from the 200s." Being optimistic in those days—and having great confidence in the money I thought my grandfather still had—I had thought that Sarah and I just might be interested in one of the places sometime—the location was certainly ideal for us—unless we found someplace better.

But Sarah and I hadn't lasted, and Grandpa's money turned out to be gone. These places might be a heck of a bargain to somebody who had a five hundred thousand dollar check rolling in every year, and that left me way, way out.

I found 2811 and, still interested in making that good impression on Maggie, parked out of sight down the block, silently apologizing to the Mercedes on the left and the BMW on the right for hiding my elderly Oldsmobile between them.

Then I headed briskly for Maggie's front door, trying to get there before the car air-conditioning wore off.

After I rang the bell, a glance around told me one thing: Maggie almost certainly hadn't called me about security. The door lock was a Timmons Z-Bolt. The windows were fixed up with Savalli vibration detectors. The little glass marble set into the plate just under the light above the door was the lens of a Millercom video surveillance system. She already had about as much security as she could use.

She answered the door, and I made a great impression on her, all right. As soon as I stepped into the entryway, she said, "You look as if you don't know we live in the climate from hell. It's August. Get rid of that tie. If there's anything I hate, it's trying to talk business with an uncomfortable man."

I pulled off the tie and stuffed it into my pocket.

She lifted a forefinger and pointed decisively. "Unbutton the shirt collar."

I did.

"The next button, too."

I unbuttoned another one.

She looked at me with faint approval. "That's better," she said. "You can dump the jacket, too, if you want to." Turning, she headed out of the entryway.

"Nice to see you, Maggie," I said, pretty lamely.

She didn't hear me.

I gave up and followed her into the living room. The look was uncluttered. There was a powder-blue leather-covered sofa and a matching chair done in dark blue. And a coffee table. Period. Not much to fill up a room I could practically have fitted my whole apartment into.

"I'm working on it," she said, in answer to my perplexed expression. "Picking up what I like when I see it." Then she moved into rapid-fire. "Tony, how are you doing? It's really good to see you. Have a seat. What can I get you to drink?"

I sorted things out and started with what was apparently the most important thing—most important as far as my getting a real paying job, anyway—keeping up the front. "I'm doing just great, Maggie. How about you?"

"Oh, you don't even have to ask," she said, with a huge grin. "I'm going to have a drink. What'll you have?"

"Coffee'll be fine."

"Would you just go ahead and sit down?" she said impatiently. "I didn't call you over here to check out your manners. And don't say 'coffee' trying to impress me with how sober you are in the daytime. I'm going to have a drink-drink. You might as well, too."

I sat down in the chair. The leather felt like butter. It smelled like a new Rolls Royce. "Well, a beer, then."

Maggie planted her feet and shook her head. "No beer. I served my last beer at one fifty-nine a.m. on July twenty-fourth."

"Scotch-and-water?"

"That's better. Scotch-and-water, I can manage just fine. I didn't exactly overdose on serving up scotch-and-waters in that place."

She went across to the wall and opened a couple of doors in the paneling to reveal a bar. It was furnished much more completely than the rest of the living room. Lots of nice-looking crystal. Lots of nice-looking bottles. Refrigerator. Sink. The works.

Clattering ice around, Maggie said, "Not like the old days, is it?"

"I guess not!"

I settled deeper into that nice chair and checked her out. It had been maybe two weeks since she was on the TV news looking like a slightly bewildered aging female coal miner. Apparently, money agreed with her. Her hair was softer-looking now, and shiny. Her face seemed much less harsh, and she must have dropped at least ten pounds. Her voice still made you think of gravel roads, though.

Now I noticed something I'd missed when I came in: a lawnmower.

Yeah. A lawnmower.

Sitting over in the corner of that big, elegant, practically empty living room.

A ratty old beat-up, rusted-out rotary lawnmower. Once it had been shiny red-and-black, but the paint had faded and turned dull and powdery long ago.

A lawnmower?

I told myself not to worry about it. Maybe she collected

them. Maybe porcelain birds weren't enough of a challenge to her.

"Here you go," she said, setting a very respectable chunk of Baccarat crystal on the coffee table in front of me. Settling onto the sofa, she lifted up her own glass in a toast. "Here's to old times, Tony."

I picked up my glass and waved it in the air in return, and then took a drink. Great scotch. So smoky and thick I could practically hear bagpipes.

My turn for a toast. "Here's to the sweepstakes."

Maggie grinned and looked much younger. With a reverence that made the gravel in her voice sound more like sand, she said, "Right. The Sweepstakes," definitely saying it with a capital letter.

We drank. Then I said, "Something like that must be great."

She really grinned now. "It is great. You know how great it is? It's like falling face-first into a pile of doo-doo, and coming up with a rose in your teeth. That's how great it is."

I tried not to be too envious.

In a moment, she said, "Well, you look just as much like a kid as ever, Tony."

I realized that I needed to get tough and businesslike. If she maybe wanted Rambo for a bodyguard, or something, coming across as a wimp wasn't going to help at all. Sitting up straight, pitching my voice lower, I said, "You're looking pretty good, yourself."

She practically blushed. Then she said, "Are you keeping busy? Do you have lots of exciting new cases?"

It wasn't easy to keep sitting tough. This chair was too comfortable. I was beginning to like it a lot. If I shaved about ten years off the age of my car, I could probably trade it in on one of the armrests. I said, "Here and there. You know how it is. Somebody's always got a problem."

"Doing any 'domestic reconnaissance' these days?" Not giving me time to answer, she laughed. "Lord, how people get the jargon going. I still remember when you sprang that one on me. Must have taken me a week to realize it meant sitting around waiting for somebody to sneak into the wrong motel with the wrong person."

I chuckled. I felt kind of kicked in the gut by that reminder of my least favorite business activity, but I chuckled.

"We had some good times, Tony. Once in a while, in all those years I was working in the bars, nice people like you would come along and almost make it worthwhile."

I smiled. "Well, you almost made it worthwhile going in there."

"Good lord! Listen to us."

We chuckled with each other.

Then she said, "Let's get serious. How's your schedule right now?"

I hated to lie, so I hedged around by saying, "Well, if you've got something in mind, there's always room for an old friend."

She reached down and opened a drawer in the side of the coffee table and brought out a manila file folder that must have been half an inch thick, and looked at it thoughtfully.

For a moment, that female coal miner was back.

For a quick moment. During which I reminded myself never, ever to cross this lady.

Then she looked at that damned old lawnmower. I thought she might be about to explain it to me. Instead, she said, "Okay, Tony Private Eye."

Opening the folder, she brought out a check.

Handing it across to me, she said, "Two weeks in advance. Then we'll figure out if we want to keep things going."

I stared at the check. Seven thousand dollars! It took me a while to figure it out. When I did, I also figured out that I had to be messing with a crazy woman. Two weeks—fourteen days—at the full five hundred dollars a day.

"Is something wrong?" she asked. "Have your rates gone up?"

I pulled myself back together and said, "No," as calmly as possible.

She raised an eyebrow. "By this time, Bob Mitchum would at least be trying to find out what I was hiring him for."

I held the check tightly, so it couldn't get away. "Okay. What are you hiring me for?"

She reached out and pulled the file folder close to her. "To investigate my husband's murder."

That puzzled me. She had never talked much about herself, and I was sure she had never mentioned a husband. "Your husband?"

"They found him dead in his car. They said it was suicide, but I know it wasn't." She pushed the folder across the coffee table to me. "It's all in there."

I leaned forward and opened the folder. The first thing I saw was a Xeroxed copy of a newspaper clipping. A small, inside-pages-unimportant headline said, "MAN FOUND DEAD IN CAR ON BUFFALO SPEEDWAY." The beginning of the text was, "A man identified as George W. Hawk . . ."

I looked at the top of the clipping.

Then I looked at Maggie.

She was staring at that lawnmower. Her eyes were shiny, right at the edge of tears.

I looked at that damned clipping again.

I knew for positive now that I was messing with a crazy woman.

At the top of the clipping, there was printing that said, *HOUSTON CHRONICLE.*

The date was Tuesday, June 9, 1966.

THREE

But It Sure Sounded Like Suicide while They Dragged It in Bumpety-Bump

I couldn't stop staring at that clipping.

I had a case and a check. And I had a murder that was older than I was.

The doorbell rang.

Maggie jumped up excitedly. "Delivery!"

I told myself that, if it was somebody dropping off another old lawnmower, I was going to run like hell, check or no.

But it was furniture. Her new dining room table and chairs.

"Just look over the things in the folder," she told me. "While I take care of this. Help yourself to the bar. Then we'll talk."

I tried to concentrate on business, but I couldn't help watching her operate. She glowed like a little kid, running out to the truck to look inside to make sure everything was there and carefully packed. And then walking each and every piece inside, guiding the sweaty truck driver and his helper through the entryway so they wouldn't bump into anything. Then she went over every piece after it was set down in the dining room and unwrapped.

The delivery guys put up with it. Amazing! If they'd

been delivering the stuff to me, they'd have been snarling at me and describing me to each other in Spanish while they dragged it bumpety-bump up the stairway. With Maggie, they acted as if they were walking around with their pockets full of black widow spiders and didn't want to wake them up.

Back to the folder: according to the newspaper clipping, George W. Hawk's body had been found at about nine o'clock at night in his car stopped on Buffalo Speedway. Death was by gunshot. The weapon was a .38 caliber pistol, which was found in the locked car. It was obviously suicide; a note to that effect was found on the car seat. He was twenty-two years old, a student and part-time gardener. He was survived by his wife, Margaret Hawk.

Behind the copy of the clipping, there was a photograph. Five-by-seven. Black-and-white. From the suit and the stiff pose, it was obviously a yearbook picture. In it, George Hawk didn't look much like a bird of prey. He looked like the original nerd. A big, blondish, flat-topped, farm boy '60s nerd. He was wearing a tie about the width of my thumb tied onto a shirt collar that was too tight, under a suit jacket that he'd probably had since he was about sixteen. But his eyes seemed intelligent and, although he was probably boring as hell, he came across as a nice, pleasant, sincere guy.

What came after the photograph was several pages stapled together. Photocopies of police reports. From two different cops. Handwritten.

I wondered how Maggie had gotten these. Then I looked up as she shepherded the two delivery guys inside. Each of them carried a wrapped-up dining chair as if it was a time bomb—or a newborn baby. Yeah. I could see how she could talk somebody out of a police report.

The first report was that of a patrol cop named Hanley Moss. His handwriting was schoolboyish, and the report looked as if he wrote it with a ballpoint pen that weighed about twenty pounds:

> *8:50 PM. Responded to a citizen call—officer needed backup in the 2900 block of Buffalo Spdway. Found Det. J. Newhouse investigating a stopped 1955 Plymouth. Det. Newhouse reported ~~he was on his way home~~ he was driving north on Buffalo when he saw the stopped car in southbnd lane. He made a U. saw citizen in obvious distress in car . . .*

Maggie and her burly admirers tramped through to get another load, and I went on to the next police report. This was done by the detective who had discovered the body. His writing was beautiful. Geez, if you were having a wedding, you'd want this guy to address your invitations, if you didn't mind some weird abbreviations. The J stood for Joseph, and he was a homicide detective. Joseph Newhouse. Joseph Newhouse?

I stared at the name for a second. Why should the name of somebody who was a cop thirty-three years ago, and had probably retired before I was out of high school, seem even remotely familiar to me? Oh, well . . .

> *8:50 pm. Drvng N on Buff Spdwy. Obsrved 1955 Plym stppd in S lane 2900 blk. Lights on. Turnd arnd. Apprchd from behnd. Man in drivr's position. Appeared slumped. Apprchd left side of car. Doors locked. Wndws up. Saw blood on driver's chst.*
>
> *Tappd on wndw. First no respons. Tappd again. Driver's head moved. Car was passing. Flagged down.*

Told citizen to find phone & call disptchr & get ambulnce & backup.

Went back to Plym to rndr aid. Kickd in back lft windw. Reachd in unlockd driver's door. Opend it. Subj strted fall into street. Pushd him back. He fell towrd passngr side, dislodging gun that fell to florbrd. Checkd for pulse. No pulse. Waited for backup.

Maggie and the boys carried in more chairs and she left them unsupervised long enough to go to the refrigerator in the bar to get them a couple of Cokes. As she passed me, she beamed at me because I was already hard at work.

Next, there was a copy of the note that was found in the car:

Maggie—
I can't take any more of this. Nothing's working out like we wanted it to.
I'm taking the easy way out.

Newhouse's report continued with the information that the police had determined that the pistol belonged to the deceased. And a paraffin test on his hand showed gunpowder residue.

Next there was the autopsy report—lots of medical jargon which, with the help of a photograph of the body taken on the scene from the passenger side of the car, said that death was caused by massive trauma to the heart. The photograph was just a Xeroxed copy of the real photograph, but even so, it was nasty as hell. It's scary what a bullet fired from just two or three inches away can do to your clothing—and your body. Included was a note about the results of the paraffin test. It was in chem lab jargon, but there was the word, "nitrate," which even I knew was a component of gunpowder.

Of course, the big stickler—and the thing I kept coming back to every time I came back to the folder after looking up and grinning at Maggie babying her new furniture inside—was that the dates on this stuff kept coming up the same: antique.

Next in the folder were pages of Xeroxed notes. Handwritten. I made the guess that they were Maggie's. Finally, there was a bunch of copies of newspaper clippings.

Jeez! I wondered if Spenser sat around and daydreamed about getting antique murder cases.

Maggie's new furniture was finally all inside. The delivery guys, for some reason, were thanking her for turning a hot fifteen-minute job into a sweltering hour-long one. They weren't even expecting a tip. When she handed each of them a twenty-dollar bill, they practically genuflected.

After they left, she had to show the stuff off to me.

It was nice. I'm not exactly a consultant for *Architectural Digest*, but even I could see that it was nice.

It was a long dining table and eight chairs. Oriental. Black lacquer that looked like glass. Intricate carving. Upholstery on the chairs that had to be silk and was what I think was plum-colored. Beautiful stuff! More beautiful than that.

Maggie's voice was sandy again as she stood in her dining room looking over the new furniture, one hand resting caressingly on the deeply carved back of a chair. "I can't count up how many times I came home after closing down that bar at two a.m., and sat down at a card table with my feet in a pan of ice water and ate corn flakes."

She brought herself back to normal. "Well. We have to talk, don't we?"

"Sure," I said, meaning, "We sure as hell do!"

She got a huge grin on her face. "But first—when did you have lunch?" She gestured toward the beautiful table. "Let's break it in."

We did.

It was fun. It was only about four o'clock in the afternoon, but we ate by candlelight in her dining room that was bare except for the new table and chairs. Maggie might not have accumulated a whole house full of furniture as yet, but she had picked up a lot of the trimmings. The silverware was sterling. The napkins were linen that felt like marshmallow and the tablecloth was pure white lace. The china was good enough for Nancy Reagan. The glasses were about ninety dollars a stem. The wine was about sixty dollars a bottle. The pizza ran fifteen-fifty, delivered.

When the pizza was pretty well demolished, Maggie daubed delicately at her lips with her napkin and glanced around and said, "You know, I still can't believe all this."

"You seem to be enjoying it okay."

She rolled her eyes. "Enjoying it? I guess you could say that." She tapped a fingernail on the side of her wineglass and sighed at the perfect bell-sound it made. "Almost the first thing that popped into my mind was that now I could go places—see the places I'd always wanted to. I even went to a travel agency and loaded up on brochures. I was going to travel until I dropped. Then I got practical."

Picking up the wine bottle, she came down to my end of the table and poured about half of what was left in it into my wineglass, and then went back and poured the rest into hers.

Settling into her chair again, she continued. "I wanted to travel, but I wanted someplace nice to come back to, too. Mostly, I didn't want to end up blowing all my money like a lot of people do that win lotteries and things. So I went to see a lawyer and a CPA. Then I sat down and budgeted things out. I bought myself some nice clothes and a nice car, and I bought this place. And some of the little things—dishes, and things like that. And now, I'm buying my furniture bit by bit, whenever I see something I can't live without. I put some money away, too. Thank God I don't have any family left that all think I owe them something." She grinned at me. "I also budgeted in some to hire you.

"Next summer, when the next check comes, well, then's when I'll take my trip." She started to toast to that, but hesitated and set her glass down. "This must sound so crude to you—me sitting here talking about money. Your family was well-set, and you didn't have to go without anything, and you've always been successful and had money. You don't know what it's like to have to worry about money all the time. You've always been secure."

Her expression turning bitter, she said, "Nice, secure people who don't have to worry always think it's crude because people like me—like I used to be before I had my luck—think about money all the time. Well, when you don't have any money, what else can you think about but how are you going to pay the rent, and whether you can afford to run the air conditioner, and will the car hold up for a little longer?"

Standing up, she waved everything away. "Anyway, sorry about that. I guess I'll get used to it after a while. Then I can stop thinking about money, too. And think it's crude when people who have to worry about it do their worrying out loud."

I was discovering that I liked Maggie-the-sweepstakes-winner even more than I had liked Maggie-the-bartender.

That would have been true even if she hadn't hired me and overpaid me. She was definitely choice.

It got me to thinking that maybe there's some justice, after all. If somebody like her could win a sweepstakes, there was definitely at least a moderate amount of justice in the world.

That still didn't change the fact that her case was thirty-three years old.

She cleared the table and we settled down in the living room with snifters of brandy.

After we had sipped a bit, I tapped the file folder with my forefinger. "I guess you wrote those pages of notes. I didn't get a chance yet to get into them very thoroughly."

She nodded. "For years, every time I thought of anything new, I wrote it down." She thought back, with an expression of regret. "The police didn't pay any attention to me, and I always wanted to hire a detective to look into it. From the start. But I didn't have the money. I saved up for it, but every time I got something ahead . . . well, something would come up and there it'd go."

For a few moments, Maggie was sad. Then she brightened. "But now, I've got money to spare. I can finally get a professional to work on it."

That skewered my conscience more than somewhat. To the point that I had to be at least a little honest with her. "Maggie, I've got to be honest with you. So far—from what I've seen—it doesn't sound much like murder."

Obviously, this wasn't the first time someone had said that to her. She raised a finger. "One: that note. You notice it's not dated. George wrote that note to me a few days before. We'd just been let go from our jobs because the man we worked for said he had to cut expenses, so we were going to have to move, and things were rough for George at school, and he wrote me that note. Somebody cut off the bottom of the note and put it beside his body. Originally, it ended with, 'So I'm going fishing. See you tomorrow. Love, G.'

"And he did go fishing. Down in Galveston. The next morning, he brought back two nice flounders that I cooked for our supper."

She held up a second finger. "That paraffin test, showing he fired a gun. Well, that stumped me for a long time. Then, just a couple of years ago, I read somewhere that lots of other things can put nitrate on your hands, chief among them being fertilizer. He was a gardener. That's how we were working his way through engineering school. He was a gardener, and I was a maid. And don't look down your nose. Being a maid was different then. People did whatever jobs they could. Nobody'd heard of Yuppies and public assistance then. When George and I got married, I just had a year of community college, and I had to drop out to help keep him in school. Being a maid was about all I was qualified for."

Finger Number Three: "And there's that picture of his body. Did you look at it? He was shot through his shirt. People don't shoot themselves through their clothes. They open them up and go for skin. He wouldn't have hurt that shirt. It was his best one. I gave it to him for his birthday."

I didn't point out to her that Number Three was extremely weak. I said, "What about you and him? Were you having any problems between you?"

"I told you he signed that note, 'Love,' didn't I?"

"All right. What was he doing out in his car alone the night he was killed?"

"He was going to go see a lawyer that the man we'd been working for had talked to George about—a friend of his. This lawyer finally called George and told him he'd talk to him about his invention. Told him to get his invention and all his drawings together and come over to his house. George was all excited, and he got dressed-up after supper and went to see him."

It was now time for my big question: "Okay. If you're sure he didn't kill himself, then who killed him?"

Her expression went completely bitter now. "Who killed him? It was the son-of-a-bitch that stole his invention." She pointed over my shoulder toward that rusty old lawnmower sitting there in the corner of her nearly empty living room.

I'd been right there with her, ready to pick up rocks and fight on her side, no matter how outdated the cause was. But now, here we were: smack in the big middle of Daffy Duck Land.

She didn't seem to notice my reaction. "George took all his drawings and his invention with him when he left to go see that lawyer—drawings that'd prove his invention was his—in one of those brown paper grocery sacks. When they found him, the sack wasn't in the car. It never turned up."

I could practically feel that check beating in my jacket pocket like another heart. It was breathing space. It would get Sarah and the apartment manager off my back. It was also starting to make me feel like shit. I felt like I might just as well have sneaked it out of Maggie's purse.

But I needed it!

Carefully, I said, "Maggie, this sounds like a case I'd really like to get into. It's a terrific challenge. But I keep coming back to the fact that it all happened thirty-three years ago. That's a long time. That's an awfully long time."

She straightened up and stared at me as if I had just jarred her awake. "A long time? Of course, it's a long time. But we're going to do it. Don't you think I've gone crazy for years because I knew what happened, but didn't have the money to look into it? Well, I've got some money now, and I'm going after him."

She slumped back into the sofa. "George was going to patent his invention and then graduate and, by then, there ought to be some money coming in. The first thing we were going to do was travel. He'd never been anywhere but Texas, and I'd been out-of-state just one time, to go to my grandmother's funeral in Shreveport. We were going to go see the world. It was right around the corner. And then that son-of-a-bitch killed him."

Everything about her looked old and broken now, except her eyes. Her voice didn't sound broken, though. It sounded like hard, coarse gravel. "I don't care how long it's been. Now, I'm finally going to make him pay for what he did."

FOUR

Sarah Hadn't Minded Having a Private Eye in The Family, but She Hated Having to Tell People She Was Divorced from One

Sarah kept getting better-looking. Every time I saw her, I wondered why the hell we hadn't been able to make it married. But I didn't wonder too seriously. We had tried it twice and, both times, we had both turned unbearable practically before the flowers wilted. The fact was that the only thing that kept us friends was divorce.

Well, "friends" wasn't exactly the right word. I'm not sure what was. The best thing I could figure out was that we had the kind of semi-combative, semi-dependent relationship that most people achieve only after many painful years of less than happy marriage.

After I told her about Maggie, I waited for her to say, "I don't believe a word you're saying."

"I don't believe a word you're saying," she said.

"Fine. Then give me back that check I wrote you."

"Well, I'm trying to believe that much. Enough that I'll take it to the bank tomorrow."

"Not until I've had time to deposit Maggie's check."

"I'm also trying to believe that her check's good."

"It is."

"Not if somebody gives her a sanity test." Twisting

around on the sofa, she straightened her back and sat on her legs—the tip-off that one of her lectures was coming—a reminder to me that one of the big reasons we couldn't make it married was that I couldn't cope with more mothers than the one I was born with.

Her lead-off was "Getting this case seems great, Tony. It's wonderful. But it's just luck. Why won't you give up and get a job?"

"I have a job."

"You know what I mean: a real job."

I said, "Is there any more beer?"

She snorted in disgust. "Yes, there's more beer. I have a real job. So I can stock up on beer more than one can at a time. And other things. Because I have a job, I also have a credit rating and a car that's not the logo of the American Junkyard Association." She pointed toward the kitchen. "Wait on yourself."

I went to the kitchen. It was high-90s Yup like everything else about Sarah. There was a bottled-water cooler and a window box herb garden and a shelf of cookbooks from around the world. And of course, a full line of exotic food-processing machines. From scratch, she could make anything from angel-hair pasta to sourdough bread. She usually barely had the time and energy to tear open a Stouffer's frozen dinner and stick it into the microwave.

She worked for an advertising agency owned by a couple of nuts who, in the real world, would have been locked up in a padded room with a box of Crayolas. When things were going okay, they acted like Donald Trump. If things turned down and they lost an account or two, they turned into Leona Helmsley's wicked step-siblings. Sarah spent most of her time, when she wasn't trying to remake my life, bitching about them, unless it was a good period and she was waving a bonus check under my nose. She was always saying that she was going to bail out, but when there was a downturn, everybody she could go to work for was having a bad time, too. When things were jumping in the ad world and the jobs were out there, she was afraid that she'd miss a bonus check if she left. She was definitely a career woman. She kept a stack of *Fortune*s on her coffee table and a childproof bottle of Tagamet in her purse.

I got a beer out of the refrigerator and then remembered that her wineglass was almost empty.

"Gallo?" I said, when I came back into the living room, waving the jug.

"Don't hack my wine, Tony. I like it. And whatever kind it is, I bought it with the money I make in my real job."

I sat down on the carpeting with my back against the sofa and drank some beer. Then I said, "Did somebody turn on the TV by mistake? Are they doing a rerun of 'Masterpiece Marriage,' or what?"

"Just fuck off, Tony."

I laughed at her.

She leaned forward and reached down and tousled my hair and laughed at me. Then she reached down again and clicked her wineglass—maybe ten dollars a stem—against my beer can—four forty-five a six-pack. "All right," she said. "Here's to your case."

"Yeah. Here's to my case. Do you know how many lawnmowers were sold in the United States last year?"

"No, of course not."

"About seven and a half million."

"How nice."

"Maggie's got that thing sitting there in that big, empty, plush living room of hers. This thirty-five-year-old lawnmower that her husband modified, and thought they'd get rich on."

Sarah stretched out her legs and relaxed her back against the armrest, and I shifted sideways against the sofa to face her. Sometimes we slept together. But not tonight. She had already signaled that. Right after I turned up at her door, she had excused herself and gone to change out of her real-job suit into a blue oxford-cloth shirt that used to be mine, and a pair of leotards the color and consistency of gun-metal. And me, without a can-opener.

Anyway, I just dropped by to give her a check and get some mild companionship. And maybe a little help.

I continued. "Maggie said that when they first came out with rotary lawnmowers, they were a big hit, but people were always getting cut by the blades—getting their feet and hands mangled. And the blades would pick up rocks and sticks and shoot them out like bullets."

Sarah was checking her nail polish, not even remotely interested. Well, tough. I wasn't necessarily talking just for her benefit, anyway. And I couldn't count the hours I had sat and listened with no enthusiasm while she went on-and-on about the advertising agency wars.

I said, "That's what George's invention was—that he worked out while he was working as gardener for this rich guy. A rotary blade that wouldn't cut your feet off and shoot rocks.

"The great thing about it was that, once he got the design down, he knew he could patent it, and it'd be so great that the lawnmower makers would have to use his blade and pay him a royalty. Seven and a half million lawnmowers sold last year at three and a half bucks a pop royalty figures out to about twenty-six and a quarter million dollars."

That got Sarah's attention.

I tried for more of it. "Since 1968, when GRASSBUSTER Blades started showing up on all the new lawnmowers—and they were exactly identical to George's blade—just figure if maybe an average of only five million lawnmowers was sold every year. Thirty-one or -two years. More than a hundred fifty million blades. That's more than five hundred million dollars."

"My God!" Sarah said.

"That's not all. They're using the blade design in a lot of other places, Maggie says. For royalties, too. In kidney dialysis machines, agitating the blood they're purifying without making it bubble, and in those soft ice cream machines, like Dairy Queen, and in frozen yogurt machines. We're talking big bucks here. Humongous bucks."

Sarah was frowning. "Wait a minute. What about patents? You can only patent something for seventeen years, you know."

"Yeah," I said. "Right. Something like that."

I got a very superior look from my ex-wife.

And quashed it with, "But licensing agreements can go on forever, can't they?"

"Licensing agreements. All right. I suppose so."

My turn to look superior now.

Sarah shrugged it off and pushed up straight against the armrest of the sofa and took a sip of her wine. She looked down at me, making sure she had my attention in her "Read-my-lips" attitude. "Over five hundred million dollars? Are you telling me you're going after somebody that's made *half a billion dollars?* Do you have any idea how touchy somebody with half a billion dollars can get, if somebody bothers them?"

I showed her that I could shrug, too. "What can he do? He'll just point at himself, if he tries to do anything."

"Oh, Tony. Damn it! Why couldn't I be divorced from a damned CPA?"

"Fine. All right. I'll be careful."

Her expression was high skepticism. Then she said, "All right. Just who is it your Maggie wants her revenge on, anyway?"

"Revenge? I hadn't exactly thought about it like that. But that's good."

"You can be so naive."

We'd had character-sessions lots of times. But I certainly didn't want one now. Quickly, I said, "Well, it was the rich guy she and George worked for—except he wasn't so rich then—his family had oil, but he made some bad investments and he was about down to his last guesthouse. So he needed a big new source of income."

I picked up Maggie's file folder from the coffee table and put it in Sarah's lap. I still hadn't had the chance to go over the notes in detail, but they looked very interesting.

I certainly wouldn't mind if Sarah got curious about them—and the case. When Grandpa was alive, she was fascinated by his true detective stories, but when I got into the position of having to try to be a detective, myself, she lost interest. She hadn't minded having a private eye for a grandfather-in-law, I guess, but she hated having to admit that she was divorced from one. She had helped Grandpa sometimes by digging into the research department at the ad agency to find out things for him. I didn't dare come right out and ask her to do that for me, but I hoped that some of her old habits would emerge now that I was working on a moderately interesting private eye case of my own.

I said, "Along with all kinds of notes, Maggie's got a list of everybody that worked in the place—the cook and housekeeper and everybody, and some of the people that were close to the rich guy and ought to have known what was going on with George's invention. And George's advisor at Rice University—Dr. Potter. Some of them are dead now, but not all of them. Maybe they won't know anything, but just talking to them will get things moving."

Sarah wasn't interested in the file folder. Moving it off onto the cushion beside her, she said, "Fine. The 'rich guy.' Just who are you talking about, Tony?"

I didn't think she'd ever ask.

Drama time.

Except that, suddenly, right there at the climax of it all, I had a brain-flash. Who knows how those things work? It's just that out of nowhere, some kind of connection gets made in your head, and *Pow!*

"Joseph Newhouse!" I blurted out, suddenly and unaccountably focusing on the name of that cop who found George Hawk's body. "Joe Newhouse. Vegas Joe Newhouse."

"The barbecue guy?" Sarah said unbelievingly.

"Yeah. Vegas Joe's *BRBQ*," I said, trying to pronounce it as it was done on his big neon signs.

"Are you crazy?" Sarah said. "He's not worth anything like a half billion dollars."

"He's not who I'm talking about. But don't you know Newhouse? Didn't his barbecue places used to be one of your accounts?"

She looked at the ceiling and went into her *humoring Tony* mode. "He's a former account," she said, using the tone she reserved for those misguided enough to have dumped her agency.

"I've been trying to place the name, and it just came to me. Joseph Newhouse. Vegas Joe. You know him. He used to be a cop, didn't he?"

She hated to be reminded of those who had gotten away,

but she was humoring me. "All right. Fine. I think so. Before he opened those barbecue places."

"Okay," I said. "Great. That's why his name stuck in my mind."

"Could we go back to your case? Please?"

I tried to get the drama going again. Reaching into the shelf under the top of Sarah's coffee table, I pulled out today's *Chronicle*. Fiddling out the "Lifestyle" section, which is what they call the "Society" section in these egalitarian times when everyone's equal except the too rich and the too poor and about two-thirds of the people who've managed to wangle Handicapped Parking tags, I whipped it open to page three.

"You're not going to believe this," I said.

Sarah sighed. "Bet me."

I folded the newspaper section to feature a photograph of a bunch of people in suits standing around giving each other self-satisfied smirks. The headline was, MAJOR CONTRIBUTION TO RICE UNIVERSITY.

Holding the newspaper up toward Sarah I said, "Just by coincidence, he got his picture in the paper again today. He's the one handing over the check—giving them twelve million dollars of George Hawk's money to build a new classroom building."

With mild interest, Sarah looked at the photo.

Drama was rekindled. Her mouth practically dropped open.

She grabbed up Maggie's file folder and held it like a shield. "Him?" she said. "Jason Woods? Good God, Tony! You can't possibly be talking about Jason Woods!"

FIVE

The Video King's Girlfriend Strikes Again

Somebody was knocking on my door.

The cat had been sleeping in his usual spot next to my feet, but he had jumped straight up, and now sat quivering on the corner of the bed, every hair on his black body and tail sticking straight out, his eyes looking as big as dimes.

The clock showed a couple of minutes before seven.

Knocking! Loud, insistent knocking!

I had a bathrobe somewhere. But a pair of old jeans crumpled up on the end of the dresser was easier to find. I yelled, "Just a minute!" toward the front door, and pulled them on and hurried toward the living room to make the noise stop.

Showing me how brave he was, Spooky galloped ahead—to about ten feet from the door. There he stopped. Now it was my turn to be brave.

I got the chain undone and pulled the door open.

Grandpa had always warned me to look out for men with haircuts that cost more than their shoes.

He was right.

This one said, "Anthony Aapt, you're served."

And stalked away, leaving me standing there with a folded-up paper damned near sticking out of my stomach.

I slammed the door shut and twisted the blinds open for some light and looked at the thing.

STOCKPILE VIDEO, INC.
vs.
ANTHONY AAPT, dba AAPT INVESTIGATIONS

"What the hell?" I said.

The cat had shrunk down to near normal size now, and he stalked over to the door and checked to make sure he'd thoroughly taken care of the problem.

I looked over the summons. Damn! I really needed this! Stockpile Video was suing me—suing me!—to recover the pitiful bucks the Video King had advanced me while I was working my butt off for him.

Eight thousand two hundred dollars and ninety-three cents. All of which had gone to pay for equipment I used to hook up surveillance cameras in the stores to keep people from walking off with his cash and his videocassettes and his rental equipment.

Shit!

Plus court costs. Plus attorney fees.

Shitaroonie!

I wadded the thing and threw it down. Spooky thought it was play time, of course, and bounded after it and swatted it into a corner.

I picked up the telephone.

Art Morton was the manager of Stockpile Video's flagship store—the one in the Galleria. He was a retired traffic cop and a hell of a nice guy, and we had gotten to be semi-buddies during the time when I was trying to save the Video King from the shoplifters and the dishonest employees and the sneaky underhanded competitors.

I caught him getting ready to go to work. "Tony?" he said, with at least mild astonishment when I told him who I was. "You didn't tell Mavis who was calling, did you?"

His concern was valid. I was the guy starring in an intercompany memo ordering no one to let me into the stores, cash my checks, or rent videos to me. Art's wife, Mavis, was assistant manager of the accounts payable department in Stockpile Video's main office. Obviously, she wouldn't be happy about Art's getting an early morning telephone call from the company pariah.

"No, I didn't tell her."

"Okay. How're you doing, Tony? Haven't talked to you in a while."

"I'm doing just dandy, Art. Haven't had much to say. How're you doing?"

He sighed loudly. "Don't ask. Somebody walked out of the store with one of the goddamned rental video cameras yesterday afternoon."

"You're kidding."

That got him mad. "Would I kid about that? Shit, no, I wouldn't."

"Did you get anything on the surveillance tapes?"

"Are you kidding, Tony? Nobody bothers about them. The cameras weren't loaded. They spend all their time making the store pretty. I don't have any of that special tape for the surveillance cameras, but I got tinsel hanging from the ceiling now. Can you believe that? Since you left, they don't give a shit about people stealing things."

I said, "Oh, yeah? Nobody raised hell about the video camera getting stolen?"

"Oh, well, hell, yes. But it's all screwed-up. I raise hell about getting some tape for the surveillance cameras, and the office says, 'Here. Hang this pretty tinsel on your ceiling.' I tell 'em I was so busy hanging tinsel somebody walked out with the video camera, and they roast my ass."

"So. Other than that, how is everything?"

He laughed. "You mean, how's Angela? Well, Angela's doing just fine. They fired old Sparky Parsons and upgraded his job from Manager and gave it to Angela and now she's Ms. Vice President Angela Mills in charge of Advertising and Promotion."

That burned me up. "Damn!" I said. "Listen, do you remember when I got that asshole to give me a check and I went out and bought all those linkages for the surveillance cameras? And put 'em in myself?"

"Sure."

"Well, the latest thing is, he's suing me for the money."

"Shit, Tony."

"Angela's vice president now?"

"She sure is, and she acts like she's the goddamned queen."

I said, "Is she showing yet?"

Art giggled as if that was funny or something. "Showing? Wait a minute, Tony! It must of been a while since we talked to each other. You mean you don't know?"

"Don't know what?"

He sounded as if he was about to yell, but he went almost to a whisper, instead: "Just a second."

Spooky sat in the kitchen doorway, head cocked to the side, squalling for breakfast.

From the telephone, I heard Art call out, "Honey, you go ahead and take your shower first."

There was a long pause, after which he did yell, apparently confident that the sound of rushing water would cover for him. "You wanted to know if she's showing yet? Why, hell, no, Tony. She wasn't ever pregnant!"

"What?"

"She wasn't pregnant," he said again.

I stared at the telephone.

Art said, "She waited until he promoted her to vice president and signed a paper that gave her the money she stole, and got his wife shipped off to London for the summer, and then she had a big, tearful confession-session with him. Betty Ann, that works for Mavis, heard the whole thing. Angela came back from her doctor's and laid it on him. Went on for about a half hour about how she hated to disappoint him. Said it must have been a defective home pregnancy test."

"Damn!" I said.

"But don't worry," Art said dryly. "They're still tight."

"Gee, great," I said, with as much dryness as I could generate at the moment.

"She really broke it off in you, boy."

"Yeah. I guess."

"Listen, you know what I did?"

"Did?"

"After they walked out with the goddamned video camera?"

"The video camera. Okay. What did you do?"

"I went out and bought some chain and some padlocks. I chained up all the rental equipment—I'm tired of this shit. Then they raised hell: 'Listen, you're in the Galleria. You can't chain down stuff in the Galleria like you were in some strip center next door to a pawn shop. You're right across the way from Tiffany's. You don't see Tiffany's chaining down stuff, do you?' "

Art and I continued like that for a while, pissing and moaning with each other.

I guess it helped let off steam, or something.

But it didn't help much. I was about as pissed-off when I hung up the telephone as I had been when I called. Angela, the Embezzler, was Vice President of Advertising & Promotion now! Damn! Talk about equal opportunity!

This was just great. Angela had the half million bucks she'd embezzled, and I had a summons and a starving cat.

Well, at least, I could take care of the cat part. I filled his bowl with fresh water and fed him. He turned up his nose at the canned food, of course, and turned his back on me and stalked out of the kitchen. But he shut up.

I gave it up and got my damned jeans off and tried to cut my throat with my trusty Norelco.

Tough to do, no matter how determined you are.

So I got in the shower and tried to drown myself.

That didn't work, either, so I finally gave up and got out and dried off.

I did finally have a bright thought, though.

Somewhere along the way, maybe I could sit down with good old Maggie and a couple of gallons of her fantastic scotch and get shit-faced with her, and then we could tell each other war stories about getting screwed by the big-bucks crowd.

Damn!

No justice.

I brushed my teeth as if I was trying to scrape off barnacles and then, foamy-mouthed and crazy-looking, glared at myself in the mirror. "Okay, Maggie," I said. "Let's go after that son-of-a-bitch!"

I had enough pissed-off energy to go out and run a GRASSBUSTER right up Jason Woods' philanthropic ass.

But first things first.

SIX

Maggie Hawk's "Grassbuster Chronicles"

Damn it, Grandpa! I thought. Where are you when I need you? And I went on with a few choice comments about his always hogging the criminal stuff for himself. Overlooking the fact, of course, that I had always pretty consistently telegraphed the idea that I was just a tad too good for such things. I didn't mind going out and advising some fat Yup that he needed burglar bars, but I certainly avoided getting my hands dirty with the real private eye stuff.

Anyway . . . surely, I had heard enough of Grandpa's stories to know what to do.

The first thing to do was research. That was one of his lamer, but nevertheless valid sayings: "You can't show, if you don't know."

So I whipped up some instant coffee and sat down with Maggie's file folder to do some research. With Spooky, of course, who decided he needed some companionship and, besides, I was in his favorite chair where he was used to taking the first or second of his eight or ten morning naps. I wasn't up to listening to him squall, so I made room for him.

Before I got into Maggie's handwritten notes, I went through that stack of newspaper clippings.

Apparently, Maggie had saved these clippings over the

years and had made copies of them just a few days ago when she was getting ready to sit down and call her favorite neighborhood ace detective, because the earlier-dated ones showed gray smudges caused by old yellowed newsprint.

All of the clippings starred Jason Woods.

They fell into about three categories:

Number. one: He was only incidentally a sharp and successful businessman; what really thrilled him was saving the fingers and toes of all mankind with his marvelous GRASSBUSTER invention, to the point that you'd think that he practically forgot to haul the big bucks to the bank.

Number. two: Instead of selfishly spending all his time trying to enrich himself by concentrating on Jason Woods Industries, any time he was needed to help out with a public crisis, he was available.

Number. three: He was also dedicated to making Rice University, his beloved Alma Mater, strong and financially independent. He endowed scholarship funds. He built buildings. He gave tracts of land.

Argh! Five minutes of leafing through that stuff was about enough to make me gag. Damn! Didn't this guy ever belch or scratch himself? Didn't he ever run a stop sign?

Apparently not.

Lots of the clippings included photographs. About every five years, it seemed, Woods would do a new publicity photograph. The earliest photos—taken when he was about thirty—showed him as a sharp-faced, thin-lipped man, just a little on the rugged side—a bit like the Marlboro Man with sophistication. Gradually, distinguished gray wings appeared at his temples and then enlarged, and his shoulders did some sloping. But the face stayed sharp and the lips got thinner.

Pretty soon, I gathered up the clippings and tossed them

onto the coffee table. How much Cowboy-Bob-Good-Guy could I stand? Besides, there wasn't anything there that I didn't know already. I had grown up with Jason Woods being in the background of about everything that had to do with Houston except the rotten streets. He was a Texas Legend. There was Pecos Bill and there was Jim Bowie and there was Jason Woods.

About three times a month, it seemed, I'd turn on the Six O'clock News and here would be Jason Woods ascending the escalator in the Galleria and graciously delaying grappling with his own awesome responsibilities to pause in front of the grand entrance to the Jason Woods Industries Building and give the TV audience the benefit of his pronouncements about whatever crisis Houston or Texas was facing at the moment.

For a moment, I sat there staring at my coffee cup, feeling downright treasonous for thinking ill of one of our certified legends. Then a little reality set in. Pecos Bill wasn't a real person, but if he had been, he'd have been a showoff and a liar. Jim Bowie was a river pirate and a land fraud artist before the Alamo made him a dead hero. Where did that leave Jason?

Anyway, he wasn't making my payment to my ex-wife; Maggie Hawk was.

I dove into her notes.

She apparently started writing them practically as soon as they told her George was dead. The notes were more of a diary or journal than just random jottings and, as I read through them, I started to appreciate her mind.

She was sharp.

She hadn't missed much.

There were the names of the cops who came to tell her George was dead: Detective J. Newhouse and Officer

Hanley Moss. The name of the cop—J. Newhouse again—who had spent about fifteen minutes investigating the obvious suicide, paying little attention to what she tried to tell him about George's invention or his non-suicidal frame of mind because she was, after all, not exactly reliable since she was the grief-stricken and obviously distraught widow.

The cop mentioned the suicide note that had been found in the car but apparently didn't tell Maggie exactly what was in it. He went on at some length about the fact that George had used his own gun. Maggie couldn't believe George owned a gun, but the cop told her the old .38 caliber pistol had to have belonged to him because "G.W. Hawk" had been scratched into the handgrip years ago.

Maggie's total perplexity shouted from her notes. Who could have done this to her husband? Maybe he picked up a hitchhiker, who killed him and left it looking like suicide. But that seemed unlikely on a relatively short urban trip between River Oaks and North Boulevard. Maybe he gave some friend or acquaintance a ride, and some sort of argument arose. That seemed even more unlikely. Slightly more possible was that someone jumped into George's car at a stoplight and then killed him.

But if that were so, wouldn't there have been some sign of a struggle? Where was the brown grocery store bag with George's drawings and his prototype blade in it? And what about that gun? How could it have been George's gun? Maggie didn't even know he had one.

That George might have killed himself was absolutely impossible, as far as Maggie was concerned.

Wasn't it?

Could he possibly have killed himself?

Had she—Maggie—done or said something awful to him without even realizing it?

If he could have killed himself, what happened to his drawings and his lawnmower blade?

Would George have killed himself?

No.

No! NO!

There was a nearly word-for-word recounting of Maggie's conversation the day after George's death with "Mr. Woods," as she referred to him in those days, in which he was very nice and sympathetic and kind.

Maggie was trying to keep herself too busy to think, and going ahead with packing to get out of the servant's apartment. When "Mr. Woods" knocked on the door, she was pulling down the colorful travel posters with which she had decorated the grim and tiny place. They were of places she had dreamed of seeing when George sold his lawnmower blade and got rich: the Eiffel Tower; snowcapped Alps; Ayers Rock; the Pyramids; the Taj Mahal.

Maggie's side of the conversation with Woods showed an almost pathetic appreciation of the fact that, although he was "nearly strapped for ready cash," as he put it, he gave her four hundred dollars to help with the funeral expenses. She was also moved by his offer to recommend her for a wonderful job with a friend of his. The friend traveled all over the world, and took his family along, and needed a nanny to travel with them and take care of his two small children.

Maggie was very tempted by the job. But after only a little agonizing, she turned it down. She couldn't just walk away from George's death.

In that conversation with "Mr. Woods," she brought up the missing drawings of George's invention, and the lawnmower blade he had made:

I told Mr. Woods that the policeman said that George's drawings and the blade weren't in the car, and he said that was a shame because, without them, George's idea for a cutter-blade couldn't get developed. He said that, if I found any drawings, to be sure and let him know and, if it was worth developing, he'd make me an offer for it.

I told him that was nice of him, but what I'd do was what George had wanted to do and that was to get it patented and then see about getting somebody to use it. I asked Mr. Woods if maybe he'd be interested in that. He said of course he would, if I found any of the drawings, but he didn't really sound very interested. Why should he? He's practical. He doesn't want to waste time talking about something that's lost.

After he left, I remembered George's advisor at school—Dr. Potter. Maybe George showed him his idea. Maybe he even has some drawings.

Maggie called Dr. Potter, with this result:

I asked him about George's drawings. He wasn't very nice. He tried to be, I guess, but he wasn't. I guess I can understand. George was his most favorite student ever, and he didn't like it when we got married because it took George's time away from school. He blames me for George dying. I could hear it in his voice. He said he doesn't have any drawings of a lawnmower blade.

I guess all of them, for sure, were in that paper sack that George had with him in the car.

In Maggie's notes, there was a lot about the situation at the Woods place in River Oaks—it obviously was not a happy one. Jason Woods' older brother had been disowned and disinherited by the family years ago after numerous scrapes with the law. Then he totally disgraced himself in Jason Woods' eyes by marrying a Mexican girl. A few months before Maggie and George went to work at the estate, the brother was killed and Jason Woods reluctantly took in his widow and two small children because they had no money and nowhere else to go.

So now I was finally finding some belches and scratches. According to Maggie, Jason treated his sister-in-law and her two children like dirt. Well, another Texas Legend . . .

One of Maggie's notes cleared up a minor mystery for me—the old lawnmower sitting in the corner of her living room:

I'm almost through packing. There's not much, but it's been hard. Mr. Woods had somebody clean up the car and even put in a new front seat, but I can still just barely stand to get in it. I put George's lawnmower in the trunk of the car this afternoon. Took off the handlebars and it fit just fine. It was an old lawnmower of Mr. Woods' that he told George to throw away, but he kept it and fixed it up and got to experimenting on it and that was how he got his idea for the cutter-blade. He'd make drawings and then make a blade from them in the garage in his spare time and put it on that old lawnmower and see if it worked. I remember the first time he got the blade to work. He wheeled that old lawnmower out onto the lawn out by the tennis courts and threw down a bunch of rocks and sticks and then cranked up the lawnmower and ran right over them. You could hear the blade hit the rocks and sticks, but it didn't throw them like a regular lawnmower did. George was so tickled that it worked like he planned it to!

Mr. Woods was playing tennis with a friend of his—John Scott—and they came over to watch. They were so impressed! Mr. Scott got down on his knees and turned the lawnmower over and studied the blade, he was so impressed. Well, the blade's gone, but I've got that lawnmower that George worked so hard on, and I'm going to keep it.

There was an explanatory note about the gun:

I didn't know anything about that gun, but George's mother told me about it at the funeral. It was his father's and George got it when his father died and to keep his brothers from claiming it, he scratched his name on it.

So he had a gun, after all. I didn't know anything about it. He must have kept it somewhere I didn't know about.

When Maggie couldn't sleep during those first weeks after George's death, she would write her notes.

Well, I've got a room to live in, and a job. George wouldn't like it that I'm working in a bar, but what else can I do? (I could be traveling around to all those wonderful places taking care of those little kids, that's what I could be doing! But I couldn't just run off and leave everything hanging.)

Bar work. Ugh! I keep waiting to see all those big tips they said I'd get. Well, I guess it's not a bar. It's a private club since you still can't just sell hard drinks over the counter in Texas. Anybody that walks in can join for $5, and that lets you serve them mixed drinks. At least, it's what they call a gentleman's club because they charge $5, *instead of just $1 or nothing, so I don't have to wear something skimpy like in some of those places. Whatever they call it, though, it's still a bar, but it's still better than being a maid. I didn't mind being a maid when it was helping put George through school, but I won't be a maid just to make my living. I'll start taking some more college classes when I can—and I tell you what—it'll sure be something more practical than Art History, like what I was taking when I met George.*

Maggie's handwritten notes must have been as much therapy for her as my swaggering into the bar and bragging about being a hot private eye was therapy for me.

A lot of them were useless, of course, but here and there, things caught my eye.

A few days after Maggie moved and started working at the club, she got a call from Bonita, Jason Woods' brother's widow, saying goodbye. Practically giggling with happiness, Bonita told Maggie that an insurance policy on her husband had turned up—one she had no idea existed. It had apparently been sizeable because it was going to allow her to take the children and move far away from her unkind brother-in-law. The two children, ten-year-old Rhea and six-year-old Carl, both of whom had adored George, came on the telephone to say teary goodbyes. Maggie was sad that they were leaving, but very glad that they were getting away from the unpleasant situation with Jason Woods.

There were lots of notes.

Maybe Maggie's the one who should have been the detective.

Here was another clipping. I grunted out loud when I saw it, and Spooky got upset at being disturbed and hopped indignantly off the chair and went over into the corner and started batting the wadded-up summons around and pouncing on it and then biting hell out of it.

"Go get it!" I said to him. Then I wondered if I'd get charged extra court costs because the thing was full of tooth marks. As if another few bucks would make any difference.

Back to Maggie's file. This clipping wasn't about Jason Woods. It was torn out of the *Houston Chronicle*'s Thursday, February 2, 1967, Restaurant section. The headline was VEGAS JOE NEWHOUSE HAS ALL THE LUCK! AND GREAT BARBECUE, TOO! The article was a frothy account of his "fabuloso" new Galleria-area restaurant that read exactly as if it had been written by Newhouse's giddy sister.

Maggie had scratched a note across the photo that showed Newhouse in his signature gaudy outfit standing in the entrance of his first "BRBQ" restaurant: "That cop! Some people have all the luck!"

More notes. These early notes were mostly grief and frustration, with something written practically every day and night. Then the notes and the ideas started getting sparse. There were just four or five short paragraphs over a three month period that were nothing much but regret over George's death and the fact that all their dreams had died with him.

Finally, there was about a four month period of no notes at all.

And then, POW!

It all became very, very clear.

At about three o'clock on the morning of March 3, 1968, Maggie got home from the club and sat down with the newspaper and found out what had really happened. The paper seemed to be full of lawnmower ads:

IT'S FINALLY HERE—
THE NEW SNAPPER LAWNMOWER
WITH THE REVOLUTIONARY GRASSBUSTER BLADE—
CUT THE GRASS, NOT YOURSELF!

And

STOP DODGING THOSE ROCKS, BUDDY!
GET A TORO WITH THE GRASSBUSTER BLADE!

And

IT'S FINALLY HERE—
THE FIRST REAL ADVANCE IN GRASSCUTTING SINCE THE GOAT—
THE ULTRA-MODERN 1968 JOHN DEERE LAWNMOWER
WITH THE REVOLUTIONARY
SAFE
EFFICIENT
GRASSBUSTER BLADE

All of the ads had *"GRASSBUSTER © Jason Woods Industries, Inc."* and *"Patent Pending, Jason Woods Industries, Inc."* noted at their bottoms.

Maggie was stunned. Totally rocked.

Now, she knew exactly what had happened to George. And to his invention.

All she had to do was prove it.

The cops weren't interested. All they needed to make their day complete was a suicide-widow waving around a bunch of lawnmower ads.

She tried to call Jason Woods. She got to talk to secretaries who acted as if they were all too accustomed to handling the crackpots that bother rich and successful people.

She did get through to the lawyer, Clinton McKenna. And here, it showed that Maggie was getting technical because she took down his conversation exactly as he said it. "What lawnmower blade? I wasn't aware that your husband was coming to see me about something like that. Frankly, Mrs. Hawk, it was my impression that he was coming to see me about . . . well . . . I wouldn't hurt your feelings for anything, but . . . about a divorce."

She called John Scott, the friend of Woods, who had interrupted a tennis game to watch George's first successful demonstration and had turned the lawnmower over to study the cutter-blade. He said, "What lawnmower? What rocks? I don't know what you're talking about, lady. I play tennis with Jason. I don't stand around and watch his people cut the lawn." A little later, Maggie found out that he was now a vice president of Jason Woods Industries.

Frustrated, she decided the only way she was going to accomplish anything was to hire a private detective. A note written in May 1968 describes that adventure:

> *I went to see this private detective that has an office down the street from the club. He looks like he ought to be in the movies. Like an old Robert Mitchum, if you can imagine that. I started telling him that my husband had been killed and his invention stolen and he made me stop. He asked me if I was prepared to hire him. I said yes, but how much. He said he didn't take anyone's case unless they paid him in advance. If I had the money to pay him fifty dollars a day for two weeks' work, then we'd be in business.*

Fifty dollars a day! I told him that when he proved my husband's murder and got the invention back for me, I'd pay him lots more than that. He told me no real detective worked that way. Then he said he was busy. That when I got the money to hire him, he'd listen to me all day.

Well, I'll get the money together. But I won't go back to him. He could have been nicer. He wouldn't even listen to me if I didn't have all that money right there!

I got that far in Maggie's notes and had to stop and chuckle with more than moderate wryness. Obviously, the detective Maggie had gone to see hadn't been my grandfather. Of all the pithy sayings he was fond of, "Pay in advance" definitely wasn't one of them.

After that, according to her notes, Maggie started saving her money. In the meantime, she got back to serious note-writing, wracking her brain to remember everything that might possibly have any bearing on the cutter-blade or on George's death.

There was this entry:

All of a sudden I remembered that about a week before George was murdered, Jason Woods had some workmen come to do some heavy tree-trimming. George talked to the foreman—he could make friends with anybody. He showed that foreman his cutter-blade. I chatted with the foreman myself when the cook had me take some lemonade and doughnuts out. Nice man. Mexican. But educated. About thirty. Mustache. Stocky. Spoke good English. WHY CAN'T I REMEMBER HIS NAME? OR THE NAME THAT WAS ON THEIR TRUCK? He'd remember about George's cutter-blade. WHAT WAS HIS NAME?

There were revelations:

JESUS GARCIA! JESUS GARCIA! THAT WAS THE FOREMAN'S NAME! It's 4:25 in the morning, June 2, 1968. I woke up out of a sound sleep remembering that foreman's name! Jesus Garcia!

There was a laugh or two:

*June 2, 1968—How can there be that many Jesus Garcia*s *and J. Garcia*s *in the phone book? I've been calling them all day, trying to find one that does tree-trimming. I sure know a whole lot more Spanish now than I did this morning. But I bet most of it I'd better not say out loud.*

Disappointment:

June 5, 1968—I talked to Mrs. Ynez Garcia. Mrs. Jesus Garcia. Her husband, Jesus Garcia, did tree-trimming. He's the one. But he was killed in a car wreck last January. Damn! All the wrong people are getting killed.

Accomplishment:

January 3, 1969—$700! Got it saved! That's a lot of letting drunks pat your butt and not smacking them in the face. But I've got that $700. Tomorrow, I hire a private detective! I wish my stomach didn't hurt. I ought to be celebrating, but my stomach hurts. When I hire my private detective and start getting the goods on Jason Woods, I'll feel a whole lot better, though! George, we're going to get him!

Despair:

January 10, 1969—Out of the hospital. Appendix. There went my $700. And then some. Damn it! Damn! Well, there's not any use bawling over something that can't be helped. All I can do is start over. Damn appendix, anyway! Next time, remind me to get the damn detective paid, and then keel over.

More despair:

May 23, 1969—Mom had a stroke. Only 52, but it hit her just like that. The only thing I can do is try to take care of her. I sure can't afford nurses. I'm getting this two-bedroom apartment and this colored lady to stay at night with her while I work. Lucky I had the money I'd been saving for a detective.

The next note page was puzzling. It started out with Maggie's writing about her mother on October 10, and again on October 16, 1969. The notes sounded optimistic because her mother seemed to be getting better. Then at the bottom of the page there was:

October 19, 1969—Why! Thought I was through with that. I'm so stupid! After what I did. And then all of a sudden, I wake up out of a dream about L! Damn! I'm not . . .

That note should have continued on the next page, but it didn't. It stopped in the middle. I leafed through to see if pages had gotten out of order.

They hadn't. So I went back to where I had left off. And found:

December 18, 1969—Another stroke. She was getting better, and then it hit. This time she's paralyzed on her left side. The doctor said she won't ever get much better. But maybe she will. She's got to.

After that, there were only scattered entries in the "journal" for years. Maggie mentioned that she changed private club jobs several times until finally, Texas did away with the private club laws, and regular mixed drink bars came in. Then she waitressed at several different places.

And then:

April 17, 1985—2:45 AM—Can't believe who came in the bar last night—Hanley Moss, that patrolman that came to tell me George was dead. He was the one they sent to George's car to help that detective that turned out to be Vegas Joe. Must have taken me twenty minutes to figure out why he looked so familiar. Lucky it was Tuesday night, and not very busy, and I could take time to talk to him. He's still nice-looking. And nice, too. Not like that sarcastic Vegas Joe Newhouse was. He remembered me. At least he said he did.

I think he likes me, but I'm not going to lead him on. Even if I could. He's got a wedding band, and I know how that goes. Boy, do I! He said he'd look around and see if there was anything there about George. We'll see. He said he'd come in again tomorrow night—tonight. Well, I've heard that before, haven't I? Wish he didn't have that wedding band on—I guess. But he does.

Then came disappointment again:

April 18, 1985—Well, no Hanley Moss. What did I expect?

Then a bit of surprise:

April 23, 1985—Couldn't believe there was mail for me at the bar when I got there last night! An envelope with no return address. Inside were some copies of police reports—police notes, actually, I guess—about George, and a copy of some of his autopsy report. That Hanley Moss must have sent them. He didn't come back in the bar, but he at least kept his word. Probably a good thing he didn't come back, since he's married. Yes, it is. Don't know what good this stuff will do, but it's something, anyway. And it's nice that somebody promised something and then did it.

Now I knew how Maggie had gotten those report copies that were in her files. They obviously hadn't done her any good as far as proving anything, but at least she didn't have to wonder about them anymore.

Or about George's suicide note.

That suicide note! Why didn't somebody tell me then what it said so I could have told them about it? Damn! There's a copy of the note in the stuff Hanley Moss sent me.

Maggie—
I can't take any more of this. Nothing's working out like we wanted it to.
I'm taking the easy way out.

Yeah, George wrote that note. But that wasn't all of

it. He wrote it right after Jason Woods told us he couldn't afford us any longer, and the bottom got cut off. It used to end up with

So I'm going fishing. See you tomorrow.
Love, G.

Damn! Damn! DAMN! Why didn't I make them show me the note way back then so I could have told them somebody just cut off the bottom and made it look like a suicide note? I never even thought about that fishing note until now. Last I knew of it it was in a bowl on top of the refrigerator in that place we lived in at Jason Woods' place, along with a Valentine and a birthday card. DAMN!

Then there was:

June 8, 1986—I woke up this morning feeling so blue, and didn't know why for the longest time. Then I finally realized it's been twenty years since George died. Twenty years! Where did they go? I cried myself out. I never cry anymore, but I did today. Twenty years!

There were only scattered notes after that. They covered Maggie's getting the chance to manage a little bar on Alabama Street. It wasn't much, she said, but then she said she wasn't much anymore, either.

Then:

October 8, 1998—Buried Mom today. But she'd been gone for years. First thing I thought was I could start trying to save up to hire a detective again. Who am I kid-

ding? You know what a private detective costs now? And I sure can't work the tips like I used to. Jason Woods just keeps getting richer. He's beaten me, George. He's beaten me.

And then, finally:

July 25, 1999—I'm numb! Numb! Money! $10,000,000! ! ! ! ! I almost didn't even mail that silly sweepstakes entry. Oh, my God! George, are you out there anywhere? I hope you didn't give up on me. It's been a long, long time, but we're going to get him now! We're going to get that son-of-a-bitch Jason Woods now! One way or the other.

This nice young fellow's been coming in the bar, and he's a really hot-shot private detective. I've kept listening to him talk about his cases, thinking if only I had the kind of money he charges, I'd sic him on Jason Woods.

Well, I've got it now! I'm going to do it!

And she did.

I stared into my coffee cup for a while. Was my conscience feeling kind of blistered? Yeah. More blistered than that.

Damn!

There was one more sheet of notes. Before I read it, I let myself fantasize a little. Maybe this last note would say something that would make me feel better, like:

August 9, 1999—I'm about to call Tony Aapt. I realize he was kind of embroidering his private detective stories to entertain me and make himself feel good. But I like him. After all these years, there's no hope of getting the goods on Jason Woods, but I'm going to hire Tony, anyway. Just because he's been nice to me, and maybe he could use the business. Why should I worry about ancient history, anyway? What I should do is just kick back and enjoy myself.

But the note didn't say anything like that.

Damn again!

It was a list:

UPDATED LIST OF PEOPLE WHO MIGHT REMEMBER SOMETHING ABOUT GEORGE'S INVENTION

Hilda Guttman—JW's cook—retired now—3122 Tangley Road
Bonita Woods—died in 1991
Rhea Woods—Chatham now—2704 Le Mans Drive
Carl Woods—lives in Chicago
Dr. Melvin Potter—Rice University
Aurora Delgado—JW's housekeeper—died in 1992
John Scott—died in 1982
Clinton McKenna—3301 San Simeon
Hanley Moss—4103 Peterson Way

Not a very long list.

But it was about ten times the size of my self-esteem at the moment.

SEVEN

Just Practicing

Time to get going.

The first thing I needed to do was deposit Maggie's check.

Going to the bank hadn't lately been a whole lot of fun. I thought the tellers probably made bets on whether my ugly old car would make it out of the drive-through without a tow truck, and I was certain that they bet on whether my typical minuscule deposits would clear.

But this morning was different. Seven thousand dollars different.

I pulled poor old Hizzie into the slot and gave the teller a big grin as I stuck my deposit slip and Maggie's check into the plastic cylinder and sent it on its way. I grinned even bigger when I saw the teller's eyebrows go up in surprise when he opened the cylinder and saw the amount of the deposit.

Life seemed unusually nice at the moment. Adding to the niceness was the fact that, because Maggie banked at Texas Commerce, too, there wouldn't be any delay for clearing. Yeah. Nice!

Until the paranoia to which I'd gotten all too accustomed lately struck. What if Maggie had come to her senses and stopped payment?

It was no help at all when I saw my teller step away from his spot and go show my deposit to somebody else—another teller, or a supervisor. Geez! Suddenly, I was sure that everything had gone wrong. At any second, a gang of security guards would burst out of the tellers' enclosure and drag me out of the car.

I think I jumped about two feet when the pneumatic tube started wheezing and the plastic cylinder plopped down. I grabbed it. There was nothing in it but a deposit receipt.

My deposit receipt. For seven thousand dollars!

The speaker hummed. "Is there anything else we can do for you today, Mr. Aapt?"

Wow! It had been months since a teller had asked me that.

"No, thanks," I said.

And the teller said, "Have a nice day. And thank you for banking at Texas Commerce, sir."

Paranoia be damned! A bank teller had actually called me "sir" again!

I was grinning bigger yet as I steered Hizzie's bulk out of the drive-in and took off. It was really nice to be a "sir" again.

Some realization set in pretty quickly, though. I wouldn't be a "sir" for long if I didn't produce at least something to earn Maggie's money.

So I drove about eight blocks west of the bank branch and started practicing.

There was no possible way that the patrol cop who had been only somewhat involved in George Hawk's death scene thirty-three years ago, and chanced onto her at a bar years later was going to be any help. Yeah, he had sent Maggie some documentation, but that didn't mean much.

He might be some good private detective practice for me, though. And God knew I could use all of that I could get.

Hanley Moss.

Forty-one-oh-three Peterson Way was one of the hundreds of smallish two- and three-bedroom houses that had sprung up in this area to answer the housing shortage after World War II. Once, they must all have looked pretty much alike, but over the years the owners had made them different with built-ons and paint and plants. In some parts of town, areas like this had started toward ruin. But this area, which had once been far west boondocks Houston, was now Inner-Loop, and the homeowners knew that reasonably well-kept-up places that had cost three thousand dollars in 1947 were now being snapped up by traffic-weary commuters for fifty times that.

As I walked up the sidewalk, I guessed at Moss' age. He must have been at least twenty-one in 1966, so he'd be about in his mid-fifties now.

Wrong. When he answered the doorbell wearing an explosive Hawaiian shirt, I revised that guess to mid-sixties, at least, even though he still had most of his hair.

"Mr. Moss?" I said.

He glanced at the papers in my hand. "Are you from the real estate company? You're not supposed to start 'til next week."

"No, sir." I abandoned all caution and reached inside my jacket, pulled out my wallet and showed him my P.I. ID card. "I just want a few minutes of your time."

"Hmmm," he said. He pushed my wallet and hand away to far past arm's length so he could get his eyes focused. Then he snorted, meaning that he was about as unimpressed as I had expected a retired cop to be. "A few minutes about what?"

"About a detective named Joseph Newhouse you worked some with a while back."

Moss snorted again. "Newhouse!" He waved an arm around so dismissively that it made the Hawaiian shirt shimmer like fireworks.

I was going to say something else, but he started stepping back and closing the door. "Maybe some other time. I'm real busy right now."

"I'm kind of pressed for time, Mr. Moss."

That was the wrong thing to say.

He said, "Well, son, so am I," and stepped farther back, swung the door nearer to closed.

There was no doubt about it; I had totally flunked out on my first real attempt at private-eyeing.

Grandpa, though—wherever he was—came to my rescue.

Suddenly, Moss stopped shutting the door and frowned and said, "Wait a minute. Let me see that ID again."

I fumbled it out and held it up and far enough away for him to see it.

"Aapt?" he said. He squinted at me. "Any relation to Wilbur Aapt?"

"He was my grandfather."

"I'll be damned. Heard he died. Sorry about that. He was a good man. Met him once or twice. People respected him, not like most of 'em."

"Thank you, sir."

"Were you close, you and your grandfather?" Moss asked, and didn't wait for an answer. "You were, weren't you? I can see that. It's hard when you lose somebody close to you. I know that. Lost my wife in February. It's hard."

The door was wide open now, and Moss said, "Why in hell would anybody want to talk to me about Joe Newhouse?"

"Just to see what you might remember about an incident you worked on a while back. With Detective Newhouse."

A sudden grimace. "Newhouse! That'd be a long while back." He snorted. "Not long enough, if you ask me."

I unfolded the papers from Maggie's folder, and held them up to him. "You and Newhouse wrote these reports about the death of a man named George Hawk. Later, you sent these things to Hawk's widow, Maggie Hawk."

Moss tilted his head back this time to make some vision distance. "Hell, that's my writing, isn't it?"

"Yes, sir. I'd really like to hear anything you remember about it."

A big frown of concentration. "Maybe I do remember something." He stepped back and opened the door all the way. "Come on in, and let me put on my glasses and think.

"So you're Wilbur Aapt's grandson," he said, as I followed him through the living room.

"Right," I said, looking around, thinking that Spooky and I—and Sarah, too—must definitely have let a new decorating trend pass us by.

There was a stack of maybe a dozen neatly folded Jockey shorts sitting on the end of the sofa. Next to it was a stack of folded handkerchiefs. In the middle of the sofa was a stack of six or seven Hawaiian shirts, all at least as gaudy as the one Moss was wearing, all of them done up neatly in dry cleaner packages. On the easy chair were dry cleaner packages of white dress shirts. The coffee table held three pairs of dress shoes and a pair of walking shoes and a pair of running shoes.

Shaking my head, thinking that to get trendy, maybe I should start decorating my living room with the empty cans of the motor oil that good old Hizzie, the Oldsmobile, sucked down, I followed Moss into his kitchen.

"Want some coffee?" he said.

Great! If he was offering refreshments that meant he wasn't going to rush me out and that meant I must be doing at least some of the private eye stuff right.

He poured coffee into a couple of mugs and then picked up a pair of eyeglasses from the window sill and sat down across the kitchen table from me. "Oh, my," he said, picking up the police report copies. "Yes. That boy that shot himself on Buffalo Speedway." Suddenly, then, he stood up. "Just a minute."

He hurried into the living room and came right back with a yellow legal pad, and sat back down at the table. "Got to make sure I take all my meds along," he said, making an addition to what I saw was a list.

"Shorts" and "Handkerchiefs" and other things were checked off, but lots of things on the list weren't. What he had just written was "Prep H."

Setting the yellow pad aside, he tapped it with a fingertip. "Got to get everything together so I can pack," he said, "I'm taking a cruise. All over the Caribbean. Ten days. Leave on Saturday. Flying to Miami. Get on the ship there." He frowned and pulled the pad toward himself for a moment and apparently found that he had already written down something that had just come to mind. "Taking my wife along. Don't look at me like that. Her ashes. That's what I'm taking."

He sat back and shook his head sadly. "Ada always wanted to go on a cruise. We were always trying to plan to, but something'd come up. Finally, though, after the kids were on their own and I retired, I got a job doing bank security and started rat-holing part of my pay. Finally got enough. Got the tickets. Just in time to surprise Ada with 'em on our fortieth anniversary. Valentine's Day. She was beside herself. And then, a week later, she just keeled over dead. Just like that, she was gone. Heart. I didn't know women died like that. They do."

I tried to think what to say.

He waved me silent. "I'm just glad Ada knew about the cruise. So she got a little happiness out of it. I was going to wait and surprise her at the last minute. Changed my mind. Real glad I did. After she died, thought I'd cash in the tickets. Then I thought by damn, I'll just go ahead and go. Ada wouldn't have talked to me for a month, if I didn't. So I'm going. My old buddy, Wash, is going with me. I'm taking Ada's ashes along. All the way. When we get back to Miami, I'm going to put 'em in the sea. Stupid, isn't it? Well, I'm going to do it, anyway. I'm putting the house up for sale. Going to move into one of them assisted-living places—but not too damned assisted. Going to sell this place and take it easy. Going to get me a computer when they get all this Y2K-stuff fixed up, and learn how to use it." He grinned suddenly, and for just a moment, looked like an evil, gleeful elf. "Going to look for some of that porn they're always talking about on the TV news. Hell, I talk too much. I'll shut up. You talk."

"Well, I just wanted to see what you remembered about George Hawk's death."

"Ah, not much, to tell the truth. That was a long time ago." He shuffled through Maggie's photocopies and found the photograph of George when he was alive. "I know one thing. That boy had no business killing himself. Had everything ahead of him. Had a real pretty wife." He shook his head sadly. "Oh, yes. I had to go tell his wife he was dead. With that fool Joe Newhouse. They call him Vegas Joe now. Did you know that?"

"Yes, sir."

He made a rude noise. "That Joe Newhouse. Show-off. Big mouth. Wasn't three months after that when he went to Nevada and came back with all that money he won. Blackjack, I think. Yeah. I heard it was blackjack."

I shuffled through the photocopies until I found Moss' report. "How about this? Why was 'he was on his way home' marked out?"

"Oh, yeah. We wrote out these reports by hand back then, you know. Then one of the girls'd type them up. That's what Newhouse told me at first. We wrote out our preliminary reports at the same time to make sure we agreed on things. Newhouse saw I was writing that. Said he didn't say that. Told me to mark it out. Hell, maybe he didn't say it. Wouldn't have made sense if he did. Because he had an apartment over somewhere around Westbury, as I remember, and he moonlighted doing security down south on Mikawa Road somewhere. Wouldn't be going home from there on Buffalo Speedway. Everybody was glad when he won that money and quit the force and opened up that high-falutin' barbecue place."

"Why was that?"

"Hell, he was an asshole. In and out of trouble. He was in Vice. Then got moved over to Homicide. I don't know why, but there was lots of rumors. Then he got in trouble in Homicide."

"Yeah? What kind of trouble?"

"Shot some kid. Couple of fifteen-, sixteen-year-old kids were breaking in cars in the parking lot at that place he moonlighted at. Newhouse saw 'em. Stealing radios and eight-track players out of cars. You know what those were?"

I had to chuckle. "Yeah. I know about eight-tracks. Grandpa still had an eight-track player and a bunch of tapes he played."

Moss chuckled, too, and then went serious. "One of the kids got away, but Newhouse shot and killed the other one. Said the kid had a gun, pointed it at him. Wasn't any gun on the scene. Newhouse said the kid that got away picked up the gun and took off with it. It got in the papers, of course. Then the other kid came forward, said there wasn't any gun. Newhouse was in for some bad trouble. Then he got lucky somehow."

"How?"

"Well, it got to the grand jury and, all of a sudden, Newhouse got no-billed, and he was back in Homicide. Always seemed fishy as hell to me. But who am I?"

This was interesting, but it wasn't really getting me anywhere. It was fun listening to Hanley Moss, but so far, I didn't think I'd even started earning Maggie's seven thousand dollars.

To start to wrap it up, I said, "Back to when George Hawk died. Did anything seem strange to you? Or out of place?"

Moss shook his head. "Just that that young fellah would kill himself. But people do that all the time."

I said, "Fifteen or sixteen years later, you ran into Maggie Hawk and then you sent her copies of the reports on George's death."

"Oh, yeah. Sure did. You know, that was one of the luckiest things ever happened to me—running into her at that bar."

"How was that?"

"Well, Ada and I'd had a big argument. She jumped on the bus and went home to her mother's in Dallas. I was mad, and figured the hell with her. She was mad, and figured the hell with me. We was both stubborn as mules, you know. So I went out on the town. This good-looking cocktail waitress started talking to me. That was Maggie Hawk. I thought, well, the hell with Ada, bring on the girl. Then the waitress reminded me of who she was. Reminded me I told her her husband was dead. Hated when I had to do that. Hated it bad. Anyway, Maggie Hawk wanted to know if I knew anything about her husband's death. They always do, you know. I wish people that kill themselves'd think about what they do to people. I told her I didn't remember much, but I'd look into it. Thought maybe she and I'd get together and talk about it, if you know what I mean. Something I'm not proud of, but you know how it is. Well, all of a sudden, I just stopped and looked at myself. Thought about how dumb I'd feel if I got a call from Dallas from some cop telling me Ada was dead. I guess I was a little drunk, but that hit me hard. Real hard. I could of really got going with Maggie. But not after I thought about that. I got out of there and went to the first pay phone I saw away from that bar and called Ada and just about bawled my eyes out. So did she."

He paused and took a big drink of coffee, and a couple of big breaths. "I felt bad about Maggie, though. So I checked around the department and found this paperwork. Sent copies to her. Maybe helped her a little bit." He shook his head. "Probably, it didn't help her. Helped me, though."

Time was wasting. I stood up and set one of my business cards on the table and started gathering up the papers I had brought. "Mr. Moss, thanks a lot for your time. And for the coffee. I enjoyed talking with you."

"I talk too much," he said.

"You can maybe talk some more when you get back from your cruise. Maybe we can go to lunch and you can tell me all about it."

Moss picked up my card. "I imagine that boy's widow's still working things over. They do that. When somebody kills himself."

"I imagine she is."

"That boy should have thought of that before he shot himself."

"He sure should have."

"Wish I knew more. Wish there was more. Kind of late for you to be checking on that Newhouse fellah. Asshole, if I ever saw one. Wish I knew something else."

"Well," I said, "if you do happen to think of anything, give me a call."

EIGHT

Beware of Old Ladies with Birdbaths, Burglar Bars, and Ugly Cats

I'd practiced about as much as I could, and had survived it. Now it was time to go to work for real.

Hilda Guttman. Not a bad name for a cook.

3122 Tangley Road, her address according to Maggie's list, was on one of those Robin Hood-name streets in West University Place, this funny, smug little separate town that sits right in the middle of Houston, but acts as if it's on another planet. It's got twenty-mile-an-hour speed limits. Ordinances against big threats like Sunday garage sales. Trees so old that their tops had grown together over the streets while Harry S Truman was president. It had gotten ultra-trendy lately, for some reason, and its tiny, cramped 1930s houses had current price tags so high they made your teeth hurt. Yuppie heaven.

Normally, I tried to avoid the place. The people of West U. loved old houses, but the cars they were partial to were new and shiny and European; they looked on twenty-year-old Oldsmobiles as if they had just waded across the Rio Grande.

But this morning, I drove in trying to act as if I belonged there, using only enough good sense to park down the street from the Guttman residence. A half-block walk through the dark tunnel the trees made out of the street brought me to 3122.

The house was utterly West University. It looked as if it had stepped right off the cover of an old *Saturday Evening Post*, except for the burglar bars on the windows and totally enclosing the wide front porch, testament to the fact that, no matter how many ordinances they might pass, the occasional drug-crazy wandered in—from evil Houston, of course.

Lying in the sunshine on the second porch step was a huge and apparently extremely self-satisfied cat, that seemed at least half-again as big as Spooky. I guess his design was what you'd call tortoise-shell, but the way the colors ran together, he looked as if he'd picked up a bad case of toadstools.

Luck was with me. I thought. Standing on the lawn in front of the house was a three-thousand-year-old woman using a garden hose to fill a birdbath.

I paused for a moment in front of the house next door, running Maggie's notes about Hilda Guttman through my mind. First, there was one she wrote the night after George died and she couldn't sleep and wrote down whatever came into her mind:

> *Mrs. Guttman is Mr. Woods' cook, and she says she's forty-one, but she looks older than that and acts as if she's about a hundred. Someone said her husband died 3 or 4 years ago and left her with nothing but a pile of bills, so she had to go to work as a cook to support herself, so I guess she's got a right to be bitter. Her specialty is her own secret recipe for homemade peach-and-raspberry ice cream, and Mr. Woods always has her make it when he's entertaining. Sometimes, there's leftovers and she'd give*

some of it to George and me because she was nice to him because he fixed things in the kitchen for her. But she never would give any of it to Bonita and Rhea and Carl. She'd throw it out first. She's one of those people who's nice to somebody only if she has to be or if it's going to do her some good.

Then Maggie mentioned her in the note she wrote after Bonita called to say goodbye:

Bonita sounded so happy about leaving! She tried to raise my spirits by saying that maybe it would turn out George had an insurance policy, too. Then she asked me if I needed any money. That was so nice of her. But I told her I'd get along okay, and I will. Rhea said she'd write to me and send me her address and said she'd miss me. Carl said he'd write, too, and then said, Guess what? Uncle Jason has started acting nice. He even got Mrs. Guttman to make some of her peach-and-raspberry ice cream just for him and Rhea and their mother. But Carl said that, ice cream or no, he was going to be glad to move away from that place.

I took a deep breath of upscale West University air and said to myself, "Okay, be a private eye, Tony," and headed for that birdbath.

Getting closer didn't change my age estimate. According to Maggie's notes, Mrs. Guttman wouldn't be much more than mid-seventies now, but one look at her and you knew that she had to be at least three thousand. She was wearing a granny dress and plastic thongs made in Taiwan. Even though the name was right for a cook, her size wasn't—she looked as if she couldn't have outweighed the thongs by much.

I stopped on the sidewalk in front. "Mrs. Guttman?"

She glanced up, checked the birdbath, decided it was full enough, and creakily bent down to lay the hose on the grass. Then she turned and peered toward me, all wrinkles and false teeth and owl-glasses with lenses about half an inch thick. "Yes. I'm Mrs. Guttman." She peered harder. "Who're you?"

I didn't know what kind of correction the glasses were supposed to do, but they cut the size of her eyes by about two-thirds. As she peered at me, something I heard my grandfather say a few times sprang into my mind: "Mean as a snake." He hadn't said it often, but I knew for certain that he would definitely have said it about Mrs. Guttman. It made for quite a combination: moderate skin-and-bones face, humongous lenses, tiny little black eyes that seemed about the size of a pencil lead. And real honest-to-God meanness. Not exactly someone I'd want to show off at the Grandma-Grandkid Banquet.

This seemed to be the wrong time to start off with, "Okay, lady, I'm a private eye. Where were you between eight and nine p.m. on the night of 8 June 1966?"

Grandpa has always talked about "connections," like when Hanley Moss talked to me because "Aapt" rang a bell with him. Chances were pretty good, though, that Mrs. Guttman had never met Wilbur Aapt—and probably would have hated him, if she had. Well, Grandpa also said that a bad connection was better than no connection at all. So I'd try a bad connection. Maybe it would work. People's memories tend to fade over the years. And the meaner someone is, the more he—or she, in this case—likes it when someone else remembers only the good.

"You probably don't remember me, Mrs. Guttman. But I sure remember that peach-and-raspberry ice cream of yours."

She really peered now. I knew it wasn't happening, but it seemed that her eyes got even smaller behind those deep lenses, because she was checking me out so hard. "My peach-and-raspberry? How would you know about my peach-and-raspberry?"

I walked over and leaned on the edge of the birdbath and smiled big. "Summer Sundays out on the verandah. And that nice homemade ice cream of yours. Mmmm!"

She gave me a pretty good idea of how an amoeba feels under a microscope. "You're talking about Mr. Woods' place." She shook her head mournfully. "That was such a long time ago. Just who in the world would you be to be reminding me of that?"

I shook my head, too, doing it more slowly, giving it the old-home-week move. "Carl Woods, Mrs. Guttman. Jason Woods' nephew."

"Little Carl?" she said. "Rhea's little brother? My goodness! Why, you've certainly grown up, haven't you?" She stood back and marveled. "Carl Woods. After all these years."

"Well, now, it hasn't been all that long, has it? Seems like yesterday to me."

"Just excuse me a minute," Mrs. Guttman said. "I'm wasting water." Scuttering her thongs through the grass to the edge of the porch, she reached through a bank of ferns and twisted off the spigot.

The birdbath was new, I saw. And it was incomplete, being so far just a big concrete bowl supported by a steel post sunk into concrete poured into a hole in the ground.

While I was checking it out, I realized the cat was watching me. Not just watching—*glaring*—with his tail jerking in the air. I had the definite feeling that he was telling me to move my ass—the birdbath was his private territory.

"What in the world brings you by to see me?" Mrs. Guttman asked as she backed out of the ferns.

"I'm visiting from Chicago, and I was close to West University and I remembered someone telling me you lived over here. I remembered Tangley Road, and that you lived in the thirty-one hundred block, and here you are, right out here in the yard."

"Isn't that nice? Isn't that such a coincidence? My goodness, you know I haven't made any of that peach-and-raspberry ice cream for longer than I can remember."

"That wonderful ice cream," I said. And decided to try a little self-pity, constructing it wholly out of Maggie's notes. "You know we weren't very happy living at Uncle Jason's. But that nice ice cream of yours made up for a lot."

Mrs. Guttman comforted me. "Well, now, everybody has some bad times. But your mother took you and your sister to Chicago and made her own way. It was quiet when you left, though."

"It was nice getting away," I said. "I didn't miss Uncle Jason much, but I missed some of the people at his house."

"Oh, that's been . . . how long? Thirty years ago, at least, hasn't it?"

"Thirty-three. 1966 was when we moved. In June."

"Thirty-three years!" Mrs. Guttman said in astonishment. Then she moved up close to the birdbath, giving it all her attention.

The cat, I noticed, had relaxed again. I had the distinct suspicion that Mrs. Guttman was having the birdbath installed for him, rather than in an effort to keep the birds of West University clean and, that as long as she was staying close to me, he wouldn't worry about my trying to snatch any of his goodies.

Mrs. Guttman said, "Such luck, you coming along just now."

I was confused.

She put as close to a sweet helpless old lady smile on her mean face as she could manage. "You grew up to be such a nice, strong man, Carl. So you can do me a favor while we chat."

I was still confused.

"They didn't get my new birdbath all finished, and I never know whether that old man that cuts my lawn and does odd jobs is going to show up or not." She pointed toward the side of the porch next to the driveway, where there was a pile of concrete shapes.

That cleared it up. I was going to do physical labor.

"You wouldn't mind helping me out, would you?" she asked.

Of course, I wouldn't.

I went over and squatted down and looked things over. The long pieces with a concavity running down the insides must fit against the steel post. The pie-shaped pieces would be sections of the base. I picked up one of the long pieces. It was heavy as hell.

I lugged it over and coaxed it into place against the steel post. It fit nicely.

Mrs. Guttman beamed crinkle-faced at me.

I went back for another section and said, "Funny, coming back to Houston after all this time and remembering things. And people, of course. Whatever happened to Uncle Jason's housekeeper? Aurora, I think her name was."

Obviously, the housekeeper had not been one of Mrs. Guttman's favorites. She sniffed. "Oh, that one. She stayed on at the River Oaks place. I heard she retired about ten or eleven years ago. Then I heard she died. She was one of the reasons I was glad to leave the house and go to work running the executives' dining room in Mr. Woods' nice big building."

She looked brightly at me while I fitted the second pedestal piece into place. "You knew I retired, didn't you? Eight years ago." Almost whispering, she added, "And you know, ever since I did, I don't think I've cooked anything at all that I can't take out of a box and stick in the microwave. Right now, though, you almost make me itch to get busy and make some of that nice ice cream."

"Mmmm! That was wonderful stuff, Mrs. Guttman," I said, getting the third and last section of the pedestal assembly niched into place.

Then I went over and heaved up one of the pie-shaped pieces. Heavy as hell! Covered all over with ivy leaves in relief.

The cat watched me. He definitely approved of what I was doing. This nice wide base I was fixing up would give him much better footing than plain old grass. He was getting so self-satisfied that I practically had to spit feathers out of my mouth.

I stood up, and Mrs. Guttman said, "Now you take off that jacket and let me hold it for you, Carl. I don't know what I was thinking about to let you get all perspired."

Gratefully, I took off my jacket and handed it to her and went for some more concrete, saying, "Somebody else that worked at Uncle Jason's—the maid."

Another sniff. "Maid? They had maids in and out of the place."

Two chunks of birdbath base remained. "This maid's husband worked there, too. He was the gardener."

"Oh," Mrs. Guttman said, her wrinkles compressing into

a disapproval that far transcended sniffing. "You mean those Hawk people."

"Hawk?"

"Last name. Hawk. Molly, was it?"

"Molly? No. That's not quite it. Maisie? No. Oh, I remember now. It was Maggie," I said, grunting a little as I chivvied the new concrete section into place. "That was her name—Maggic. And George was her husband's name. He was always in Uncle Jason's garage, trying to invent things. You remember, don't you, Mrs. Guttman? He died just before Mom and Rhea and I went off to Chicago."

Coldly, she said, "Oh, that. Of course, I remember that." More coldly yet, her wizened face twisting into a sneer, she said, "He didn't die. He killed himself. You don't forget stupid, cowardly things like that."

I stood up and looked over my work, using the pause to remind myself that it was considered bad stuff to backhand nasty old ladies, even for speaking so contemptuously of someone's dying. "Right," I said, finally. "He did kill himself, didn't he?"

Getting the hell away from her, I went to pick up another section of birdbath base.

She wasn't finished. When I brought the piece back and knelt down to ease it into place, she said, "Killed himself in his car with a gun, like the coward he was."

The piece fit nicely. I thought about it, not about the old woman's malice. The birdbath didn't look too bad. I hoped she wouldn't suddenly remember that she wanted a swimming pool dug.

Trying not to sound too challenging, I said, "I liked George. He was nice to Rhea and me when most people weren't. And he was always talking about inventing things. I was only a six-year-old kid, but I thought he'd invent something really great. He was always tinkering around in Uncle Jason's garage."

"He was just one of those dreamers," Mrs. Guttman said, twisting her face into twice as many wrinkles. "A visionary. Just a visionary. A big talker. I don't remember any tinkering. Just loafing. What could he invent? He couldn't even keep himself alive."

I stood up and went for the last section of base. "He did more than just dream, didn't he?" I said over my shoulder. "Seems to me that I remember he was working on something. A lawnmower, wasn't it? I'm sure I remember him inventing something on a lawnmower."

"That man didn't invent anything. All he was good for was to shoot himself."

I set the last piece into place, using as many muscles as I could on the job, to keep them from doing something they—and I—would regret. It fit perfectly.

Then I looked up into that mean old lady's sweet smile. Hugging my jacket to herself, she caroled, "I can't tell you how nice you were to help me with my birdbath, Carl." She glanced toward the house. "The least I can do is invite you in to have some iced tea."

I got my teeth unclenched and said, "That sounds great to me."

Mrs. Guttman started toward the porch steps.

I moved to step ahead to pull the wrought-iron gate farther open for her.

She waved me off. "Oh, don't fuss, Carl. I've been making it up onto this porch and getting in and out of this gate for more than thirty years now without any help."

I stood aside and let her go up the steps. She draped my jacket over one arm and, with the other hand, pulled the gate all the way open and stepped onto the porch.

I started to follow.

She slammed the gate in my face. Its heavy lock engaged with a vibrating clang. So much for connections!

Glaring those tiny eyes at me through the bars, she spat, "Carl Woods? You're no Carl Woods! What do you take me for, anyway? Carl Woods and that sister of his and that leech no-good mother of his that wasn't any better than to try to live on her brother-in-law, all had black hair—she was a Mexican. How stupid do you think I am? You thought I was just a stupid old woman and you'd sweet-talk me into saying bad things about Mr. Woods, didn't you? That's what you're really after. Well, you think some more."

I stared at her. What else is there to do when you've gotten terminally blindsided? Not a damned thing.

She started digging inside my jacket. "Let's see who you really are." She pulled out my wallet. Fingered out my driver's license. Holding it about two inches away from her glasses, she cackled shrilly and then announced, "You're somebody named Anthony Aapt! I knew you weren't little Carl Woods."

She threw the license through the bars and rummaged deeper into my wallet.

I watched helplessly. It was moments like this that really made me love the private eye business.

"What's this?" Mrs. Guttman said.

It was my P.I. ID card, of course.

That gave her a goose. "A private detective! I knew you were something like that."

"Now, Mrs. Guttman . . ."

"Hmph!" she said, hurling my wallet through the bars, following it with my ID card and, like falling leaves, other cards and the junk you accumulate in your wallet. "That's what I think of private detectives." After I had picked up the debris and stuffed it back into my wallet, she peered at me some more. "Who sent you over here to spy on me?"

"Can't tell you that, Mrs. Guttman."

"Well, you just tell 'em it didn't work. You just tell 'em, if they want to nose around about Mr. Jason Woods, they better nose around somewhere else."

"What makes you think I'm interested in Jason Woods? Is there some reason I should be?"

Her face screwed up with wrinkled anger. Fumbling her hands around, she stuffed my jacket through the bars. "You get off my property. You better not let me catch you around here again. I ever see you nosin' around here again, I'll call the police on you."

I picked up my jacket and picked up as much pride as I could, and got the hell away from there.

Before I was off her walk, I heard her front door slam shut.

Looking around, I saw that ugly cat of hers sauntering out onto the lawn to check out his big new concrete feeding dish.

"I hope you have better hunting than I did," I told him.

It was a lie.

NINE

Looking for Elvis Presley

Among my grandfather's many interesting qualities was his ability—if you wanted to call it an ability and not just a bad habit—to quote or manufacture a saying for any conceivable occasion. Right about now, he'd be telling me, "Okay, boy, if you get knocked on your ass, you've got to get right up and climb back on."

Pithy platitudes. Enough to make you sick. What I really wanted to do right then was to check out on Maggie Hawk and pick up the want-ads and start looking for a new career.

But if I did that, Grandpa could say, "Don't start something you can't finish." Also, I'd be even broker than I was yesterday.

I gave up and got back on.

And drove over to Rice University.

The Harvard of the South.

Not named for a small grain plant with wet roots, but for a turn-of-the-century Houstonian who got himself killed in mysterious and bizarre circumstances and left his money to higher education to frustrate the plotters.

I found Dr. Potter's name in the University directory, listed as "Potter, Melvin Ph.D., Professor Emeritus, 621 JWAB."

The JWAB was short for The Jason Woods Administration Building. And that was short for the official full name: The Jason Woods Administration Building of the George R. Brown School of Engineering. Typically Texan. We tend to marry women with one- or two-syllable names, but we don't scrimp when it comes to hanging titles on our important edifices.

The JWAB was a nice building. About what you'd expect at a major down-home Texas college—you could set it next door to the Trump Taj Mahal and it would look right at home.

That was nothing, though. Just inside the entrance, there was a glass case holding an architect's model of the soon-to-be-built Jason Woods Mechanical Engineering Classroom Building. It would make the Trump Taj Mahal look like . . . well . . . like just the Taj Mahal.

Dr. Potter's office was on the sixth floor. It was small, but it had nice corner windows. There was room for a wooden visitor's chair and a beat-up old wooden desk that looked as if it had been handed down from Abraham Lincoln's first job. The long interior wall, except for the doorway, was all bookshelves from floor to ceiling. The other was covered with framed degrees and honors and photographs of buildings and people. Dr. Potter had been around for quite a while, so a lot of the photographs were black-and-white. Through the windows, there was a wonderful southwestern view: green treetops stretching for miles, broken only by the tall buildings of the Medical Center on the left and, on the right, bulging up like an immense high-tech breast, the Astrodome.

When I entered the office, an old man was struggling to replace a thick book in the bookshelves; for a moment, I thought I must have walked in on the cleaning man. He was tiny, with white, wispy hair. His skin had that pink delicacy that exists only on babies and the very old. He wore the first seersucker suit I had even seen except in reruns of those old Tennessee Williams movies about the decadent South.

"Dr. Potter?" I said. I stepped to him and rescued the book from his fragile hands and shoved it into its place, pausing only to realize that it was even heavier than it looked and had a title that was about a paragraph long in German.

He stood back and looked at me through eyeglasses which could only be called spectacles—silver-rimmed, the kind people wore before designer plastic came along. "Yes," he said. "I'm Dr. Potter."

"I wonder if I could talk with you for a few minutes?"

He thought that over, sparing a moment to peer into the shelf and reassure himself that the book was all right. Then he reached up and patted it just enough to get it perfectly straight. Looking back at me, some kind of discomfort showed suddenly on his face.

That bothered me. Until he moved away and his discomfort eased. Then I decided that he wasn't afraid of me; he was simply aware that he was old. I don't exactly awe the average fullback, but I was young and therefore capable of rambunctiousness, and he was frail and old.

"Are you a student?" he asked, moving around the side of the desk toward his chair. He showed more wariness as he went, looking out for the sharp, hard corners of the desk, feeling of the chair as he approached it, gathering himself against the shock that would come as he sat in it and its springs adjusted to his slight weight.

It scared me for a moment. I barged through buildings and offices and life. So once had Dr. Potter. But now, everywhere he went, everything—and virtually everyone—he encountered was harder and stronger than he was.

I took a deep breath and reminded myself that that kind of thing was at least forever far away from me, and said, "No, sir. I'm not a student."

He waited.

I had already decided I wasn't going to get cute and risk another blow-up like the one with Hilda Guttman, and I pulled out my wallet and reached across the desk to show my ID card.

When you do that, you can always tell the people who don't watch much TV. The TV watchers take one look at your P.I. card and yawn or make a joke. Dr. Potter took it seriously. "Private Investigations? Why in the world would a private investigator want to talk with me, Mr. . . . Aapt?"

"It has to do with someone I've been told was a student of yours some time ago. A young man named George Hawk."

Dr. Potter reacted to the name with deep and sudden pain and, for a moment, I was afraid that I had harmed him. Then he turned his faded blue eyes toward me. "George Hawk? Why in the world would you want to talk about George? That's been so long ago."

"He was your student, I believe."

"Oh, yes. George was my student," Dr. Potter said. He smiled sadly and showed, not the dentures I had expected, but probably the most beautiful mouth of teeth I had ever seen. "George was the student a teacher hopes he'll encounter at least once in his career. He died so long ago. More than thirty years ago, I believe. Yes. More than thirty years ago." Moving his old hands around the desk top, he nudged a pad of notepaper into place and then pushed a couple of pencils into exact alignment with the edge of the leather desk pad.

The word "prissy" leaping into my mind, I said, "I realize that it's been a long time, Dr. Potter. But I'd appreciate it if you told me about George Hawk."

For long, sad, old-man's moments, he stared through the windows at the hot, blue summer sky. Finally, he said, "Of course. I'll be glad to help you in any way I can."

This certainly beat Hilda Guttman's attitude, I thought, trying to settle into the visitor's chair, which somehow managed to be even more uncomfortable than it looked. "You said, 'The student a teacher hopes he'll encounter at least once,' Dr. Potter. Would you explain that?"

His face seeming suddenly to be at least another hundred years older, he turned toward that wall of framed photographs. "George was such a fine young man. Dedicated. Hard-working. Brilliant in so many ways. He would have had such a wonderful career, had he lived."

Looking away from the photographs, he suddenly began to study me. "Did you go to school, Mr. Aapt?"

I wasn't quite ready for the jump-shift. "Uh, school, yes. I went to Texas A&M."

On his scale, that was obviously somewhere between nowhere and questionable. "I see. What discipline?"

I had never felt so completely frivolous. Sitting there surrounded by books in German on bridges and books in French about tunnels and in some kind of Scandinavian about calculus, I felt even more frivolous than that when I admitted, "Communications."

"Ah," he said, obviously finding it even more frivolous than I did, but doing his best to hide it. "Communications." Sparing a moment for silent regret that we weren't going to be able to enjoy a nice chat about tensors and cosines, he said, "Coming from such a radically different . . . discipline, I'm not certain that you'll be able to understand when I say that George had an innate understanding of engineering. He thought in an engineering way, in terms of balance and force and tension. It's something we can teach only to a slight degree. It's such a great joy when we find it already present in a student."

I said, "Then you expected great things from him. New designs. New structures. That sort of thing."

Dr. Potter waved a pale, blue-veined hand at me. "Oh, no, no, no. Nothing like that. George wasn't tied to the practical. There are a thousand practical men for every one like George. No. He was that great rarity—a theoretician. He wasn't tied to detail or purpose. His mind worked at the theoretical level—he was a visionary, you might say. His worth was in his vision. He would have been such a fine, fine theoretician, had he lived."

Once more, Dr. Potter turned toward the wall of photographs, and I paid more attention now. The larger photographs were of campus buildings, including one of this god-awful administration building when it was under construction, before most of the trendy and wholly garish decorations had been tacked on. The smaller photographs were mostly of people, apparently his memorable students.

One of them, black-and-white, was a photograph of George Hawk—that same yearbook-style photograph that had been in Maggie's file folder.

Turning back to me, Dr. Potter flashed those teeth. They were perfect. Every time he smiled, I wanted to ask him for his dentist's name. He said, "George was competent with the math and the basics. But application was his short suit."

He peered at me for a moment, trying to estimate at what elementary level he might be able to communicate with a communications major. "I suppose what I'm trying to say is that George could, for example, see the need for a bridge in a certain spot, and even know intuitively what sort of structure it would need to be, but for the actual design, one would have to turn to someone more practical."

That was elementary enough to get through to me, all right. And it stabbed right into the heart of Maggie's contention that George had been murdered so that his practical and marvelous invention could be stolen. In other words, George's mentor was telling me there was no way George Hawk could have invented the lawnmower blade that saved the world.

I said, "Then you wouldn't have considered George to be inventive at all?"

Showing me some more of those teeth, Dr. Potter made an old man's small dry breathless laugh. "Oh, no. I'm afraid not. George's brilliance was far removed from such practical things. He was no inventor."

In the face of such sincerity, I was starting to feel like a total fool.

This whole thing was patently foolish, anyway.

What I was involved in was another Spindletop Heirs fantasy. Next thing, I'd be running around telling people that my grandfather had actually been the Lindbergh Baby, or that the old lady who did filing and telephone-answering out at Hull Airport back in the days when I could afford flying lessons was really Amelia Earhart. And the fat old guy who hummed under his breath while he stocked canned peas at Kroger was Judge Crater.

I wanted to take my communications degree and get the hell out of there. Instead, I said, "Well, Dr. Potter, did you know George Hawk's wife?"

The reaction once again was pain, but not nearly so deep

this time, and much mixed with consternation. “His wife? Oh, yes. I knew his wife.”

I waited.

He waited, too.

Finally, I tried some more. In a different direction. “Was Jason Woods also a student of yours?”

The abrupt shift surprised him. But he liked it. “Jason Woods? Oh, yes. Some years earlier than George, of course.” Settling back comfortably, he flashed those blindingly white and perfect teeth at me. “Jason was the opposite of George. George was a visionary, as I told you. But Jason was all practicality. The word, ‘inventive,’ arose a few moments ago. Jason Woods was truly inventive. As he has so well demonstrated. You are familiar with his remarkable lawnmower blade innovation, are you not? It’s been in use for some years now, and is very much taken for granted these days. But it was a marvelous innovation for its time, and is still very much in use.” He allowed his eyes to twinkle. “I’d wager you’ve mowed a lawn or two in the not too distant past. You probably never thought about it, but Jason’s GRASSBUSTER blade made it much safer for you than it used to be.”

“Yes. I know about the GRASSBUSTER.”

“A marvelous innovation. By a marvelous man. One who’s never stinted in his support of The University [Dr. Potter’s caps, not mine]. Even years ago, before he invented his lawnmower blade, when Jason was going through some very difficult financial times, he did what he could for The University by providing work for some of our students. George worked for him, you may know, while he attended Rice.”

I nodded.

“Mr. Woods is such a splendid man. Very practical.

Down-to-earth. Public-spirited and giving."

"Back to George Hawk's wife," I said. "From your reaction a little while ago, I'd have to assume that you didn't approve of her."

Dr. Potter sighed and then decided to bare his soul to me. "George's wife," he said, as if repeating a title. "She was a distraction when George needed no more distractions. It was not a good match. I was always certain that she married him solely to escape a life of poverty." He made a lost, sad smile. "You know how it is. Some women marry doctors to better themselves. Others marry engineers."

"You think she married George just because he was going to be successful?"

No smile now, sad, lost, or otherwise. "I know that's why she did it. I was always certain of it. She confirmed it before George was cold in his grave. Telephoning me. Making the absurd claim that George had some marvelous invention that would be worth great amounts of money—as if George had been the inventive sort. Coming near to accusing me of hiding his drawings of this invention from her."

For long moments, Dr. Potter was lost in a silent reliving of the awfulness that Maggie had done him.

I waited.

Finally, he recovered himself and continued. "I knew later what it was, of course. She was in close proximity to Jason Woods—she worked for him as a maid, you know, while George worked as a gardener—time he should have been able to spend on his studies, if there were justice in the world. From her proximity, she must have known that Jason was working on his GRASSBUSTER invention. I've always suspected that she was attempting to involve George in a plot to steal it—something he was entirely too honest and honorable even to consider. I've always had the awful suspicion that it could have been that—her avarice—that drove George to take his life." Mournfully, tiredly, Dr. Potter shook his head. "George would have died before allowing himself to become involved in something so reprehensible. It was a terrible, terrible thing. Such a brilliant mind to waste."

I sat up straight, about to take my leave. I had heard more than I wanted to hear. It was time to go.

But then, Dr. Potter began talking about his history at Rice, and Rice's history, and I didn't want to leave.

He started by telling me that the whole engineering school at Rice was about six hundred square feet and a couple of used slide rules when he came in as a freshman back in 1936. And how it had grown and prospered since then, until now it was one of the great engineering schools in the world.

Boring stuff.

Really boring stuff.

But told by Dr. Potter with so much passion and love that I wanted him to go on all day. This prissy old engineering professor could certainly have taught three or four of my communications professors a thing or two.

He must be terribly lonely, I realized, hanging about the university with no classes in which to involve himself, and little to do but sit in this office and browse through old books. It would certainly cost me nothing to sit here with him for a half hour.

After a while, he rambled off history and into theory. I didn't understand half of what he was saying, but he spoke with such passion and eloquence that it was fascinating just to sit and listen.

He spoke of shapes and stresses. He spoke of the integrity of form and function.

As his voice went on, I got into it almost as if it were music. For a while, I watched his old face which was now animated by a marvelously youthful glow. Then I moved on to look out over the mass of green treetops that flowed to the rounded top of the Astrodome, shimmering silver in the hot late morning sun.

After a little, I began to study that wall of photographs. One black-and-white photo was of a partially completed bridge. Another showed a group of thirty or so black-gowned and mortar-boarded young men standing stiffly in front of a wooden building—graduation day at the upstart college in the '30s.

I moved on to that photograph of George Hawk, fastening onto it across the distance of eight or nine feet and thirty-three years, trying to trick my eyes into telling me if he was really a visionary or a practical man, a victim, or an idealistic young man driven to take his own life by the greed of his wife.

Dr. Potter was speaking of the integrity and beauty and correctness of shape; of the relationships of structure to structure and form to form.

Almost, I thought I understood. Almost, concept was coming to me. With a moment of near dizziness, I glanced over that wall of framed photographs, close to really understanding—and *feeling!*—the scheme of their arrangement . . .

Suddenly though, I was staring because a true and absolute understanding had come to me. But not the one, I think, about which Dr. Potter had been speaking.

There was George Hawk's old black-and-white 1960s nerd farm boy yearbook photograph.

And just below it—positioned *exactly* below it—although all of the other photographs on the wall were offset from each other, as if someone with a mind full of precision and a deep understanding of the relationships of structure to structure and form to form had carefully calculated the perfect random positions for them—was another photograph of the same size, framed identically.

It was black-and-white, also. George would be fifty-five years old now. The man shown in his youth in the photograph positioned exactly below George's was now sixty-four.

I had noted the evolution of that man's appearance in the five-years-or-so interval newspaper photographs in Maggie's collection of clippings. Now, I saw the youth who had preceded those.

Jason Woods.

Jason Woods' photograph in a carefully *un-random* position exactly below George Hawk's on a wall where everything else was studiedly random.

In the last few moments, Dr. Potter had veered toward talking about the upheavals at Rice during the Vietnam War. Just a little while ago, what he was saying was unendingly fascinating. Now, I wondered if this, too, was a lie.

Perhaps the only thing about this entire building that wasn't a lie was the way Dr. Potter had arranged his photographic mementos on his office wall.

Looking suddenly at my watch, I bolted out of my chair. "Dr. Potter, I'm sorry," I said, and used the first excuse that popped into my mind, prompted no doubt by his perfect white teeth: "I'm late for a dentist's appointment. You were telling such interesting things that I almost forgot about it."

He gave me a perfect smile of forgiveness.

And I got the hell out of there.

Going down in the elevator that Jason Woods had bought for the university with money he had made from

George Hawk's stolen lawnmower blade, I found myself shivering and sweating at the same time.

I didn't want anything much but to get out of this place.

But when I got to the lobby and stepped out of the elevator, I had to stop and stare.

I would have sworn that the heavyset old man with a beard, who stood near the entrance admiring the architectural model of the new classroom building, was Ambrose Bierce.

TEN

Among Maggie's Souvenirs . . .

Libraries are wonderful places.

Books. Silence. A gentle mustiness, even in this day of industrial-strength air-conditioning.

If it happens to be a college library, like the Fondren Library at Rice University, there's a collection of old yearbooks.

When I walked into the library, passing under a gallery of portraits of various Rice benefactors, including, of course, a smiling Jason Woods, a pudgy little middle-aged man sitting behind the front desk started to give me eyebrow. But I waved at him and tried to look like an engineer and went on past. He looked a little stuffy, but didn't stop me.

In a corner of the second floor, I found the yearbooks. Including the Rice *Campanile*, vintage 1966, which would have covered George Hawk's junior—and last—year.

In the Junior Class section, George Hawk's photograph was there with the others.

It was the same photograph I had found in Maggie's file folder; the same one that hung on Dr. Potter's wall: the farm boy nerd.

But I wasn't too much interested in the class photos. I wanted to check out the activities.

Except for the geeky 1960s clothing and a profound absence of quasi-military uniforms, the activities photographs in the Rice yearbook were practically like the ones in my Texas Aggie yearbook: stiff, formal organization membership shots, and stupid, silly party shots.

I looked through them all with no luck—there wasn't a shot of George Hawk anywhere except in the rogue's gallery of the junior class. He didn't appear in any of the activities photos, or in the silly party-shot section.

I turned over to Faculty and found Dr. Potter easily enough. Without the name under his photograph, though, I'm not sure that I would have recognized him, even though he seemed to be wearing the same suit he had on today.

There's a point somewhere in their late seventies, usually, I think, when people stop looking like themselves and start looking just generically elderly.

Grandpa had made me aware of that. He had been very much aware of it, himself. On a day when he was in an especially good mood, he'd likely as not explain it as being because, when he looked in the mirror as he shaved that morning, he had still recognized himself.

In this faculty photograph, Dr. Potter would have been in his late forties, and still looking like himself—stern, unsmiling, somewhat prissy, marginally less delicate-appearing.

Interesting in a historical sense, I supposed. But not very useful to me. So I replaced this yearbook in the shelf and pulled out the one for 1965 when George would have been a sophomore.

Same results. The only place George appeared was in the sophomore lineup, looking slightly younger, but just as nerdish, and wearing the same suit.

I went back to 1964.

And had more luck.

Lots of luck, as a matter-of-fact.

In his freshman year, before marriage, before having to go to work part-time, George must have had more free time, and he appeared in the membership shots of a couple of clubs. The first one I found was the Boolean Algebra Club, obviously either very exclusive or not a hot item, since there were only six people in the photograph, along with the note, "Not pictured: Harmon Lewis Jones." I wrote down the names of the members.

George was also pictured with the members of the Slide Rule Club. There were forty-odd members of this one. I wondered idly if they called it the Electronic Calculator Club now, but didn't drag out the current yearbook to check.

Forty-odd was a lot of names. But the uneven rows in the photograph suggested that the members hadn't been posed according to height, and the names weren't in alphabetical order, so I made a guess that George would have been standing with a buddy or two, and wrote down the names of the five guys closest to him.

That was all the organized activities I could find for George so I went to the party-shots.

On the first page—Bingo!

But not Bingo! for George.

In a snapshot taken at some college Halloween party, I found Maggie.

She practically leaped out of the photograph at me. I realize there's no way you can see the sparkle in somebody's eye in a thirty-five-year-old black-and-white snapshot, but I'd swear that was what hit me: the absolutely great look in her eyes. Just like the look that had been there when she told me how great it had been to win that sweepstakes.

She was very pretty. Prettier than that. And slender and smiling and sexy. Even though her hair was ratted all to hell and she was wearing bobby sox and a long, full, Terry Moore skirt, she was sexy.

She was also with a guy.

That was some more surprise: he wasn't George. According to the caption, he was somebody named Larry Milburn—"Larry Milburn & Best Gal Maggie Rand—looking for ghosts?" was the cute caption.

He was nice-looking. Probably handsome. He was the guy you'd cast, if it was 1963 all over again, and you were making a movie about a heroic Midwestern college quarterback, and you figured out that Tom Cruise was only one year old.

Larry Milburn?

Wait a minute!

That was ringing some kind of bell.

I pulled out the notes I had made about the Slide Rule Club and checked them over. Yeah. Here it was: Lawrence Roth Milburn. I had written down his name because he was standing next to George, on his left.

Very interesting.

I underlined the name in my notes.

And turned the page.

Bingo! again.

On this page, there was another snapshot from that Halloween party. This one included George. Looking momentarily too cracked-up laughing to be his characteristically nerdy self, he was pictured ducking "his (erstwhile) buddy, Larry Milburn," in a tub full of apples and water. In the background stood Maggie, smiling and happy.

Going back to my notes, I underlined Lawrence Roth Milburn again.

I found nothing interesting on the next page of the yearbook.

Or the rest.

So I turned back to that first page of party-shots.

I stared at Maggie's smiling face in that photograph for about ten minutes.

Then I performed one of the really shameful acts of my life—I tore out the page and folded it and stuck it in my inside jacket pocket.

Talk about guilt!

But I consoled myself with thinking that good old Jason Woods could always use some of his stolen money and replace the yearbook.

Looking over my shoulder to make sure that the cops—and my mom—weren't already after me for book-mutilation, I leafed back and checked to see how the faculty had been doing in 1963.

And discovered something more than marginally intriguing.

Here was Dr. Potter. He was wearing that same seersucker suit. It wasn't his clothing that made me stare, though—it was his mouth.

The photographer had obviously caught him off guard and snapped the camera when he was grinning, because he had that thin-lipped, ill-at-ease expression that people get when they don't want to smile and you chivvy them into it. He was grinning. And his grin showed teeth that were crooked and misshapen—a good reason for keeping the mouth closed. Teeth that were nothing like the marvels I had stared at just twenty minutes ago.

I told myself that lots of people had gone to the dentist since 1963.

But I pulled over my notebook and wrote, "Dr. P—Teeth?"

Then I closed the yearbook and shoved it back onto its shelf.

Libraries also have telephone directories.

And there, it looked as if my luck was running out.

The Houston book had a listing for Thomas A. Hitchings, one of the guys in the Boolean Algebra Club, but no listing at all for any of the people who had been standing close to George in the Slide Rule Club photograph, including primarily, no listing for Lawrence Roth Milburn.

Well, as Grandpa would have said, "Life is rough, but you work with what you have." I passed the pudgy little man at the front desk again, waving goodbye to him, and went to the pay telephone near the entrance.

More bad luck.

I called the Hitchings telephone number. A woman answered. Yes, she was Mrs. Hitchings. No, Mr. Hitchings wasn't available. He had passed on in 1982. No, she had never heard him mention anyone named George Hawk. Or Lawrence Milburn.

I apologized for bothering her. And looked up at Jason Woods' portrait.

Its smile had turned into a smirk, and it was all for my benefit.

Damn!

Pudgy, at the desk was looking at me. Maybe real engineers didn't stand around staring at the benefactors' portraits. I gave him another friendly wave and he looked quickly away and got busy neating-up his desk and straightening his nameplate, looking at it intently for a moment as if to remind himself that he was the "Harry M. Langston" it proclaimed him to be.

I went over to the water fountain and got a drink.

Damn! Who the hell was Lawrence Milburn, and where the hell was he?

Suddenly, I had a brilliant thought and went back to the pay telephone and pulled up the directory and checked in it. Then I stuck in a quarter and dialed.

A sweet young girl's voice answered with, "Good morning, Rice University Alumni Association."

I said, "This is Harry Langston, at Fondren Library. We need some information, please."

"Oh, certainly, Mr. Langston."

"Would you look in your files for the current address of a former student—Milburn, Lawrence Roth? Class of 1967."

"Milburn, with an I?"

Trying to sound as stuffy as Pudgy looked, I spelled the whole thing for her.

"Just a moment," she said.

I looked up at Jason Woods and gave him back a smirk of my own. Then I happened to glance over toward the water fountain.

And about fell over.

The overweight, aging fellow pausing for a drink was undoubtedly, irreproachably, absolutely Elvis Presley!

In my ear, the helpful young lady was saying, "Mr. Langston? Mr. Langston? Are you there?"

"Of course I am," I said, even though, at that moment, I wasn't entirely positive.

ELEVEN

This Was Not My Grandfather's Oldsmobile

I headed southwest.

It was hot as hell, but I went with air-conditioning off and windows down because Hizzie was already sucking gas enough. She was going great, though, allowing for the fact that her long-ago-used-up shock absorbers and Houston's pitiful streets made her lurch along like a drunken bathtub.

Good old Hizzie.

We had a history, Hizzie and I.

She was Grandpa's car that he bought after one of the Mideast Oil Crises when the American public was thumbing its nose at high gasoline prices by snapping up major gas hogs that hogged even more gasoline than their size and weight required because of their socially responsible pollution control devices—use twice the gas to cut emissions by one-third? Uh-huh.

Anyway, she was a gorgeous boat when she was new, and Grandpa used to love enraging my dad by sneaking me out for under-age driving lessons in her.

As impressive as she was new, though, she aged rapidly and gracelessly—her paint turned to powder, her imitation chrome peeled and flaked, her vinyl top went fungoid—and Grandpa soon moved on to new and shinier wheels.

But he kept Hizzie because of her practically nonexistent

trade-in value, and used her for fishing trips and for surveillance work in the seamier neighborhoods.

I started driving her shortly after he died. At about the time I finished scaling practically everything down to nothing and took a breath and reminded myself that things could have been worse, they got that way—the leasing company lost confidence and picked up my nearly new Lexus company car.

In Houston, you can't operate at all without a car of some kind. And the only car available to me was unhandsome but faithful Hizzie.

She didn't thrill me nearly as much as she had when I was fifteen and cruising around, hoping the girls would see me, but that Dad and the cops wouldn't, but she certainly came in handy. And she was, after all, about the sum total of my material inheritance from Grandpa.

Over a period of time, I got more or less accustomed to her and, in a perverse way, almost liked her, in spite of all of her obvious faults. She never saw a gas station she didn't like. Her upholstery was infected with terminal psoriasis. She rattled. She wheezed. She jounced. The only way you could get the passenger window to close from the driver's seat was to jam your thumb on the button as hard as you could and say, "Shit!" three times. But she got me there and back. Most of the time, anyway. And as Grandpa would have been sure to say, "Well, the only game in town is the best game in town, whether it is or not."

Today, she gulped gas happily, and we went south on Buffalo Speedway and pretty soon, jogged over to another improbably named street: Stella Link. Why was it called Buffalo Speedway? I don't know. And why Stella Link? Was it the link between something-or-other and Stella-something? Or was it named for some lady named Stella

Link? Who knows that, either?

Mostly, I just knew that I'd been here before.

It had turned out that Larry Milburn was practically a next-door neighbor of my old girlfriend, Polly, better known to connoisseurs of locally made TV commercials as Miss Houston Waterbeds.

The young lady at the Alumni Association had been very helpful. And she talked as she went.

"Lawrence Roth Milburn," she had said. "Yes. Here's his folder. Oh, my goodness. This is too bad."

I stood at the pay telephone and gritted my teeth, gearing up to get the bad news that George's old buddy had gone to join Thomas Hitchings in some Rice graduates' version of heaven. Up on the wall, Jason Woods' portrait was starting to smirk again.

In a mournful voice, the young lady at the Alumni Association said, "We have a change-of-address notice from Mr. Milburn that says he started a new job in Kuwait in 1990. Ooh. That wasn't a very good time to go to work in Kuwait, was it?"

"No," I said, about three seconds from thanking her and hanging up.

Then she said, "Wait!"

"What?"

"Wait just a second. Yes. Here's another notice from him. Yes. Oh, good. Wasn't he lucky? When Iraq invaded Kuwait, Mr. Milburn was in Egypt. Wasn't that lucky, Mr. Langston?"

"Of course. Yes. That's very wonderful. So, where is he at present?"

"Well, here's another change-of-address card. From just last year. It says he got a job in Nigeria, to work on their oil fields."

"Nigeria?" I said. "Aren't they having problems in Nigeria now?"

"Oh. Are they? That's just awful. Poor Mr. Milburn. He's always in the wrong places, isn't he?"

I stared at Jason Woods' portrait. He was looking as confused as I was.

"Seems like it," I said. And started to end the conversation and go back to square zero.

But then the young woman giggled. "Oh, look here. I just found another change-of-address card, way in the back of the folder—somebody hasn't been doing their filing very conscientiously, have they? This one's dated July 30, 1999, and it says that Mr. Milburn was coming back to Houston. To his permanent address, 6218 Braescreek Place." She giggled some more. "It has such a cute note on it: 'I quit. I'm too damned old to get shot at anymore!' Isn't that funny?"

"Yes, it is," I said, proving it by grinning all over myself. Thanking her, I got off the telephone and headed out, pausing only long enough to shoot a heartfelt smirk of my own at good old Jason's portrait.

By now, I'd had about enough of the Stella Link washboard, and I turned off onto Beechnut. Its surface was marginally better and Hizzie stopped some of her lurching.

Beechnut.

Along here, it was more commercial than residential. Restaurants. Tropical fish stores. Supermarkets.

And a big sign that said, VEGAS JOE'S BRBQ.

Yeah. This was one of former homicide detective Joseph Newhouse's barbecue restaurants.

Geez! He had had about as much luck as Maggie Hawk. Just years earlier. Lots of people considered the barbecue produced by his wonderful and very secret cooking method and slathered with his also wonderful and very secret sauce to be the best in the world. Rock and film stars and magnates and politicians had tons of the stuff flown great distances for their parties. Dignitaries of all stripes couldn't visit Houston without stopping by Vegas Joe's BRBQ for lunch or dinner.

Even I had to admit the stuff was great. Back in my days of solvency, Sarah and I had dined at Vegas Joe's a few times, usually at this very one. Only once had I gone to the first and biggest Vegas Joe's, the one he had opened with his Las Vegas winnings. That one was located on Westheimer Road, in the shadow of the Galleria, and Vegas Joe, himself, held court there.

He was quite a showman, parading around the place, sucking up to any patron sporting at least five carats of diamonds or a Rolex, in his trademark chartreuse silk shirts and his custom-made jeans that were exactly like Levi's Button-fronts, except they were made from white velvet. Oh, boy. The Liberace of the Short Rib. No telling where an ex-cop might turn up.

More commercial places. A Bed-and-Bath. An Eckerd's drugstore. A new car dealership.

A new car dealership.

I stopped looking at new car dealerships months ago. Momentarily, after things started looking as if they were coming together for me with the Video King, I had sneaked an occasional glance. Not since that deal fell apart, though. No way!

But today, I wasn't watching myself and, suddenly, here was a Chrysler dealership and I screwed up and looked at the showroom window as I drove past. There was poor old beat-up Hizzie's reflection, and right behind it . . .

Uh-oh!

I went eyes-front. I told myself I hadn't seen it. I told myself it didn't make any difference whether I had seen it or not. I told myself to be tough.

Sure, Tony.

At the corner, I slowed. Turned. Circled the block.

Damn!

I told myself to use some willpower and keep eyes-front and drive right on past. My willpower turned instantly into corn flakes.

I stopped.

I got out and heard Hizzie's door rattle like old tin as it closed. Cussing myself with every step, I walked into the showroom.

There it was.

The Car! Twice as pretty up close as it had been through the showroom window.

A new candy-apple red Chrysler convertible.

It was gorgeous. It was at least three times more gorgeous than that.

A sexy saleslady came sauntering toward me with love in her eyes. She was smiling. She was practically salivating. She knew meat when she saw it. One glance at my credit application and she'd drop me like a dead fish. But at the moment, I was meat.

She came close and took a dip and a deep breath to get me involved with her cleavage and said, "Beautiful, isn't it?"

I tried to sound blasé. "It's okay, I guess."

"More than okay," she breathed.

I yanked myself back to reality and said, "Well, the truth is, I just bought a new Honda convertible, and my wife jumped me for not buying American, so I dropped by to get some argument for her."

End of the affair. The cleavage went decisively back into storage. "Well, you just help yourself," the sexy saleslady snapped as she walked off.

I looked at the car. I circled it. I did everything but salivate on it. The interior was butterscotch. I caressed the door open, eased myself down behind the wheel. The leather seats smelled just like Maggie's chair.

Damn!

I got back out. Beautiful car. Fantastic car!

Self-defense set in. It had air bags, of course. I told myself that was all I needed—to drive this thing on Houston's ratty streets and wait for the next pothole to explode the steering wheel in my face. It had all kinds of computer-operated stuff in it, too. If the air bags didn't get me, Y2K would undoubtedly cause the computers all to blow out at the stroke of midnight on New Year's Eve.

Hizzie might be a little dumpy, but she had all the kinks ironed out of her. And she was paid for.

Yeah.

Yeah!

I grabbed myself by the scruff of the neck and got the hell out of there and got in Hizzie and drove off.

I didn't look back at that candy-apple red brand-new Chrysler convertible.

But I wanted to.

Three or four blocks along, I drove through an amber light, as it's customary to do in Houston unless you want the car following you to end up in your tailpipe.

A second later, there was a crash behind me. I looked into the rearview mirror and saw two cars crammed together in the intersection. They had been approaching each other on the cross street. One was intent on a left turn; the other wasn't intent on much of anything. Bang!

I slowed for a moment, long enough to see a woman get out of one of the cars, her white hair shining silver-blue in the sunlight, and start pointing and yelling at a baldheaded man who got out of the other car and started pointing and yelling at her. Obviously no grave injuries. Just a hell of a mess in the intersection.

I drove on.

A couple of blocks later, I turned left onto Braescreek Place. Six or seven blocks more, and there was Polly's apartment complex.

Polly.

She was an aspiring actress, of course, but made her living being the luscious TV spokesperson for a local chain of waterbed stores, along with doing an occasional commercial for somebody else. She was an awesomely good-looking woman. A Wow! on anybody's scale. It did wonders for my ego to walk into places with her and have all the men stare and all the women drape napkins over their heads. I also thought it was great that we got our pictures in the paper a couple of times and even made TV once—my fifteen minutes of fame.

The problem with her was that the design was a whole lot better than the realization—along with all that lush blonde beauty, she had the common sense of a canary and the mind of a cocker spaniel. She also wasn't nearly as good in bed as she demanded that you tell her she was.

We dated for a month or so, during which I kept thinking that, surely, things would improve. They didn't.

I was a rebound situation for her. The forever-to-be-nameless and highly married Houston Astros star, with whom she had been carrying on, had gotten a crisis of conscience and started staying home with his wife, and I was handy and reasonably presentable and suitably upscale because of my connection with Stockpile Video, for whom she'd just done a commercial. Besides, she could go out in public with me, for a change. And she loved Hizzie. I told her that, when I wasn't busy protecting videotapes, I still did some private eye work, and Hizzie was perfect for undercover. Every time we went out, she acted as if she thought she was on a mission with James Bond. One more comment on her intelligence. And on my ego.

The big breakup occurred when we got into an argument that started off centering around some old Bette Davis movie. It moved on to my admitting that, in my personal concept of the great scheme of things, the well-being of the world probably depended more on Sally Ride's work than on Bette Davis' and Polly's combined. It sputtered to a climax when Polly spilled it that the baseball player, apparently having changed his mind about the sanctity of his home, had called and was due in about twenty minutes. So much for my ego.

And now, it turned out that the address I had conned out of the Rice Alumni Association for Lawrence Milburn was practically across the street from Polly's apartment complex.

For old time's sake, I put Hizzie where I used to park when I was seeing Polly, and walked from there.

I discovered on the way that Polly-and-I really was finished—what I was thinking about as I walked along toward Lawrence Milburn's house wasn't Polly. It was that candy-apple red convertible.

As Grandpa would say: "Life is short; romance is shorter."

TWELVE

The Cauliflower Man and His Electric Pencil Sharpener

Lawrence Roth Milburn was about half-sloshed. He was also the size of Milwaukee; there was no way he'd fit into a Halloween party apple tub these days.

His place was somewhat on the neglected side. The lawn could have used the ministrations of a GRASSBUSTER or two. The house windows were dirty. There were spider webs in the corners of the overhang that formed the roof of the small front porch. Inside, the living room was decorated in bazaar Arabic. Through a doorway, I could see packing cartons stacked along a hallway, their drab cardboard exteriors splotched all over with exotic customs stickers.

Larry was very pleasant, and glad of some company, I think. I told him—mumbling—that I was "kind of doing some research on Rice alums," and he stuck a can of Schlitz in my hand and popped a new one for himself and motioned me onto a sofa that smelled of mothballs while he settled back into his green Naugahyde Barcalounger.

Thinking of that torn-out picture in my jacket pocket that showed Maggie with the quintessential Midwestern college quarterback put me into kind of a time-warp. That good-looking guy had gotten flabbed-out long ago. Today, sitting there in that shiny green chair next to a table covered with bags of Fritos and cheese balls and cookies in front of a TV set on which the Cubs were blowing a day game with the Phillies, he looked like a huge stale cauliflower.

It was probably the easiest interrogation possible. All I had to do was mention something, and he'd spill his guts about it. First, though, I got the History of the World—and the State of Cubs Baseball—as seen through the eyes of Larry Milburn, Peripatetic Engineer.

"Algeria. Now that was something. You wouldn't remember the old Algeria, boy—before your time. What's the matter, you're not drinking. You don't like real beer? You used to that Lite-beer-shit? *Shit! Walked him! Damn!* Yeah, Algeria was something! Went over there right out of school. Worked on pipelines. Figured I'd stay there forever. And then they nationalized everything and ran us the hell out. *Throw a strike sometime, will you?* I scrammed back to the U.S. and bought this house and got a job with Warren Petroleum—you remember them? No. I don't guess anybody does. Gulf swallowed 'em up. Now, Chevron's swallowed up Gulf. Thought I'd stay here for a while. *C'mon, Ump! What kind of blind-ass call is that? Shit! Did you see that?* Then I got bored, and so I got this job in Libya. Hot place, but nice. Nice people, then. Thought I had it made. Oil out the ass. *Don't walk another one, babe! Argh! Damn, how come they don't have any relief pitching?* I'd of stayed in Libya forever, but then Khadafi took over. Crazy man. Nationalized everything. Got out of there and went to Iran. Great place. Thought I'd found a home. Oil everywhere. Great people. *Shit! Couldn't anybody catch that thing? Damn! How come the Cubs can't win more than once a week?* Loved Iran. Then here came the Ayatollah. Screwed up my life again. Moved over to Iraq. Got going good. And then they got in a war with Iran. So I went over to Saudi Arabia. But I got bored, and got a chance to go to Kuwait. Best job I'm ever going to have. But I hadn't been there hardly even six months when the goddamned Iraqis moved in. I was just lucky I was over in Egypt having a good time. Then old Stormin' Norman kicked Iraq out of Kuwait, and I went back and helped 'em put out those goddamned oil fires. After that, I got a new job in Qatar. Thought I was set up for life. And then damned if they didn't go to hell. Coups and bombs.

"So I got a new job in Nigeria. Nice place. Real nice people. And then, sure enough, they went to hell, just like everybody else where I got a good job. I'm too old to get my ass shot off anymore. My house back here in Houston wasn't rented, so I figured I'd come home and retire for a while. Got my stuff out of storage, and here I am. Makes you wonder, though. I was halfway afraid to come home to the USA, for fear it'd go to hell, too. *Hold on to that goddamned baseball! Damn! Damn it to hell!*"

Since Larry seemed to have run out of both world history and baseball for the moment, I said, "In college, you were buddies with a fellow named George Hawk, weren't you?"

"George Hawk? Damn! I haven't thought about old George for a hundred years. Damned nice guy. My best buddy—you know that? Damn, I have to tell you, we got in some scrapes together."

"But he got married, didn't he?"

"Oh, hell, yes. And then he had to work, too. Had a little scholarship of some kind, but he had to work. He wasn't married the first year, though. We got into some scrapes together then. *Look at the way he holds that bat. Can you believe that?*"

I said, "George was married to a girl named Maggie, wasn't he?"

My saying her name cut the decibel level in Larry's living room by about sixty percent. I wondered if I was about to get the answer to why there hadn't been a single mention in Maggie's notes about George's buddy, Larry Milburn.

"Maggie," he said, lying back suddenly and looking up at the ceiling, missing seeing practically the only hit the Cubs had had since 1945. "I introduced Maggie and George. Did you know that? Listen, boy, let me tell you: don't go introducing your girlfriends to your buddies. Hell, I thought I was going to marry Maggie, and then I showed her off to George and, next thing I knew, she was marrying him."

"Yeah. I guess you can break up a lot of friendships that way."

He waved his hand. "No, no. Didn't break up anything. Just showed me how lucky I was not to have got any more mixed up with her than I was. She just wanted an engineer, and she met George, and thought he was going to do better than I was. Showed me I was lucky, that's all. George was still my buddy. Tore hell out of us running around together, of course. She kept him close. But we were still buddies."

He seemed to have completely forgotten the baseball game, and was looking around, stopping his gaze momentarily on the three intricate hookahs that sat on top of the low bookshelf across the room, and the coffee table made from a huge and intricately engraved brass tray, and the string of camel bells that hung from the mantel. "You know about George?" he said. "You know he killed himself, don't you?"

"Yes."

"Did it because of her, I always figured. Must of found out she was just looking for a meal ticket. I was damned glad I was out of the country when he did it—had a summer job up in Calgary that year—or I'd of told her exactly what I thought about her. I was cooled off when I got back to Houston for senior year in September. It was spilled milk then. Damn, boy, don't ever let a woman get that much hold on you."

I said, "Did you know Dr. Melvin Potter?"

Larry liked the change of subject. Glancing at the television, he saw it was commercial time, and gave me most of his attention. "You mean Dr. Potty?" He chuckled. "About a hundred and thirty pounds. Twenty pounds of brains, and the rest asshole."

"How did he and George get along?"

A Schlitz can got shifted from right to left hand, and two pudgy fingers went up, waggled sausage-like for a moment, and then slammed together. "Like that—George and Dr. Potty. He thought George hung the moon. Kept trying to get him scholarships so he wouldn't have to work. Damned near killed him when George got married—then he had a job *and* a wife to distract him from classes. Old Potty always blamed me for fixin' 'em up. I did, you know, but I sure as hell wasn't happy about it. Damn!"

"So George was sharp, huh?"

"Sharp? Man, you don't know sharp. George was so sharp you wouldn't even believe it. Listen, if that guy had lived until computers came around, we'd be buyin' real estate in Tokyo right now, and sellin' 'em Chryslers, instead of the other way around."

Thinking his idea over, Larry liked it a lot, and laughed appreciatively.

Suddenly, then, in a blur of white, fat, hairy legs and faded plaid Bermuda shorts straight out of the '60s, he erupted from the Barcalounger. Squatting down beside a low brass-trimmed bedouin-style wooden chest, he looked more than ever like an immense cauliflower. He must have been an object of endless fascination to those people in the Middle East, who had grown up with the thin and stately camel.

On the television screen, the Cubs were all of a sudden hitting the baseball as if they were pros. Larry was too busy to realize it, though. He was digging into that trunk.

Treasures came out of it. Gorgeous alien-looking fabrics, some of them embroidered with gold and silver. Brass vases. Glass vases. Ornate daggers. A couple more hookahs. Inlaid boxes. Fabulous colors. Scents of exotic incense and spices.

Finally, he heaved back and sat on the floor, holding up something about the size of a baking potato wrapped in yellowed tissue paper. "Back in school, doin' all that mechanical drawing, you know how much time we spent sharpening pencils?" He pantomimed sharpening a pencil in a hand-cranked schoolroom-type sharpener. Then he went through the motions of sticking a pencil in one of those little devices that you hold with one hand while you twist the pencil with the other. "Pain in the ass. So George made this for us." He pulled away tissue paper and revealed an ancient, cracked and curling electric cord dangling from what looked like nothing so much as a brown metal egg.

"An electric pencil sharpener!" Larry exclaimed. "In 1963. You ever hear of an electric pencil sharpener in 1963? George made it out of this little electric fan and an old hand-cranked sharpener. It worked great. I couldn't believe it. An electric pencil sharpener way back there in 1963 was like an electric toothbrush—unheard-of, outlandish. But it worked great. I told him he ought to patent it, but he told me he couldn't because all he'd done was adapt stuff to make it. What he was after was something he could patent and make a million on." Shaking his head mournfully,

Larry said, "This thing wasn't worth anything, but it sure helped out with the goddamned pencils."

I said, "Did you ever know of George doing anything with lawnmowers?"

"Lawnmowers?" He frowned and thought about it. Then he shook his head. "No. I don't remember any lawnmowers. But if there was something to be done with 'em, he would of thought of it and worked it out." A thought struck him. "Maybe he did. After he and Maggie went to work for that fellow over in River Oaks. George did the gardening. So if he was going to think of something to do with lawnmowers, he would of done it there."

He looked off into the distance. "Funny, thinking about George and Maggie. Haven't thought about them in a long time."

He picked up a folded piece of fabric that was all embroidery—scarlet and yellow and pale blue and gold and silver. Running his hand over it tenderly, he said, "Maggie. I used to think a lot about Maggie. I was too hard on her. She was something, you know? I blamed George killing himself on her, but I got to thinking about her after I got to Algeria, and she wouldn't do that. George wouldn't of let her, anyway. Not George. If he ever got it in his head to kill himself, nobody could have stopped him. And if he didn't want to, nobody could have made him do it."

His hands were clenching hard into the fabric. His face was tight with old remembered pain. For a moment, peeking out from under the fat, there was that good-looking kid from the Halloween party.

"I was too hard on her," he said. "Finally figured that out. I didn't blame her because of George. I blamed her because she was the only girl I ever really wanted to marry. And George killing himself fixed it for sure that was never going to happen. How could Maggie and me ever get by something like that? No way. But I should of done something. I should have tried to talk to her. Or something."

He dropped the fabric and laughed nervously. "Shit! You get out in the boonies on these jobs, you get to thinking too much—get yourself all screwed-up rehashing things."

He stuffed the fabric back into the trunk. Then he picked up George's pencil sharpener. Tenderly, he wound the ruined cord around the fan motor. Tenderly, he said, "I ought to get off my ass one of these days and put a new cord on this thing. Shame to just let it sit here and rot."

Rewrapping it in the tissue paper, he set it down into the trunk. "I've got other stuff that George made around here somewhere. He was always doing that. He'd think of something, and then sit down right there in the dorm and make it. Marvel that way. Not like me. I kept bitchin' about the damned pencils; George did something about 'em."

In the last few minutes, things had changed on the television screen. The Cubs had had their glory. Now the Phillies were batting again and, every time a baseball came their way, about two seconds later, the Cubs were watching it sail away into home run land.

Larry stuffed things back into the trunk and closed it and turned to look at the TV just as another ball went out. "Shit!" Turning disgustedly away from the set, he said, "Okay. Who the hell wants to watch baseball? What was it you wanted to talk to me about?"

I stood up. "Nothing, really. Just dropped by for a beer. Thanks a lot." Bending down, I shook his hand.

He looked mildly confused. I felt mildly guilty for having caused him to miss the only five minutes of good baseball the Cubs had had this month.

I guess that's why they call it a game.

THIRTEEN

River Oaks and Thuperthiliouth

After I left Larry Milburn's, just for kicks I walked through the courtyard of Polly's apartment building. No big reason, except for the scenery. And there was some. Polly wasn't out by the pool, but some of her neighbors were. Nice. There's nothing quite like boobs and butts baking under the Texas sun.

When I got back to Hizzie, it was about ten after one and, damn, it was hot! The only good thing about summer in Houston is that, if you're in Buffalo, New York, in January, dreaming about Houston summers gives you the strength to face the next six months of winter.

The inside of the car felt and smelled like a Naugahyde's armpit, and I left the door hanging open until I could get the engine started and the windows down. The steering wheel burned my hands. The little chrome jobbies on either side of where you stick in the ignition key burned my fingers when I twisted them to start the engine. The seatbelt latch felt red hot.

But finally, I got buckled-up and legal, and got her going, and got a breeze moving through. Two or three blocks away from Larry Milburn's house, I stopped at a convenience store.

The pay telephone that was partly shaded by the

building was out of order. The other one, in full sunlight, practically shimmered with heat, but I got a quarter fed into the slot without completely cooking my fingers and called home to check my answering machine.

Maggie had called: "Hi, Tony. Just checking in. Call me when you can."

So had someone else: "Mr. Aapt, this is Hanley Moss. Found out something else about that Newhouse fellow you were checking on. Maybe you already know about this. Anyway, call me if you're interested."

I thought I probably wasn't. I figured I'd call him later on.

I stuck in another quarter and got Maggie's answering machine. I told it, "Hi, Maggie, it's Tony. At about one-fifteen, time and temperature. It's been an interesting day, and it may get more so. Talk to you later."

I replaced the handset and got back in the car. This time, I headed northeast.

River Oaks.

A couple of things I've always wondered about: first, why did they call it "River Oaks" when practically everything in the entire Houston area that could possibly qualify as a river is called a "bayou"? Maybe "Bayou Oaks" just didn't seem to have an expensive enough ring to it. I don't know, but it seems silly to me. After all Beacon Hill used to have a beacon, and Beverly Hills had a Beverly.

Second, why are River Oaks streets even worse than in the rest of Houston—crummy enough to shake the liver out of the average moose? Maybe it's because of the years of wear and tear from heavy vehicles like Rolls Royces and Mercedes, and buses carrying maids and gardeners in and out. Or maybe it's because they're afraid their taxes will go to hell if they get the streets fixed. Maybe along with your deed, you get a thousand shares of stock in the wheel alignment and shock absorber cartel. I don't know. But I do know that, if I had a ten million dollar house, I'd like to be able to drive home to it without losing my gallbladder.

Anyway, I drove jouncingly deep into River Oaks, trying not to look too much out of place, trying to appear haughtily unconcerned, as if both of my Ferraris were in the shop and I had borrowed the cook's car and my daddy was so rich that I didn't care whether anybody saw me in it or not.

Deep into River Oaks. Into the land of pillars and monster oaks and big lawns and Mercedes and BMWs and Rolls Royces.

I found Jason Woods' place with no problem. Walled and gated estates that take up a whole oversized block are kind of hard to miss.

There was a TV pickup beside the gate, and a monitor. Color, no less. I pushed the button. In a moment, the most supercilious guy I had ever seen, on TV or off, was looking out of the monitor at me. "Yes?" he said, making it into about a four-syllable word and putting "th" where the "s" should be.

"I'd like to see Jason Woods," I said.

He looked at me as if I were pond scum. "Do you have an appointment?"

"No."

I got eyebrow and mutilated S's. "Mister Woods sees no one without an appointment."

"Fine. I'll make one."

More eyebrow, but marginally less lisp. "Just what is the nature of your business with Mr. Woods? If I may ask."

I shoved my ID card up toward the camera and pulled it back. "I'm a private investigator."

"Oh?"

"I'm investigating the death of George Hawk."

He gave me boredom and "The death of whom?"

"George Hawk. H-A-W-K."

"And your name?"

"Tony Aapt. A-A-P-T."

"What interesting thpelling, Mr. Aapt. At what telephone number might you be reached? If one were to find that Mr. Woods was interested in seeing you."

I gave him my number.

"Thank you tho much," he said, and the screen went blank.

I sat there in the car looking around for a moment. The gate appeared to be plain old decorative wrought-iron, but the overly solid joints in it, and the industrial-strength roller mounts suggested to me that it was really high-grade steel, good enough against about anything but a tank. The foot-wide steel plates that ran across the concrete drive about ten feet in and about thirty feet in looked like drain covers, but I'd have bet anything they were spike-sets ready to pop up and further discourage anything that made it through the gate still able to motor. The little aluminum doodads sitting at about twenty-foot intervals on top of the ten-foot-high brick wall were receptors for a Savalli Motion Detector System. They probably wouldn't notice if a pigeon plunked down for a visit, but anything much bigger would set off all kinds of alarms in the house.

Nice equipment. Some of what I'd set up around my own house if I had more money than I knew what to do with, along with a moderate case of paranoia.

Good old Jason Woods might be a philanthropist and Mr. Houston Nice-Guy, but he obviously wasn't too keen on having people drop in uninvited.

I punched the button again.

After a long pause, Supercilious came back, letting more than a little genteel miff show on his face when he saw it was still me. "Yeth? Was there something else?"

"Have a nice day," I said, and flipped a little wave at him and then backed out onto the street.

In the next block, I checked my watch. One forty-five. Early yet.

"It'd be a shame to waste a good trip to River Oaks," I told Hizzie, and took a right.

FOURTEEN

Wildebeests, Beware!

She had the mouth of a meat-eater.

If I were a baby wildebeest, I'd have been heading straight for my mommy or the middle of the herd, whichever was closer, peeing on myself with every step.

"A private detective?" she said. "Now, isn't that interesting."

She was Rhea Chatham. Jason Woods' niece. Carl Woods' sister. By my math, she was forty-something, but expensive upkeep and cosmetics and/or surgical magic, plus several rich husbands had kept her looking very smooth and tight and youthful.

She looked lots different in person. It seemed that every time you leafed through the Lifestyle section of the newspaper, if Jason Woods wasn't pictured giving another architectural oddity to Rice University, Rhea Chatham—or whatever her last name was at the moment—was pictured wearing some designer masterpiece and hanging onto Baryshnikov or Prince Charles or whatever other celebrity happened to be passing through town. In those newspaper photographs, her patented toothy smile made her appear glamorous and vivacious. But standing in the library of her house with her, all I got was a chill and the hope that she'd had a large and satisfying lunch.

She asked, "Why in the world would a private detective want to see me?"

Coming up the driveway, I had given her house about a four on a River Oaks scale of one-to-ten. No gate. No wall. And it shared the block with two others. There was another vehicle in the driveway—a Mercedes station wagon done in metallic burgundy lacquer and bearing a discreet but very elegant logo: "Nathan—Design." After I hid Hizzie behind it and was invited inside the house, I had to raise its score to a five. The entryway was guarded by a couple of porcelain Foo dogs the size of baby elephants, and the walls were covered with green watered silk above wainscoting enameled in the color of fresh cream. The Lalique chandelier hanging in the majestic curve of the grand staircase probably weighed more than my apartment.

Here in the library, there were lots of books, of course. Some of them were the required impressive-looking leatherbound jobs that I think must be delivered by the case to new River Oaks houses on chandelier-hanging day, but there were a lot of others, too. Enough of them in enough variety that it made you think that maybe somebody in the place could actually read. There were some very nice trinkets, also, including a Baccarat crystal horse's head the size of a rottweiler, and an antique ivory chess set that practically made my mouth water.

Rhea and her little brother, Carl, and their mother had been poor relations of Jason Woods back when Maggie and George Hawk worked for him. I didn't know anything about Carl Woods—except that he had black hair—but Rhea wasn't anybody's poor relation any longer. A talent for marrying well and getting out with the community property had taken care of that small problem.

She was waiting.

I said, "I'm investigating the death of a man named George Hawk."

"Who?" she said, and cocked her head in her patented newspaper-photo pose and added, "Aren't you just a bit young for this?"

She was really something. It was hard to think of her as a senior citizen. Shiny, black hair in a casual toss that probably didn't take more than a couple of hours a day to maintain. Flawless skin. Small, tight, high breasts, and an extraordinarily aerobicized body. If only her mouth didn't look as if she was about ready to chomp down and start feeding.

"He was an employee of your Uncle Jason's," I said.

Eyebrows. "What in the world would that have to do with me? Jason and I aren't exactly close, you know," she said, and immediately followed with something off the wall. "Do you work out, or do you just have good genes?"

This was getting to be a bit much for me; I'm partial to women who look as if they like roses, not human haunch extra-rare. Maybe if I really got down to business I could keep her distracted and get out of here alive. "This is a rather unusual case. George Hawk—and his wife—worked for Jason Woods when you and your mother and brother were living in his house."

Her eyes went wide. "When we were living there! His wife? Was she a maid? Oh, my God! Maggie? Are you talking about Maggie and George?"

"Yes."

"You can't be talking about Maggie and George. Why, that must be . . . well, a very long time ago."

I waited.

"George? But he killed himself. Good God, I haven't thought about Maggie and George for . . . longer than I care to remember. How could you possibly be investigating his death?"

"There seems to be some thought that it might not have been suicide."

"Isn't it a little late to be worrying about something like that?"

"Not for my client."

"Who is . . . ?"

I didn't have to tell her—or anybody—but sometimes confidentiality loses out when it's put up against impact. "My client is Maggie Hawk," I said.

"Maggie?" She got up and circled me. "Is this some kind of joke? People don't just decide years later that they'll hire a private detective to check into a suicide."

"She hasn't been able to afford it until now."

Going back to sit down, Rhea said, "This is incredible." Then she leaned back and gave me that meat-eating grin. "All right. Maggie was nice to me when I was a little girl—and to Carl. Not many people were. Dear, sweet Uncle Jason didn't like for people to be nice to us. What do you want from me?"

"Do you remember much about George?"

She arched her eyebrows. "Oh, well, yes, I thought he was handsome. I was just beginning to get an inkling that men were men." She arched her eyebrows at *me*. "And George was different from men like Uncle Jason. He wore such interesting clothes. And he perspired. I thought that was very nice." Pause. A little smile that would have shaken an entire herd of wildebeests. "I still do."

I was afraid that I was about to do some perspiring of my own. Quickly, I said, "Do you remember George's inventing things?"

She laughed. "Well, yes. I remember that, too. He was

always tinkering with things in Uncle Jason's garage. I remember he made a new kind of flour sifter for that nasty old cook of Uncle Jason's. It didn't make dust."

A thought struck her. "If it wasn't suicide, what was it?" Suddenly, she realized that wasn't exactly a multiple choice question. "My God! Are you serious? Murder? Somebody murdered him?"

"That's the theory."

"You can't be serious."

I waited.

"Who would have murdered him?"

I wasn't ready to elaborate too much on that. Jason might not exactly be her favorite uncle in the whole world, but jumping right into accusing him of murder could tend to wake whatever small amount of family loyalty she still had. "Well, that's kind of open."

"My God!" she said. "What can I tell you that would help? I liked Maggie and George. They were the only nice people in that whole place." She thought over the situation and added, "Do you think Uncle Jason knows anything about it?"

"He might. But he's not exactly the easiest person to talk to. He doesn't answer his own door, you know."

"He'd surely talk to you. He was so broken up when George died."

I wondered if she could really be that naive. Possibly. But I was going to leave it alone for now. Let her think about it.

From somewhere close, there came a terrific scraping noise. It was followed by a sound like cloth ripping, except about twenty times as loud.

Seconds later, a grinning young man stepped into the library. He was wearing a red body shirt and blue jeans that were faded almost white, and carelessly—just a tad too carelessly—stained here and there with paint and glue. His thick dark hair was gathered into a short ponytail that rode fashionably high on the back of his head. He could have been the poster child of the Association of Intensely Butch Interior Designers of America. He was holding a ragged swatch of that nice green watered silk wall covering.

He was just a bit crestfallen to find that Rhea wasn't alone. He also was a bit miffed. Intensely butch poster children are prone to seeing rivals everywhere. "Oh," he said to Rhea. "I didn't know somebody was here." He waved the torn silk. "I couldn't stand this stuff a moment longer."

Rhea seemed to have forgotten about murder mysteries. Looking even more like a meat-eater, she almost purred, "In a few minutes, Nathan."

He showed his own teeth in a quick, cute, lip-biting grin. "Sure." With a flourish of the torn silk and a smirk that he obviously thought meant something to me, he vanished through the doorway.

"You must be redecorating," I said, when he was gone.

Rhea looked as if she was thinking about dinner. "Oh, yes."

I stood up. "I won't take any more of your time. You've been a help. If you think of anything, you have my card."

She stood, also. "Oh, I will."

Sizzle and rip! There went some more of the entryway silk.

"When I finish redecorating," Rhea said, "I really must try to think of some use for a private detective."

I glanced around to make sure I knew where the doorway was, and quickly said, "Just one more thing—do you remember anything about George inventing something that had to do with a lawnmower?"

For a moment, she was puzzled. "A lawnmower?" Then her eyes went wide. "A lawnmower! Oh, my God!" She touched her mouth in shock. "You can't be talking about Uncle Jason's lawnmower blade. You are! You're talking about his GRASSBUSTER." Suddenly, she looked very, very hungry. Maybe those latent family ties weren't so strong, after all. "You're talking about Uncle Jason! Aren't you?"

More silk wall covering died.

I said, "I'd rather not get too specific about that."

"Oh, this is wonderful! Wait until I tell Carl."

"Your brother?"

"Yes. My dear little brother. You're going to talk to him, too, aren't you?" she asked, doing an odd little smirk as she said it.

"I understood he lived in Chicago."

"Not anymore. In June, he moved back to Houston. Do let me give you his address." Smirking that odd little smirk again, she reached onto the table and picked up a pen and a piece of heavy cream-colored note paper. Writing on it with a motion that looked like clawing, she handed it to me.

I glanced at it before I put it into my pocket. Seeing the address she had written, I understood her smirk.

"Thanks very much," I said, and left her in the library.

There was a ladder in the entryway now—that first big noise had been its legs scraping on the marble floor. I interrupted Intensely Butch just as he was getting ready to scrape it around some more to remind us that he was waiting.

When he saw me, he gave me his smirk again, to remind me that I was leaving, and he was staying.

I gave him a smirk of my own. "Just remember—they have their best luck around the water holes."

"Huh?" he said.

"Huh, hell," I said back, and left.

Outside, there wasn't a smirk in sight—mine or anybody else's. The afternoon Houston summer air smelled like hot fish sweat.

I liked it.

FIFTEEN

The Payoff Concept

Things were getting interesting.

I was practically enthusiastic now.

Reassuming the my-Ferraris-are-both-in-the-shop attitude, I got back into Hizzie and drove to 3301 San Simeon.

That was the address of Clinton McKenna, the lawyer George had been on his way to see when he died, except that McKenna had lived on North Boulevard then, a somewhat less exalted neighborhood.

I was a little disappointed in the place. There was the required expanse of manicured green lawn and there were pillars, but the house looked like the stodge version of Rhea Chatham's.

There were no cars in front. The garage doors were closed.

I parked and went up the steps and rang the bell. I could hear it pealing melodically behind the narrow beveled glass panes beside the door.

No one answered. I rang again. No one. It must be the maid's day off, I thought. I went back and got in good old Hizzie and drove away.

Just for the hell of it, I swung back by Jason Woods' place and nosed Hizzie up to the gate.

Supercilious popped onto the TV monitor and, when he

saw it was me again, looked as if somebody had stuck a jalapeño pepper up his nose.

"Just checking," I said. "Have you got my appointment set up yet?"

Sniff. "Mr. Aapt, you're fast becoming a nuisance," he lisped.

"Just keep after 'im," I said. "And let me know. In the meantime, you ought to do something about that cold."

Fun. Stupid as hell, but fun.

I chuckled a little as I headed out of River Oaks and back to the real world. Things were definitely getting interesting.

Hilda Guttman had been managing to make it up her West University front steps—which were attached to a house which seemed at least somewhat beyond her means—without any help for more than thirty years, she had said.

Dr. Potter had the teeth of an alligator in 1963. Today, he had a mouthful of caps that Bruce Willis would die for. He said George Hawk was an impractical "visionary," which was a word appropriate for him to use. Hilda Guttman called George a visionary, too, a word you don't exactly expect to hear tripping from the mouth of an elderly retired cook. Particularly when it turned out that she apparently owed at least some of her culinary success to the neat dustless flour sifter this visionary had whipped up for her in his spare time.

But Cauliflower-man Larry Milburn had an entirely different opinion, and he had George's cobbled-together electric pencil sharpener to prove it.

Rhea Woods Tolliver Monroe Wendel Waggoner Chatham also didn't call George a visionary. And it was refreshing to find, mixed up in all this mess, a lady who obviously thought that "family" wasn't much more than just another six-letter word. Because she'd been a help and because it might keep her from thinking about hiring a private detective for as long as possible, I wished her a good long feed on Intensely Butch.

In the meantime, the five o'clock traffic wars were still a couple of hours away, so I made a quick trip downtown to check on one of my prime conjectures.

The Harris County tax records showed that 3122 Tangley Road was owned by Hilda Joanna Guttman. There was no current lien. The only lien on record for that address was taken out in 1938 by one Richard Pollard, who had bought the new house on the property with the help of San Jacinto Savings & Loan in the form of a mortgage for four thousand dollars. The mortgage was retired in 1958. In December, 1966, Pollard sold the unencumbered property to Guttman. No lien.

That meant that Mrs. Guttman had almost certainly paid for the place in cash.

How much?

I checked the neighbors. In 1962, 3214 Tangley Road changed hands, and there was a seventeen thousand dollar mortgage. In 1966, 3002 had done likewise, with a nineteen thousand dollar mortgage.

Just to put things in perspective, West University real estate style, 3002 Tangley Road had changed hands again in 1993. The mortgage this time was for a hundred ninety-two thousand dollars. Not bad property appreciation, huh? It explained why everybody in West University always looked so smug.

I could guess that Hilda's place would have cost her somewhere between sixteen and twenty thousand dollars back in 1966—not even a year after George Hawk died.

Big bucks then.

Really big bucks for a forty-five-or-so-year-old woman who had been left a widow with "just a pile of bills," according to Maggie's notes.

There was only one way I could think of that she could have gotten that kind of money, and it wasn't as a bonus for making neat peach-and-raspberry ice cream.

I felt pretty satisfied with myself.

Maybe antique murder cases weren't so bad, after all.

SIXTEEN

"It's Damned Near Impossible to Get Decent Falsies in This Town," He Said.

When I left the courthouse, Carl Woods was next on my list. Chances were that, being only six years old when George died, he wouldn't remember much, but Grandpa would have gotten going on about an hour's worth of wise, old boring sayings, one after another, if I had given him an excuse like that.

The address Rhea had given me was 1600 Alabama Street—about halfway between here and home.

But the gas gauge was dropping toward the danger zone, so I stopped and filled up. Then I saw a convenience store and pulled in and called my answering machine. Maggie and I had missed each other again; she had talked to my machine about thirty minutes ago; I called now and talked to hers. After that, I realized I was hungry and stopped at a Burger King just off the intersection of Westheimer and Montrose for a gourmet snack of french fries and a Bacon Double.

While I sat in the plastic dining room eating, I stared at the Stockpile Video store across the street.

Damn! They were suing me!

I couldn't believe that the Video King, himself, could be behind it. He was basically kind of a turkey, but he wasn't malicious. The one who was turning the knife in me had to be ex-embezzler/Vice President Angela.

Damn!

The store across the street was second in size and sales to the big flagship store in the Galleria. The front had the standard Stockpile Video signature, which was TV screens all the way around the plate glass window showing cuts from the current big-renters, and life-sized cardboard cutouts of this summer's superstars like Julia Roberts and Harrison Ford and Gwyneth Paltrow. And sure enough, just like Art had said, the whole ceiling of the place shimmered with foot-long lengths of tinsel tacked about two or three inches apart.

Festive, I guess. But my big interest wasn't in the decorations. I had worked my butt off trying to protect these stores, and I was more interested in that.

I shouldn't have been. It wasn't my problem anymore. I shouldn't have wasted my digestion on it.

But I had spent a lot of time and sweat installing surveillance cameras and had put in a lot of hours drilling the store managers and the employees on security procedures and, as far as I could tell, it was all for nothing.

I could see only one of the ceiling-mounted Videoscan cameras from my position, but its in-operation red light was off, meaning that all of them must be off—and even if they were running, the tinsel would have screwed up their view. The late shift was coming to work, and somebody left a cash drawer sitting out on the front counter through about two-thirds of my french fries. A customer actually had to push the thing aside when he came to the counter to be waited on. Fortunately, he didn't notice what it was, or was honest, because he didn't dip into it. Just as I was about to leave, a young lady carrying her Stockpile Video green blazer over her arm came rushing from the bus stop—nearly late for work, apparently—and pulled open the side delivery door that should have been securely locked at all times, and walked right in.

Fine. It wasn't my problem anymore.

I tossed the lunch leftovers in the trash can and went out to Hizzie.

As I pulled onto Montrose and started toward Alabama, I remembered that I'd had to shake the deodorant can a little too vigorously this morning. Okay. Walgreens was just ahead. I needed some cat litter, too, and I ought to stop at a grocery store.

But I didn't stop anywhere. Suddenly, I realized what I was doing, coming up with all these side trips and errands. What I was doing was putting off going to see Carl Woods. Grandpa would have had several rather pointed sayings about this.

Mentally, I rapped my knuckles and passed up Walgreens and headed directly for 1600 Alabama.

1600 Alabama.

Rhea had done that odd little smirk as she wrote down that address.

I knew why. She had expected me to be shocked when I got there. But we had kind of a history, 1600 Alabama and I.

I was about fourteen when my cousin, Doug, who was twenty or twenty-one then, announced at Thanksgiving that he was gay.

His mother, my civic-minded Aunt Pearl, had a cow on the spot and had to be practically carried home, missing the only turkey this century that my mother didn't cook to the consistency of hot Styrofoam. The rest of the family coped in their own ways. Dad carved the turkey as if he'd heard there were hand grenades mixed in the dressing. Mom relaxed because the bird wasn't so dry that the knife blade skreeked and because, with Aunt Pearl gone, everyone wouldn't be yelling about politics all day long. Grandpa kept nodding understandingly at Doug and reciting pithy sayings. My other aunt, Aunt-Ant, cutely short for Aunt Antoinette, looked relieved because, for once, she wasn't going to have to sit there eating and listening to Pearl, between campaign speeches, make snide remarks about her weight, which had long ago gotten way past the remarks stage. I wasn't too bothered. I did wonder if this meant that, from now on, when Doug and I played football, it ought to be tag only. But mostly, it seemed okay to me. I was in high-mega-mid-puberty and anything that improved the guy/girl ratio even minutely in my favor was fine with me.

No big deal. We all took it pretty well.

Except for Aunt Pearl, of course.

She was determined to get elected to the City Council and fulfill her life, and she couldn't get over the fact that her only son had turned "funny" just to ruin her chances. Sometime later, though, she figured out that Kathy Whitmire had gotten elected Mayor with the help of a huge gay voter turnout and, when Thanksgiving rolled around again, good old Aunt Pearl practically held Doug down and hand-fed the cranberry sauce to him.

That didn't help her win the next election. But she kept on trying. She still does. To the point that, last election, one of the bumper stickers for the candidate who won said, "Pearl Ruhl for Candidate/Sheila Matuszek for City Council."

Anyway, when Doug broke the big news, he was just out of college with a new job selling copy machines for Xerox, and a little later, he moved into this big apartment complex at 1600 Alabama which was well known to be a practically completely gay place. After I got over worrying about what form of football it was socially acceptable to play with him now, we kept on being buddies.

Discos were still pretty big then and the best discos, with the best music and lights, were gay places, and I went around to some of them sometimes with Doug. Sometimes, I took dates there. They were great places. Besides the fact that they were better discos, I didn't have to worry about somebody hitting on my date. It always astonished me how comfortable those gay places were, and how relaxed. The regular places were different. At Gilley's, which was still going big then, or at Cooter's, for examples, everybody was tense all the time, walking around with stiff legs and attitude. It seemed to be house rules that you had to scratch your crotch at least once every two minutes whether you needed to or not. And if somebody looked at the wrong pair of boobs the wrong way, you had to be ready to get really tense and hit him in the mouth.

Doug was a good guy.

Then AIDS got big and disco died completely. Aunt Pearl lost a couple more elections. My dad died. Mom turned into a professional widow and, whenever you needed her, pulled out the photo albums and the guilt. Aunt-Ant became a health food freak and never wanted to talk about anything but wheat germ and organic gardening, and got fatter than ever. Sarah and I got married and divorced the first time. Grandpa was a good guy, but his sayings got older and older. Doug, though, was a rock. Then AIDS got even bigger. Doug came down with it. He died slow and hard about ten years ago. Aunt Pearl asked me to help clear out his apartment at 1600 Alabama. But that wasn't the way it worked. She sat and sobbed over how she'd gone wrong while I packed Doug's things and did a little sobbing of my own, but privately. Then she asked me to do a favor for her and call somebody and find out how long she could continue to use Doug's Handicapped Parking tag because it would be such a big help to her when she was driving around putting out her campaign signs. I kicked her out of Doug's apartment and finished the packing and watched his things get loaded onto a truck to go to her house, and then went over to Grandpa's and got terminally drunk listening to his sayings. I haven't spoken to Aunt Pearl since, and don't plan to. Not even if she starts running for President.

1600 Alabama.

It hadn't changed much. Some new paint here and there. And it seemed quieter. The guys around the swimming pool didn't look as if they were having as much fun as they used to. Carl Woods' apartment was Number 278. Doug had lived in Number 114. I went up the stairway on the west side, and didn't even have to look at 114.

At Number 278, a guy answered the door. He was too young to be Carl, and had red hair.

"Is Carl Woods in?" I asked.

"No. He's at the club."

"What club?"

He looked at me as if I had missed something. "Frenchy's Cabaret."

"Okay," I said. "Where's that?"

Now he looked at me as if I was from Mars. He told me the address in a tone that said he was wondering if he was also going to have to explain the concept of street-numbering to me: "2320 Richmond." In a moment, he added, "You're going to have to get rid of that mustache, you know."

I didn't ask. I just said, "Thanks," and started away. Back the way I had come.

But after about ten steps, I turned around and took the walkway around to the other side and went downstairs and walked past Number 114. It looked just like it always had. I wanted to knock and have Doug open the door and look at me with that crooked smile of his that meant he was wondering what his screwed-up straight cousin was screwed-up about now, and resigned to the fact that he was soon to find out.

I didn't knock, of course. Doug was dead.

I went out and got in the car and yelled at the superheated metal surfaces for a while and then drove on over to Richmond Avenue.

I hadn't used Richmond much lately. It used to be a hell of a nice street because just a few years ago, they widened it and repaved it from practically downtown almost all the way out to the Loop, and I used it all the time. It was great. It was the street the Mayor hoped you'd use on the way to vote. Then they decided to tear up the new concrete to put in a new water line. Amazing! "Your Tax Dollars at Work." With all the construction, I stayed away from it. When they tried to put it back together again, afterward, it was a mess.

Something I'd missed during the time I'd been detouring was that the overly trendy seafood restaurant that used to occupy the big corner space in the strip shopping center at Richmond and Greenbriar had closed, and something called Frenchy's Cabaret was going in in its place.

I wondered if the landlord knew it was going to be a gay place. But thinking more about it, I wondered if he—or she, of course—cared. Probably the biggest thing he—or she—was thinking about was that it would be nice if somebody would come in who could last long enough to pay some rent for a while. A surprising amount of social progress gets done that way.

Lots of construction was going on. The sign saying, "Frenchy's Cabaret," was spectacular, but a hell of a lot more tasteful than the fifteen-feet high shimmying orange neon shrimp-with-a-halo that used to proclaim that this was Herb's Seafood Heaven. In front was a small wooden sign that said, GRAND OPENING SEPTEMBER 15.

As I parked and walked across the superheated afternoon concrete toward the entrance, I was a little puzzled. The place was big enough for a disco, but I thought they were dead long ago.

The inside looked disco, too, with lots of neon shapes hanging from the ceiling and stuck on the walls—blue and white airplanes, red cocktail glasses with green olives in them, zigzag abstracts, etc.

A muscular, suntanned guy wearing paint-smeared gray gym shorts and Taiwanese thongs just like Hilda Guttman's was painting the entryway walls in some kind of DayGlo green. "Yeah," he said. "Can I help you?"

"Is Carl Woods here?"

"Oh," he said. "Sure." He motioned toward a hallway that went off to the side away from the big inside area. Then he added, "That mustache'll have to go."

I was getting kind of tired of this. But Grandpa would surely have had a saying about hassling guys with brushes full of weird green paint, so I let it pass and went looking for Carl.

It got dark back here in the hallway. It was cluttered with ladders and five-gallon buckets and stacks of acoustical tile. I was picking my way along toward a lighted doorway when a door behind me opened.

I turned around.

A woman stood there. A tall blonde woman. Around her neck was one of those old-time mink stoles where a whole mink, with glass bead eyes, is biting its own tail. She had on a long Marlene Dietrich blue-and-silver sequin-covered dress and was smoking a cigarette through a holder about a foot-and-a-half long. She went hip-slung against the side of the doorway and said, "You're late. And the ad said no mustaches. Besides, you're way too hunky."

Her voice was low. Very low. She wasn't a woman.

I held up my hand. "I just want to talk to Carl Woods for a few minutes."

"You're not here for the audition?"

"No."

He dropped the hip-slung pose and looked as if that felt much better—how the hell do women stand like that, anyway? "What's your name?" he asked.

"Tony Aapt."

He nodded. "You're the private detective."

"How would you know that?"

He did some eyebrow work that looked familiar, and confirmed it was a family trait when he said, "I'm Carl. Rhea called me."

"Hi," I said, and stuck out my hand.

He shook it. He'd done a great makeup job on himself. And even had on false eyelashes about an inch long. In the makeup, even with the blonde wig, he looked astonishingly like Rhea, except for the mouth. His mouth didn't look at all as if he was ready to eat a wildebeest. "Rhea said you're interested in our beloved Uncle Jason."

"Something like that."

He hitched at his bosom. "You know what? It's damned near impossible to get decent falsies in this town."

I tried to look sympathetic.

When he got things nudged back into reasonably proper shape, he said, "You're trying to break it off in Jason's ass, aren't you?"

For an interrogation, this was kind of a fast start. I held up my hand again, trying to slow things down.

He didn't want them slow. "Fine. Let's do it. Let's nail the son-of-a-bitch."

When things get ahead of you, jump on. "Okay," I said. "How?"

He said, "Are you straight, or what?"

"Straight."

With a toss of his blonde wig and a very Marlene Dietrich leer, he said, "Too bad. But I knew it already. Rhea said you were, and that girl's never been wrong about anything like that."

I tried to look smug.

He arched a darkly-penciled eyebrow. "Are you going to be okay to talk here? Or had I better put on my Wranglers and my cowboy boots and meet you at Billy Bob's Bullshit Bar so we can talk man-to-man over a Lone Star Beer and a chicken-fried steak?"

"Just keep your dress on," I said. "This is fine with me."

He gave me an approving red-lipped grin. "Fine." Hitching the dead mink higher up onto his shoulder, he turned and walked into the main part of the place.

I wanted to ask how the hell he managed those heels. But I didn't. There are things it's better not to know.

The bar wasn't in operation as yet, of course, but there were plenty of refreshments available, and he got us a couple of cold beers while I shoved boards and dropcloths aside and uncovered a table.

"How do you like my club?" he asked, after we sat down.

I glanced around. It was expensive. It was impressive. "Looks great. Is it yours?"

"Absolutely."

"What does your Uncle Jason think about your opening a place like this in his town?"

"Are you kidding? What can he do? He'd probably love to run me out, but then people might talk. He's leaving me alone so as not to stir up any stink."

There was a green neon airplane hanging from the ceiling practically right over us. I wondered if Carl knew how ghastly its light made him look. Surely not. I leaned forward and stared at my beer and said, "Do you dress like this all the time?"

"Auditions today. And somebody's got to show them how it's supposed to be done."

"That's why I got the mustache cracks. You thought I came in here to put on a dress."

He gave me a wry look. "Everybody else did. Why should you be different?"

"Is this what this is going to be? A drag bar?"

"Puh-leaze!" he said, in horror that wasn't entirely fake. "Not drag—*show*. There's a vast, *vast* difference."

"Okay."

Suddenly, the false eyelashes stopped fluttering. "Jason stole George's lawnmower blade, didn't he?"

"Some people think so."

Being careful not to muss his wig, he lifted the dead mink over his head and, after tenderly smoothing the fur between its glass eyes, set it down on the table. "When Rhea called and told me about you, it suddenly all clicked. I was only about six then, you know, but I knew there was something wrong. Now I know what it was."

Grandpa always told me never to interrupt a lady when

she was going good, so I just drank my beer and listened.

"I've always wondered why Jason suddenly started being nice to us right after George died, and now I finally know," Carl said. He hitched at his bosom some more, and then sat back. "The son-of-a-bitch had always treated us like dirt. My dad was his older brother and he got in trouble and pissed everybody off and got disowned and then he married my socially unacceptable Mexican mother. When my father died, she didn't have any place to go but to Jason. The way people rated with Jason, there was the help, then there was dog shit. Last, there was us.

"When George died, I said something about his gun that he kept in a shoebox in the garage, that Uncle Jason had caught me playing with one day. And I asked who was going to get his lawnmower now? Jason suddenly got real nice. To the point that he even had this old bitch-cook of his dish up some of her special ice cream for us that he usually only let company and the help have. Then he told me it wasn't nice to talk about dead people. Made me feel awful because I liked George. He told me that if I could remember not to talk about George or the things he'd been working on, and if I'd keep Rhea from talking about him, too, he'd have a big surprise for us. A couple of days later, this insurance money came for Mom, and he put us on the train to Chicago. I always wondered about that insurance money. Now I really do."

"How's that?" I asked.

"Nobody'd heard of any insurance money before that. But suddenly, there it was. I'll bet you anything it was really Uncle Jason's money, and he just came across with it to get us out of town because we knew it was George that really invented the lawnmower blade. Probably also because I knew he knew about George's gun."

"Could be," I said.

He stretched out a leg, looked at it, and squirmed around and hitched at his crotch. "Did you ever put on a pair of panty-hose?"

"Uh, no. Don't think so."

"Well, if you ever start thinking women are the weaker sex, try some."

I chuckled or grunted, or something.

He said, "I never made the connection between George's invention and Jason's money until today. I knew his company suddenly came out with some kind of lawnmower-thing, and he made a lot of money on it, but I never made the connection before."

"You were just a little kid."

He pulled the mink over close and started petting it. "Do you really think he killed George?"

I sidestepped with, "Do you think he could do something like that?"

He laughed. "In a heartbeat. That's the coldest son-of-a-bitch I ever ran into."

"Okay." I said. "If you think he could kill somebody, how did he do it?"

Carl did a big, camp "Shoo-ie!" gesture at me with his cigarette holder. "Well, you're the detective, aren't you? How the hell would I know that?"

Then he did a big dramatic pause, with lifted eyebrows and everything.

I waited.

Finally, he gave me the punchline: "I know who does know, though."

"Who?"

"That lawyer of his—Clinton-somebody. They were tight as hell, Jason and Clinton. I remember they were always acting like they were up to something. I'd be playing and get too close to where they were talking, and Jason would get totally pissed-off and run me off and yell at my mother for not controlling me better."

"Yeah," I said. "The lawyer. Clinton McKenna. He's on my list."

"You haven't talked to him yet?"

"Nobody was home."

"Keep trying. He can tell you a lot."

I already knew that, of course. I was getting antsy. There didn't seem to be much here but more old antagonisms and interesting conjectures—except for the startling news about George's gun, of course. It was almost five o'clock and Richmond would be full of maniacs trying to get home from work, but I might as well go take my chances with them. I shoved my beer bottle away and started to stand up. "I'll keep that in mind. In the meantime, I've got to be going."

I reached into my pocket. Business cards are great inventions. If you didn't have to use one to get things started, they're great to get things stopped.

Before I could hand the card to Carl, he sat back, smiling in a red-lipped way that suddenly very strongly showed that at least a few of Rhea's meat-eating mouth genes had spilled over to her little brother. He said, "Get to Clinton, and I guarantee you he'll spill his guts."

I settled back into my chair. "Oh, yeah?"

"Yeah. But you'll need an ice-breaker, you know."

"An ice-breaker?"

"Sure. Something to get his attention."

I looked at the mink. The poor damned thing must have been dead for about as long as George. "I hope you're going to tell me what that is."

"Definitely."

"Okay. What?" I said.

"All you've got to do is ask him where he spends two or three afternoons every week."

I looked blank.

"It'll be a definite ice-breaker," Carl said, looking at me very smugly from under those damned false eyelashes. "I noticed him right after I moved back to town and was scouting around the Montrose area looking for a place for my club. He looked familiar. It took me a while, but I finally figured out that he was Clinton from the bad old days when we lived at Jason's."

I looked even blanker and waited some more.

Looking even smugger, Carl did a long, long pause and waved his cigarette holder around as if he was conducting an orchestra to the grand climax. Finally, he stopped the holder.

And said, "Where Clinton McKenna spends two or three afternoons a week is over on Deep Westheimer. Cruising around in his Mercedes. Picking up hustlers. The male kind. The ones he likes best are the skinny black kids that look like they're about fifteen years old."

SEVENTEEN

Electronic Goodies and Old Memories

Maggie had been shopping.

Shopping!

Today, she had done Home Entertainment.

She had done a lot of it. So much, in fact, that guys in suits were delivering the stuff.

There were TVs for practically every room, ranging from small for the bathrooms to gargantuan for what she was calling "the study." Three VCRs, so she'd be sure not to miss something. Two CD players and enough speakers to outfit the Summit for a heavy metal concert. And of course, a whole library of CDs and videocassettes, pre-recorded and blank. Plus one of those new DVD players, and some discs for it.

Incredible. Maggie's taste—as I remembered it from her jukebox action at the Alabama Tavern—ran pretty much to Country and Western, and the CDs included practically everything Clint Black and Garth Brooks and Reba McEntire and Willie Nelson and Conway Twitty had done, with a lot of Patsy Cline and Waylon Jennings and Vince Gill thrown in, but also Frank Sinatra and Isaac Stern, Van Cliburn, Tina Turner, Meatloaf, Melissa Etheridge, Hootie & the Blowfish, Gary Barlow, etc., etc., etc. The videocassettes and DVD disks included *Air Force One*,

Indiana Jones and the Last Crusade, *Sound of Music*, *Lethal Weapon I*, *II* and *III*, *Gone with the Wind*, *Babe*, *Ghost*, *Sister Act*, *Casablanca*, *Laura*, a bunch of Cornel Wilde swashbucklers, *A Summer Place*, *Pretty Woman*, the old *Sabrina* and the new *Sabrina* and so forth. Maggie could have, right now, locked herself in, and sat here and beat her eardrums and her eyeballs off without ever repeating and without leaving the place until about 2018.

The equipment was strictly State-of-the-Bucks stuff. Some of it was so fantastic I hadn't even seen it advertised in *Playboy* yet.

Must be nice to have money.

Was I jealous?

Hell, no. Pluperfectly and totally envious, but not jealous.

I gnashed my teeth a little, and then settled in with some of that great scotch on that great Rolls Royce chair and watched Maggie in action. It probably wouldn't rank very high on most folks' entertainment lists to sit around and watch somebody accept merchandise, but starring Maggie, it was great.

Her organization was awe-inspiring. As soon as a box passed the threshold, she was ready with where it went and a reminder that they'd promised her at the store that they'd unpack it, too, and to set the empty boxes in the garage—neatly, please—in case she had to return something, "and don't throw away any of my warranty cards or manuals." She distributed the stuff around the townhouse as if she'd had the whole thing planned for years.

Me? I would have come home from Target with my marked-down last year's merchandise and set it in the middle of the living room and gotten the box off it. Then I'd try to remember to throw the box away in a couple of weeks—about the time I got a corner cleared to put the new goodie in.

At first, I felt a little sorry for the guys who were doing the carrying-in—Maggie had obviously sweet-talked the sales guys into bringing her purchases by her house, instead of going to happy hour—and they were totally sweating out their dress shirts. Then I realized that, this morning, they heaved it into work hoping that, today, please, God, just let me sell a couple of speakers, or something, and then Maggie had walked in and cleaned them out.

Some lady, Maggie.

Finally, everything was in and unpacked and in place and ready to go.

Maggie shooed "the boys" out and started a new Shania Twain album going in the nearest CD player and then collapsed on the sofa as if she'd just gone through D-Day. I went over to the bar and made her a drink and brought it to her.

She rolled her eyes in gratitude. Then she took a big appreciative slug of her drink and said, "Okay, I've been busy. What about you?"

This brought up something that Grandpa had repeated every time he told me about one of his cases: what you could tell a client about a case in progress. His answer was practically nothing, except that you were working your butt off. The exception was if something came up that the client could shed some light on. Then you got the light going, but you still didn't tell anything important about the case.

I said, "I've been busy, too. Your notes have helped a lot. I've definitely established that George was working on a lawnmower blade while you and he were living at Woods' place."

Maggie's face lighted up. She waited for details.

I said, "Tell me everything you can about Clinton McKenna."

Somewhat disappointed, she leaned back into the sofa. "It's in my notes. He was just a lawyer friend of Jason Woods. But after the GRASSBUSTER came out, I checked, and he was all of a sudden a vice president of Jason Woods Industries. Still is."

"Yeah. There's that. But what about his personal life? Married?"

"Married," Maggie said. "His wife's name is Elinor. They have two kids. I read in the paper a few months ago that they had their third grandchild."

"His wife. Just one wife?"

"Yes."

"No divorces?"

"No."

"Okay. Just wondering."

Waving off the McKennas, she said, "Who have you talked to so far?"

I said, "Did you ever meet Dr. Potter?"

Somewhat impatiently: "Yes. At some party or other at the college. He was chaperoning, and I was introduced to him."

"Bad teeth," I said. "Little prissy guy."

She smiled at my description and nodded. "Yes. That's him. 'Snaggle-tooth,' we used to call people like that." The smile left. "He didn't like me. George worshiped him, but Dr. Potter didn't like me. He didn't want George to have any distractions."

I nodded.

"Well?" she said.

I held out my hands, palms toward her, in the classic "slow down" gesture. "Don't push, Maggie. I guarantee you it'll drive both of us crazy if I give you a blow-by-blow every ten minutes. I think I'm making progress. About the time I stop thinking so, you'll get your total, full report. In the meantime, just let me do my job."

That was a little standard segment that Grandpa had inserted into practically every war story he'd ever told me. Now, I was about to see if it really worked.

It did. "All right," Maggie said. "Do it your way."

To celebrate, I fixed us another drink.

After I was sitting down again, I said, "Tell me about this," and reached into my jacket pocket and pulled out that torn-out yearbook page and handed it across the coffee table to her.

She took it with a little perplexity. The perplexity eased somewhat when she recognized what it was, except now she was wondering what an old yearbook page had to do with anything. Then she unfolded it and saw the snapshot of herself and Larry Milburn, and there wasn't anything on her face but shock.

"Who's Larry Milburn?" I asked.

Maggie set the page on the coffee table. Then she picked it up again. Finally, she said, "Someone I used to know. Before I met George."

I waited.

She looked into her glass. She took a drink. She set the glass down on the coffee table. Finally, she said, "He was George's best friend. He introduced us." She looked at me. "Why are you asking about Larry Milburn? Last I heard, he's been working in the Middle East. For years."

"I'm curious because there isn't anything in your notes about him."

"He was just an old boyfriend. He went off to Algeria after he graduated."

"Why all the reaction, Maggie?"

"Damn!" she said. She picked up the yearbook page, stared at the snapshot for a moment, and then slapped it down on the coffee table. "He must have thought I was awful. Just like everybody else did. After George died. Thinking I made him kill himself."

She went back to the snapshot. "Handsome, wasn't he? I wasn't too bad, myself." She looked at me. "All right. Fine. It doesn't have anything to do with anything, but marrying George was a big mistake. I did it because I was mad at Larry. He got a summer job in Wyoming, but I wanted him to stay here. So I was mad at him—we had a big fight over it. I was mad and lonely. George was here. We started seeing each other. It was a big mistake. But it happened."

Seeming suddenly very tired, she sank back into the sofa, still clutching that old, torn-out yearbook page. "I lied. It wasn't George that wanted to travel, it was me. Those posters in our little apartment were mine. Not George's. He thought they were silly. He had all this imagination. And all this understanding. But it was for things, not for people. I wanted romance; all George ever even knew existed was machines. It was such a big mistake. But it was done."

"That must have made it even worse for you when he died."

She gave me a pathetically grateful look. "It made it awful. Do you know what guilt is? What it really is? It's being blamed—and maybe even blaming yourself, no matter how much you tell yourself you shouldn't—for somebody dying just at the time you're about to get up the guts to leave him.

"I was going to leave George. We didn't have any real problems. But we just didn't have anything real, either. I was going to leave him and, when Larry came back to town—this time, his summer job was in Canada somewhere—I was going to try to get him to forgive me. I knew he couldn't, but I was going to crawl across Houston, if I thought it'd do any good.

"Then George was dead. And everybody thought I drove him to it."

Angrily, she finished her drink and got up and went stalking across to the bar and sloshed more scotch into her glass, not bothering with ice or water. "Is this what I'm paying you five hundred dollars a day for? I thought I was hiring a private eye, not a shrink."

"I'm sorry if I brought up bad memories," I said. "But I had to know. Something didn't fit. I had to know why."

She shook her head sadly. " 'Something didn't fit.' George and I didn't fit. And before I could do anything about it, he was dead. That's what was so awful."

Walking slowly, tiredly, she came back to the sofa and sat down. "You know, I used to have this fantasy. I'd get hold of some money and I'd hire somebody that would prove what really happened to George. Maybe not even that Jason Woods killed him. Maybe that he really did kill himself. But mostly, it'd prove he didn't do it because of me.

"And then, one night in some bar I was working in, I'd look up and there'd be Larry, just happening to wander into the place. All straight and tall and handsome. He was so handsome! And compact. You know what I mean?"

She was embarrassed for a moment, and then decided she was past embarrassment. "What they call 'hunky' now. Not like George. George's whole family was fat. Did you know that? How could you? They were gross. George was going to get gross, too." She grimaced. "I sound awful. But I couldn't stand the idea of George blowing up like his father had."

Suddenly, she waved all that away. "Larry wasn't like that. He was really handsome. In his eyes and voice and hands, as well as just in his looks.

"I'd have this daydream that he'd wander into this bar someday, and I'd go over to his table. He'd look up at me as if I was something awful. And I'd drop the detective report in front of him that said I wasn't why George died, and then I'd run like hell. In a minute, I'd be out by my car, crying, trying to get it unlocked. And Larry'd come after me. Because he'd finally found out I wasn't awful, after all, he'd come after me."

I said, "Then you'd go off to Paris and Rome and Australia and Tahiti, and all those places."

She smiled softly. "You must think I'm such an old fool."

I thought of a stale cauliflower man, chugging beer and scarfing down junk food. "No, I don't."

Now Maggie grinned. "If you were about twenty, twenty-five years older, I'd grab you up right now, and run off to Paris with you."

I grinned, too. "If I were twenty, twenty-five years older, I'd beg you to."

We chuckled a little, a little embarrassedly.

Then she looked around. "I've got all this machinery to get cranked up and try out."

I stood up. "And I've got somebody to see."

She looked at the yearbook page lying there on the coffee table. "Do you need this?"

"No."

"Good," she said. "I do."

EIGHTEEN

$500 Down—$6,500 To Go

Now, I went to the store.

Deodorant. Cat litter. Cat food.

I started to get some cans of the old cheap stuff. But why shouldn't Spooky share in the wealth? So I picked up some Fancy Feast. Then I really splurged and picked up a catnip mouse. It had been a while since I had felt like treating him to a binge.

This time when I walked into the apartment, I didn't get attitude because I was home when I should be working. I got it because I'd been out all day.

Fine. I went into the kitchen and played his song: "The Can-opener Sonata."

Suddenly, here he was, winding himself around my ankles, loving me without reservation. Oh, really? Well, you take what you can get. Especially from cats.

Fancy Feast didn't require the can-opener, of course. I pulled the handy tab-top open and dumped the stuff into one of his dishes and set it down. He loved it. He loved me. Mostly, he loved me for Liver & Giblets.

There was nothing new on the answering machine. There especially was no call from Jason Woods. So I returned Hanley Moss' call. He didn't answer. He apparently was someone who still didn't have an answering machine. I figured he must be out stocking up on Preparation H.

I sat down and scanned through my notes. Except for one more thing, one day was pretty much done. My practice session with Hanley Moss—fun but not much help. Mrs. Guttman—no fun at all, but some exercise, humiliation, and contradictions. Dr. Potter—more contradictions but enlightening, I guess. George Hawk's old buddy, Larry Milburn—great fun and informative. Rhea Chatham—scary. Carl Marlene Dietrich Woods—bizarre, and maybe the most informative of all.

Okay, what was I going to do to earn the other sixty-five hundred dollars?

The most self-satisfied cat in the world came swaggering out of the kitchen, licking his lips. He swaggered over to me and pushed against my leg. I reached down to pet him, and he let me know that he wasn't in the mood and took his swagger out of my presence.

For about the five-hundredth time, I wondered whether the old Egyptians had mummified their cats before or after their natural deaths. At the moment, I was betting on before.

I ran the Norelco over my face and brushed my teeth and changed shirts and was halfway out of the apartment before I remembered the catnip mouse.

I tore off the plastic wrapping and stepped into the living room to find the cat in our favorite old beat-up easy chair, glaring at me because I had interrupted the first of his after-dinner naps.

"Here," I said, and tossed the mouse at him. He batted it down onto the floor and then sprang off the chair and went after it. In a moment, he was just a black rag doll, rolling around on the floor, hugging and nuzzling the catnip mouse.

Once again, I wished I could get an instant high from a buck's worth of legal vegetation.

" 'Bye, Spook," I said, as I left. "Everything's okay. Knock yourself out. I'm taking the car keys."

NINETEEN

My Dinner with Sarah

For dinner, I took Sarah to this restaurant she'd been raving about, just to rub it in that, for the moment, at least, I considered myself to be a successful private eye. Well, there was another reason: I wanted to find out if she had been intrigued enough by Maggie's case to be of some help.

Eric's was Yup heaven.

Absolutely.

Attitude everywhere. Starting with the valet parking. I wasn't about to watch Sarah do her usual martyr-act over Hizzie's shabbiness, so we went in her Accord. It's amazing how put-down a guy who makes minimum wage plus tips can get when you ask him to park a car that cost less than fifty thousand dollars. Donald Trump, I'd expect to be offended. But a guy who takes the bus to work?

Inside, it kept up.

Designer jeans. Designer running shoes. Designer haircuts. Designer waiters and waitresses.

Ours was a sweet young lady with an Annie Lennox haircut, dressed in a green smock cut like a judo outfit with a little porcelain bunch of asparagus pinned over her left breast. "Hi," she said incandescently. "I'm Andrews. I'll be your guide through Eric's menu tonight."

Sarah glowed at the kindness and the originality and the

send-up of sexism with the last name only.

Andrews established a personal relationship with us—something I always go to restaurants for. "I love your bracelet," she said to Sarah with a dazzling smile. Then it was my turn to get rapport-ed. But there wasn't much to say about my old Seiko, and my shirt didn't have a pony on it anywhere, so she punted. "I'll bet it was a gift from you."

Wrong thing to say. The bracelet was Sarah's consolation present to herself after we got divorced the second—and please, God, the last!—time.

Andrews took the chill rather well. With a smile that had turned sad and apologetic, she retreated to "Could I get you something from our bar?"

She could. I ordered scotch-and-water while Sarah studied the wine list and finally settled on a glass of some unpronounceable kind of white wine, informing Andrews it was "because it's such a pleasant little *chardonnay.*"

When she walked away, I said, "It had better be pleasant, at ten-fifty a glass. Whatever happened to the Gallo girl?"

"Okay, Tony. If it bothers you, tell her we want separate checks."

It was a thought, but I was a successful private eye, so I just laughed it off. And checked out the menu.

Half of it, it seemed, was turgid, purple, misspelled prose belaboring the fact that everything about Eric's was wholly and totally organic and ecologically correct. I had to wonder about that. Presumably, he escorted cockroaches off the property with a firm grip on the carapace. Presumably, he scrubbed down the dirty dishes with a strong solution of white vinegar and spring water, and cooked on a fire fed with recycled Popsicle sticks.

The drinks came, and we ordered dinner. Sarah and Andrews had a fine social experience with that. But I was less cooperative. Andrews admiringly informed me that I looked like a raw vegetables man, but I hurt her feelings by ordering only things that were cooked. That's the main thing that disconcerts me about all this organic-stuff—idolizing plants that have had shit dribbled over them instead of good, clean chemical fertilizers. I ordered cooked stuff, and told Andrews to be sure to tell Eric to go heavy on the Popsicle sticks. She looked at me as if I'd broken her heart.

"Why were you rude to her?" Sarah asked after she left.

"She shouldn't take up with strangers so easily."

"Oh, God, Tony. Honestly!"

"Honestly. I remember when we were happy about cheeseburgers and beer."

"We didn't know about arteries then."

I glanced around. "Or running shoes instead of sneakers, and Platinum Cards and junk bonds and Fergie and designer Kleenex."

"You just love to be rude, don't you?"

"Uh-oh. Did I miss something? Did we stop by the chapel on the way over here? Did we forget and do the M-word again?"

She laughed. "God, you're a shit."

"So are you, love. I'll drink to that."

We did.

Then I said, "Do you know what I'm thinking?"

She rolled her eyes. "What now?"

"How lucky we are."

She raised an eyebrow. "Lucky, how?"

"I mean, look at us. Most people have to struggle through years of a bad marriage to achieve the kind of relationship we have. We did it with only two divorces."

She gave me a dirty look.

I reminded myself that one shouldn't get too philosophical in an organic restaurant and said, "How's your wine?"

"Well, it's wonderful, of course."

"Of course," I said.

Andrews stopped by and whispered intimately to us that Eric was working diligently on our dinners. Then she hurried over to present the check to the next table, and got a platinum Visa card in return. Obviously, all this ecological correctness didn't prevent her from appreciating plastic when it mattered.

Sarah said, "How's the case?"

"The case is fine," I said, and waited.

But instead of coming across with something helpful, she swerved suddenly into occupational therapy. "Tony, just look around."

"Look around? Okay."

"What do you see?"

"Don't ask."

"Oh, my God! I wish you could be serious and just look at yourself and your life for once." She pointed with her head. "That man over there—in the Speedo T-shirt and the Patek Phillippe watch. He can't be even as old as we are, but he's obviously successful. You can tell just by looking at him that he does something real—something he cares about—and he does it well."

"Yes," I said, and lied, "You're right. I recognize him."

"You do?"

I really lied. "Sure. He's the sportscaster with the Los Angeles Dodgers. They're in town to start a four-game series with the Astros tomorrow. Nothing but real for him. He spends every evening agonizing over whether twenty-year-old kids making fifteen thousand dollars a game are going to hit the ball tonight, or not. And his most awesome responsibility, of course, is to pop the top off another can of Bud when somebody hits a homer. How real can you get?"

She didn't know whether to believe me or not.

While she was worrying about it, someone walking past our table spoke to me and gave me a big wave and a grin. He was the kind of guy Eric was born to cook for. Stone-washed jeans. Versace shirt. Big, ugly Rolex. Italian loafers. Hair tousled just enough to tell you that he'd made the valet parking guy happy by stepping out of a BMW convertible.

"Who was that?" Sarah said, looking at me almost in awe.

"I don't know." I shrugged. "Probably the Video King's attorney."

"What?"

Quickly, I shrugged some more. I didn't want to get into that. With Sarah sitting there giving me the motherly news that I was a failure, I didn't feel like telling her that I was also getting terminally sued.

I wondered who the guy was, too. He looked vaguely familiar as he went across to the bar. After he paid the bartender four dollars to open a twenty-nine cent bottle and pour what at the outside couldn't be a thousandth of a cent worth of foreign water into a glass, he sat sipping at it, obviously waiting for someone.

In the meantime, Sarah had apparently decided that she had hassled me enough, and said, "So, how's Jason Woods?"

"Rich. Also unavailable."

"He's going to run for governor."

I stared at her.

"Sure. Word's gently seeping out. What can you expect? He's rich. He's given away bunches of money. Now he's decided to be a statesman. Why shouldn't he? He's got practically as much money as Ross Perot, and his ears are a lot cuter."

"Wonderful."

"You know, he really used his head when he brought out that lawnmower blade."

I waited for the rest of it, watching the waitresses and waiters as they moved around helping all their new-found friends. Our good-buddy Andrews wore that little bunch of asparagus. A guy with granny glasses and a Fu Manchu mustache wore a cute little porcelain stalk of broccoli. A girl who managed somehow to look exactly like Roseanne, although she couldn't have weighed much over a hundred ninety pounds, sported a sweet little red radish. Eric was definitely into food. I wondered what they'd do to the place—and the staff—when Christmas-decoration-time came around—if it lasted that long. But I really didn't want to know.

Sarah was a little miffed that I wasn't begging her for details, but she didn't let that stop her for long. "Like I said, patents only go for seventeen years. But you were right. Woods got around that by using licensing agreements. He wouldn't sell any of the lawnmower manufacturers any GRASSBUSTERS at all unless they contracted for an exclusive fifty-year supply. Neat, huh? That invention is still worth millions."

"Yeah."

"You know, I'm starting to agree with your Maggie. The guy's got to be a real crumb."

"Why do you say that?"

"Well, he's too good. Did you ever hear anything bad about him? Before Maggie, anyway."

"No," I admitted.

Sarah looked smug. "Well, believe me, that means he's got a lot to hide."

I appreciated her logic, but I thought I'd better not depend on it. I also thought I'd better not act too interested in her tidbits; if she knew I liked her information, I'd have hell getting the rest of it out of her. "Did you spend all day in your research department?" I asked. "Didn't you have any soup to sell?"

Andrews came back practically crying, and apologized for our wait and told us that Eric was so in love with food that he simply wouldn't rush. I consoled her by ordering another four-dollar-and-fifty-cent glass of water and scotch, and a new ten-fifty glass of wine for Sarah.

"So, how was your day?" Sarah asked. "Have you had any luck?"

I told her about Hilda's house. She agreed that it looked as if she might have been paid off, and got just a bit wistful, as if she were trying to think of somebody who would pay her off with a house in West University.

Then I told her about Dr. Potter and his teeth, congratulating myself only moderately for having ferreted out this obvious payoff.

But Sarah didn't buy it. "Huh-uh," she said, reaching into her purse and bringing out her trendy little eelskin-bound electronic organizer. "This time, you missed, Tony."

"How did I miss? Do you know what wall-to-wall crowns cost? These are Bruce Willis-class, at least."

She tapped at the notebook, waited for a moment, and then read, " 'Melvin Potter, Ph.D., born January 5, 1918.' Scads of honors. Hmmm. Here it is—'Brother Hilmer born in 1920, died in 1947,' and he left a widow and a three-year-old son." She closed the organizer, replaced it in her purse, and gave me her this-is-Mama-talking look. "Dr.

Potter took them in and put his nephew through college." She added a very raised eyebrow. "You didn't bother to check on relatives, did you?"

"Well, no," I said, knowing instantly that I should have.

"You should have. That nephew's now Dr. Neil Potter—DDS. Probably grateful enough to his uncle to have given him a terrific relative-discount on his dental work. That kind of tears up your Jason Woods payoff idea, it seems to me."

"Maybe," I said, without much grace.

With only slightly more grace, Sarah gave me a minor smirk of superiority. Then she nodded toward the bar. "He keeps looking at you."

I glanced around. She meant the man in the stone-washed jeans. He wasn't looking at me just then. He looked tantalizingly familiar.

Sarah said, "You should have a long talk with him. You should get him to tell you what it's like to be successful."

"Why should I? I've got you to do that."

She made a smirky kiss at me.

Andrews brought dinner. It was beautiful. It was a work of art. There were about four ounces of it, but it was absolutely gorgeous. Andrews hovered like a proud mommy until Sarah tasted one of her two sprigs of asparagus and went orgasmic. Then she went away glowing with fulfillment.

Sarah said, "Your chicken breast looks absolutely wonderful! How is it?"

"Underdone and undersized. You know what I want right now? An ugly pizza. You know what the most important thing places like this are doing for the environment? Making people think it's trendy to eat Styrofoam."

"Don't be rude, Tony. Don't be judgmental. Just relax and let yourself enjoy it."

I said, "Let me tell you what I'm going to enjoy."

And I did. Being dramatic, of course, and leading up to it slowly, I told her that I had lucked onto some information about one of the principals in the case, and that it was going to be dynamite.

She got interested.

I told her it was kind of like blackmail, but what he had helped Jason Woods do was worse. She wormed out of me that what I had lucked onto was that this guy, while being eminently straight, liked to pick up male hustlers, the younger and darker, the better.

She was shocked.

I was, too. Because just about then, I glanced over toward the bar and saw my mysterious friend in the stonewashed jeans greeting the person he'd been waiting for.

That person was male and was younger and had red hair. The waitress with the porcelain banana on her breast cooed over them and took them to a table so they could all get better acquainted.

Sarah said, "You remembered who he is."

"Yeah."

"Well, who? What does he do?"

"He's a drag queen, but he calls it 'show.' "

That pissed her off. "You can't be serious, can you, Tony? You can't just relax and have a good time. You always have to put people down."

"Okay," I said. "Fine. I'm sorry. His name is Jack Curtis. He's president of the Harris County Chapter of the Audubon Society. When there's an oil spill at the port, he bathes birds."

"All right," she said. "Why couldn't you just say that in the first place?"

"I guess hunger makes me crazy."

She shook her head in exasperation. And then said, "All right, who is he?"

I did some exasperation, myself.

She said, "Not your Audubon Society friend—I mean who is it that picks up male hustlers?"

The drama had pretty well gotten shot all to hell, I thought.

But I wanted to get every drop of it I could.

I said, "He ought to be home by now. Eat your brussels sprout like a good, organic girl, and I'll let you tag along while I go look him up."

TWENTY

I Wanted To Ask Her Why, after All These Years, the Beaver and I Couldn't Have Our Own Rooms

Sarah drove, and I directed. She had always liked River Oaks. She was never happier than when surrounded by pillars and Rolls Royces.

"Here we go," I said, and motioned her into the driveway of 3301 San Simeon.

From her expression, I could tell she was somewhat disappointed because the McKenna house was of just average opulence. But when we got out of the car and she glanced around, her spirits improved. A retired senator lived across the street behind a stone wall. Just down the street was the house of a trash-collecting heiress, the lights of its upper story gleaming through the spikes set on top of the brick wall surrounding it. It was a fairly nice neighborhood.

Lights were on inside the McKenna house.

We passed between two large white pillars and, when I pressed the button beside the front door, the vibrations of bell sounds tickled our feet through the brick porch floor.

Sarah whispered, "It's so quiet here."

"Money's good insulation," I told her.

After half a minute or so, I rang the bell again.

"They're not home," Sarah said disappointedly, bending

forward to try to peek through the narrow beveled glass panes beside the door.

Car lights washed over us.

We waited on the porch while a Mercedes pulled up and stopped at the foot of the steps.

The driver's door opened and a man stepped out and frowned at us over the top of the car. Then the front door on our side opened and a woman stepped out. A moment later, another woman emerged from the back of the car.

Sarah held my arm. We moved across the porch.

The man walked around the car. "Can I help you with something?" he said.

I waited for the three of them to get together between the car and the lower step. The man and the first woman were thirtyish. She was blonde and model-thin. He was balding and working on a belly. The other woman was older. She looked exactly like June Cleaver.

"Are you Mrs. McKenna?" I asked her.

She stepped forward into the dim glow of the porch lights. She was a dead ringer for June Cleaver!

I wanted to ask her why, after all these years, the Beaver and I couldn't finally have our own rooms. But I said, "My name is Tony Aapt. I'm a private investigator. This is my associate, Miz Warshawski. I was hoping to talk with Mr. Clinton McKenna."

The man wasn't happy about that.

Mrs. McKenna raised a hand to shush him and said, "I'm afraid that won't be possible."

I gave her an inquiring look. There was probably some sympathy in it, too. I hated to think of June Cleaver waiting supper night after night on somebody who was out buying teenaged boys.

She said, "We've just come from the hospital. My husband suffered a massive stroke day before yesterday."

Sarah's hand tightened on my arm. I felt suddenly like pelican crap. "I'm sorry. I had no idea."

"Perhaps I can help you with something."

I shook my head. All I wanted was to get out of there. "After Mr. McKenna has recovered—maybe I can talk with him then."

My eyes had adjusted enough to the low light that I could see the fatigue in the woman's face. Her hands were clenched hard on her purse. "We aren't optimistic about that, Mr. Aapt."

I mumbled, "I'm very sorry to intrude, Mrs. McKenna," and pulled Sarah along and practically ran for the car.

TWENTY-ONE

Career Guidance

We stopped at a convenience store for a six-pack of beer and a gallon of Gallo wine—during the buying of which, Sarah stayed scrunched-down behind the steering wheel for fear somebody might see her betraying the Yuppie Consumer Code.

Then we went to her apartment and ordered a pizza and settled in for a session of junk food and humility.

Humility!

Sarah started off motherly: "I can't stand to see you like this, Tony. You're bright and talented. But you're wasting your life."

"Listen," I said, "I got a setback in my case, but something else will come up. You said yourself that it's obvious that Maggie's right. So all I've got to do is keep digging."

Fact-facing was next: "Face the facts, Tony. You never had a case, anyway. You were going up against the Teflon tycoon with nothing but a former barmaid's suspicions and some conjectures. No physical proof. Nothing. Now you've got to wake up and make the best of it: put all this energy and enthusiasm into something that will pay off for you."

After that, she moved on to pizza: "Tony, this Domino's fellow had the right idea—make a pretty good pizza and get it out fast. And now, he's a jillionaire."

"Yeah, Sarah. Besides that, I'll bet he doesn't owe his ex-wife fourteen more payments of three hundred fifty dollars each."

"Besides that. Yes. That crossed my mind."

"You know what?" I said. "Something just crossed my mind, too. There's millions of guys in the world who hate their ex-wives. They'd rather be sitting here eating pizza with Janet Reno."

Sarah laughed. "Where did we go wrong?"

Then she scrunched everything all together—motherliness, faced facts, and pizza: "You don't know it now, Tony, but this case falling apart is probably the best thing that ever happened to you. Learn something from it. Get real. Get a job."

"Maybe I should start delivering pizza."

"Maybe you should. It's honest work, at least."

That was about as good an exit line as I was going to get. So I took it.

The night air was hot and wet.

I walked out from under the covered area where Sarah and her neighbors kept their cars and headed across to guest parking, wondering idly how poor old Hizzie was going to feel about having a Domino's sign strapped onto her flaking top.

Suddenly, a voice said, "Mr. Aapt," sticking in a "th" and three extra syllables.

Supercilious.

I stopped. In the semi-darkness, all I could see was a man in a dark suit leaning against a car's front fender that stuck out past the other cars parked in the guest parking area.

"Over here," Supercilious said.

I stayed where I was. Night in Houston is not a time for

going running up to people you don't really know.

Then there was a hand on my shoulder.

A big hand.

Supercilious said, "You requethted an appointment with Mr. Woods. Now, you have one."

I looked to my right. The big hand grew out of a damned big arm and shoulder. "Listen," I said, "you could have called and left a message."

"Time is of the essence. Come along now. Joe Bob, will you show Mr. Aapt to the car, please?"

Another big hand clamped down on my forearm. I came along.

When we were closer, so that the guest cars weren't in the way, I could see the rest of the car Supercilious leaned on. It was a Mercedes stretch-job, about the length of a 747.

Joe Bob brought us to a stop, but he didn't let go.

I said, "Hey, thanks, fellows. But I don't want to put you to any more trouble. Just tell me when, and I'll be there."

Supercilious smiled a wholly supercilious smile. "Very thoughtful, Mr. Aapt. But Mr. Woods likes us to take care of details like that." He glanced over my blazer and blue jeans and then smiled up at Joe Bob. "I don't see the bulge of a weapon, but we can never be too sure, can we?"

Joe Bob let go of my shoulder, but not my forearm. Moving me around as if I were a teddy bear, he patted me down.

"Good," Supercilious said, when that was over. Stepping back along the car, he opened the door of the passenger compartment.

I bent down to look inside.

I thought I might find Jason Woods there. But the compartment was empty. I started to turn to ask Supercilious if he'd forgotten somebody but, before I could, Joe Bob decisively helped me inside, and then finally let go of me and crawled in, himself. And pulled the door shut.

I was getting kind of tired of this. Scrambling across the compartment, I figured I'd scramble out the other side, and then run like hell.

The door latch didn't work. Neither did the window button. There was a black glass partition behind the driver's seat.

The car started moving, and lurched me back into the seat. Beside Joe Bob. There was room for him and me, but two of him would have crowded the hell out of the place.

The dome light was on, and I saw that Joe Bob was even bigger than I had thought. He was dressed in a very good navy blue pinstriped suit and a tie my grandfather would have killed for. He made me think of football players and professional wrestlers and Paul Bunyan.

"Okay," I said. "I want out of here." He glanced at me as if I were a mildly irritating gnat, and then seemed to forget about me while he unbuttoned his jacket and settled back to get comfortable.

The car turned.

I looked through the window.

Except that, like the partition, it was dark glass and, with the dome light on, I couldn't see through it. All I could see was my reflection and dim little pinpoints of outside light.

A speaker hummed and the car made another turn—left, this time—and Supercilious' voice sounded: "Please just relax, Mr. Aapt. And enjoy the ride." The speaker went dead.

"Damn it," I said to Joe Bob. "What's going on?"

He didn't answer. He reached inside his jacket, made crackling noises, and pulled out a cello bag of jelly beans.

Ripping the top open, he smiled pleasantly and offered me some.

I shook my head. "I'm trying to quit."

The car slowed for five or six seconds and then made another left turn and began to pick up speed. There were lots of pinpoint lights through the window. We had to be on Southwest Freeway.

I sat back and tried to relax.

Pizza delivery was looking better and better.

TWENTY-TWO

I Couldn't Help Wondering if Hillary Clinton Didn't Get Just a Tad Giggly When She Came in Here To Pee

I woke up. We were stopped. Joe Bob was hulked back in the corner, still asleep, the empty jelly bean bag clutched in his hand.

The door opened.

"Here we are, Mr. Aapt," Supercilious said.

Creakily stepping out, I said, "Where?"

He didn't have to answer. It wasn't city pseudo-darkness that surrounded us with distant sounds of traffic and a sheen of light in the air. It was country darkness, real black darkness, heavily studded with the multitude of stars that you can't see in the city.

Turning, I saw a house. A big house, with pillars and chimneys and tall, thin, brightly lighted windows. I recognized it instantly from all the times the TV news had showed Jimmy and Roslyn and, later, Bill and Hillary, dropping by for dinner parties whenever they happened to be in the area.

It was the fabled ranch house on Jason Woods' fabled W-Bar Ranch seventy-odd miles northwest of Houston. Finally, I was getting to see it in person, something usually reserved only for the noted or notorious, and the help. I'd have to remember—later—to tell myself that I was thrilled.

A plump, smiling, middle-aged woman dressed in a full skirt and huaraches that squeaked when she walked came down the steps. "Mr. Aapt, Mr. Woods will see you shortly," she said. "Would you like to freshen up first?"

Yeah, I'd like to freshen up first. I let her escort me inside.

It wasn't exactly what I had expected. It was worse. There was money here, of course—oodles and bundles and bags of money—but the style could only be described as Deep Movieland Oater Gothic. It made me think of photos and film clips I had seen of John Wayne's living room and Joel McRae's game room and, yes, there was even Norma Desmond's grand staircase.

Obviously, the person who designed the Jason Woods Administration Building had not used up all of his talents on that one. I was still half-asleep and muddle-brained, but stepping into this place, I knew exactly what Jason Woods' instructions to his architect must have been: "Here's ten million dollars. Build me a Ranch House. I love old Westerns." When it was completed, he had asked John Wayne, "Does it look like ten million bucks?" and the Duke said, "Shore 'nuff, Pilgrim," and Jason was happy.

The lady's name was Esmeralda, she assured me, grinning as if she was tickled to death to be freshening-up strangers at one o'clock in the morning. She found out what kind of coffee I liked, and then led me under a mounted buffalo head and pointed me toward a doorway.

Behind it was a guest bathroom the size of Delaware. It had to have been furnished by Cowpokes-R-Us. On the walls were fine Mexican tiles bearing hand-painted, brilliantly colored pictures of roadrunners and buffalo and armadillos and horses and longhorn cattle and horned toads.

They were exquisitely done. The problem was that the tiles were everywhere and, instead of coming across as artwork, made you think you were trapped inside the Sunday funnies. The gold-plated hot and cold water taps and spigot were horses' heads. The towel racks were gold-plated rods held up by shiny gold-plated replicas of spurs. The towels felt like cashmere and were heavily monogrammed with the W-Bar brand. They were also spotted brown and white and beige, like the hides of dead pinto ponies. The only pieces of schlock Western kitsch that seemed to have been left out were a thirty-foot path outdoors and a weather-beaten wooden door with a half moon cut into it.

As I splashed cold water on my face, I couldn't help wondering if Hillary didn't get just a tad giggly when she came in here to pee. But then, she had undoubtedly had to pee in lots of strange places over the years that she and Bill had been doing politics.

When I came out, Esmeralda had coffee for me, on a wooden tray carved with steer heads, in a heavy brown mug with a group of shiny gold coyotes chasing each others' tails around it.

She showed me to a chair in a space big enough for a hotel lobby, which I supposed was called the game room, and then hovered around while I sipped at the coffee. I'm sure she anticipated my asking her why Jason Woods had me brought here, but I didn't. People who send stretch Mercedes and oversized jelly-bean-eaters to pick up people at midnight tend to operate according to their own rules.

The room was interesting. Apparently, the decorator had started to run out of Western and decided to throw in some Kilimanjaro and a touch of Punjab. There was a regulations billiards table, complete with a long hanging light over it with a marvelous Tiffany-style shade in a Texas flag design.

In the middle of one wall, there was a huge stone fireplace. In the middle of another, a monster projection TV. The third sported a bigger-than-life-sized full-length portrait of a young Jason Woods with his foot propped up on the head of a dead lion. Stuck here and there to the various walls were the heads of various animals—cape buffalo, kudu, rhino, and elephant. Skulking on platform mounts high up on the walls were complete stuffed animals, including a lion and a warthog and a leopard. There was a zebra-skin rug in front of the fireplace. Lounging on the floor under Jason's portrait was a tiger skin, complete with snarling, glass-eyed head.

Esmeralda saw me looking at the trophies and said, "All these things date from before anyone ever heard of endangered species." Then she bent down and whispered, "Besides, Mr. Woods didn't shoot them. He bought them."

"They must be fun to dust," I said.

She gave me a long, loving look of martyrdom.

Then here came Supercilious back again. He had changed from the business suit into a tux shirt and black bow tie and a white satin-lapeled jacket. "Mr. Woods is ready for you now, Mr. Aapt," he announced.

Esmeralda smiled goodbye to me, and I went along with him, past more cowboy gaud and more dead animal parts, until we came to an elevator.

I wouldn't have protested or showed surprise if it had been a hot air balloon. Supercilious waited for me to enter and then joined me, and the door closed and we started upward. "You must work some damned long hours," I said.

He gave me a "doethn't everybody?" look. Apparently, good old Jason had bought a supply of serfs along with all those trophies.

The elevator stopped, and its door opened onto a short

hallway with a blank door at its end. Supercilious gestured me out of the elevator and to the door. He opened it to show me a small, closet-like space with another doorway at its back. "Step inside and open the outer door."

I stepped inside.

He closed the door behind me.

A bell rang softly; the light went out.

For a second, I panicked. I was sure I was trapped.

But with some groping, I found the knob of the second door, twisted it, and the door opened.

Hot muggy air. More darkness, but not quite so profound.

Stars! Sky!

I was outside. On a roof somewhere.

A hard, thin male voice came out of the darkness. "Just stand where you are until you get accustomed to the darkness. I don't want you blundering into things."

I leaned against the closed door until my vision began to adjust.

We were on the top of the house. In a sort of open box about twenty-five feet by twenty-five feet and eight or nine feet deep built into the roof. In the dim starlight, I could see odd contrivances standing here and there, parts of which were apparently metal because they reflected the stars. Off to my left, a man was bent down over one of the contrivances.

There were odd clicking sounds around me. Clickings, followed by whirrings, and then more clickings and whirrings.

Telescopes, I realized. These things were telescopes. Set up here in this weird box to avoid the lights of the house and grounds. At least some of the telescopes must be mechanized.

The man stood up and moved toward me. I knew he must be Jason Woods, but I couldn't actually see his features and be certain until he was only four or five feet away.

He extended his hand. I put out mine. We shook. His hand was dry and firm and quick. "I'll call you Tony," he said. "You'll call me Mr. Woods." He turned and waved a hand. "Let me show you my telescopes. Have you ever really seen Saturn?"

Abruptly, he stopped. "You're not night-blind, are you? You can see where you're going, can't you?"

"Well enough so I won't bump into anything," I said.

"Fine. Good. Night-blind people are a bother." He bent down toward the angled-up eyepiece of a telescope that was about the size of a beer keg. "Yes. Perfect," he muttered.

Straightening up, he motioned toward the eyepiece. "Meet Saturn."

I bent down and looked. It was Saturn, all right. Just like you always see it in pictures, with rings. Really with rings. God! It was astonishing! It was absolutely beautiful! I wanted to swim into it.

But Woods was talking to me. "Over here I've got Venus. Take a look at it. It's covered with hot gas. Seething with heat."

I pulled myself away from Saturn and went across to him and looked into the eyepiece of this telescope. Venus looked like a huge mottled pearl shimmering in the darkness.

"Mars," Woods was saying from another telescope.

I tried to see the optical illusions that people call "canals." I didn't. I saw a large reddish marble floating in black velvet.

When I straightened up, Woods was practically chuckling with pleasure. "Never seen anything like it, have you? Never knew what was hanging up there, did you? Too bad the moon's not up. Have you ever seen the moon when it really looked like a ball? No. When you see it with the naked eye, it's flat. But I could show it to you with my telescopes, and you'd see it's a ball, all right. Spherical as a basketball. Glowing like alabaster. Craters. Mountains."

I couldn't stop myself. I went over and bent down and stared at Saturn some more. It was so beautiful and real and close that I wanted to reach out to the end of the telescope and grab it and pull it in and hold it in my hand.

One of the hardest things I've ever done was breaking myself away from the eyepiece.

"She does that to you, doesn't she?" Woods said. Chuckling, he pointed toward yet another telescope. "Well, try this."

I did. He showed me nebulae and neighboring galaxies and gas giants.

My eyes started to hurt, and I stood away from a telescope and rubbed them.

The occasional clickings and whirrings were still going on.

As if he read my mind, Woods motioned toward a telescope that had a camera attached to it. "I'm looking for comets. I keep the cameras shooting and reshooting. Then the negatives are checked for squibs of light. When you discover a comet, they let you put your name on it, you know."

I was getting a headache. I was realizing that it was one-thirty in the morning, and I was on top of a house, and I was getting a hellacious headache. I'd had enough of stars and planets and comet-chases. I said, "You didn't bring me out here to look at the sky."

"No. I didn't." He moved away from the telescopes and stood suddenly very close to me.

He was an inch or two taller than I. Very thin. A wiry,

nervous thin. In the starlight, those distinguished gray wings at his temples shone silver. His mouth was a dark smudge that thinned and twisted as he talked, and his eyes were little glitters.

I was reminded of wolves. And reminded that I was very much on his territory. Wolves might have a certain fascination for lights in the sky, but they still were wolves.

Waiting, I felt the side of the enclosure against my back, and tried not to think of it as a wall. Tried also to think whether I could find the door that led back into the house.

"You've been very busy," Woods said at last. "Running to Mrs. Guttman and Dr. Potter, taking time out to visit your girlfriend, having little private chats with my relatives. Then going back to report to Mrs. Hawk before treating your former wife to a healthy dinner."

For a moment, my mind stuck on one of the things he had said—my girlfriend?

"You've been so busily interested in me," he continued, "that I thought I should certainly bring you out here to look at my stars."

Suddenly, there was a thin beeping sound.

Woods swivelled his head this way and that until he located the source of the sound and then hurried to one of the telescopes fitted with a camera. "Film's out," he said to me as he went. "Have to make a switch."

I watched him detach the camera and set it into a case below the telescope and pick up another camera and fit it to the eyepiece.

It took only a moment. Then he came back to me. "You're smart, Tony. You're talented. You need a job."

Damn! He sounded just like Sarah.

"You were treated shabbily by those video-people. My sources inform me that, until you found yourself innocently involved in their personal shenanigans, you were doing excellent work for them. Work that you have a great talent for. You should be doing that work, not running after cheap private-eye assignments."

I started to say something.

He cut me off.

Very effectively.

By saying, "Sixty thousand a year, to start."

And now, he let me say, "What?"

"Sixty K. Plus bonuses for cutting shrinkage. Your own office. Company car. Stature. That's what you need, Tony. You know that, don't you?"

"I don't understand."

"Of course, you do. Anthony Aapt, Manager of Security for Jason Woods Industries. Doing what you did for Stockpile Video. Getting paid handsomely for it."

I had to stop and breathe. I had to play some of this back in my head. Finally, I said, "You're offering me a job? Is that what this is all about?"

"Of course. It's what I do with talent. I see it going to waste, or going in the wrong direction and I grab onto it. Use it. Pay damned good money for it."

I was stunned. Maybe I'd swum out to Saturn, after all.

"I'm going to be governor," Woods said. "Think of that. There'll be plenty of work for a good security man when I get into the campaign, and after I'm elected. Well-paying work. Challenging. Open to someone who's proved his loyalty to me."

I tried to think of something to say. But my mind wasn't working well enough for that.

He said, "You'll start Friday morning. The Galleria office. I'll be in at ten-sharp. Meet me. We'll have coffee, and

I'll introduce you to Bart Schmidt. V.P. Operations. You'll report to him."

Beeping.

"Another camera," Woods said, hurrying away from me.

While he took off one camera and attached another, he kept talking. "Time for you to go. Get your sleep. Get rested. You'll do a good job for me. I'm impressed with you. Let me get this thing set, and I'll call Shepherd. He'll show you the way out."

Finished with the camera, he walked to the other side of the enclosure and put his hand to the wall. "Here's the door," he said. "Wait a minute for Shepherd."

I was still pretty much in shock. All I could think was, "Sixty thousand dollars!" I stumbled along the wall, finally making out the outline of the doorway when I was a couple of feet away.

"Wait a minute," Woods said.

I turned.

He fumbled in his shirt pocket. "Almost forgot." Reaching out his hand, he stuffed something into the breast pocket of my blazer. "Something for you. Get those video-fools off your back. Make a refund to Mrs. Hawk. And a little extra. Call it a sign-on bonus. I want my people happy and uncomplicated."

More stun. Overload, in fact. I was going to say something.

But two or three beepings went at once.

"Damned cameras!" Woods said, and scurried away from me.

That bell sounded, and the door opened. Supercilious, whose name I now knew was Shepherd, stood in the little dark space, his white jacket doing ghost-glow.

Woods was fiddling with a camera. Over his shoulder, he

said, "Ten o'clock. Friday. Day after tomorrow." He chuckled. "Day after today, actually. See you then. God-damned cameras! Good night."

I stumbled into the little hallway. Shepherd closed the door.

Lights came on. Stinging my eyes.

"Thith way, thir," Shepherd said.

I followed the sound of his voice, got into the elevator, and wc started down.

He said, "Welcome aboard, sir."

I was too confused to comment.

The elevator stopped.

Shepherd held the door for me. "I'll show you the way out, and you can be on your way home, Mr. Aapt." His superciliousness was completely gone; my name had only one syllable now, but the lisp persisted.

"With Joe Bob, of course," I said.

Shepherd seemed puzzled. "Well, certainly. If you like, sir."

I was more puzzled. "If I like? What does that mean?"

"Whatever you say, Mr. Aapt. Joe Bob and the other security people work for you now."

This was all too much to figure out. "Never mind."

Shepherd paused in the entryway beside a pair of giant mounted elephant tusks. "If you'll wait here, sir, I'll bring the car around."

"Fine."

He went hurrying away.

My head hurt even more now. I wanted about a bushel of aspirins. But I wanted even more to get away from this crazy place and the crazy people here.

Headlights. A car stopped in front of the steps. I hurried out.

It wasn't the black stretch Mercedes.

In the light from the front of the house, it glistened fiery red and shiny white. A Chrysler convertible. Just like the one I had looked at a million years ago this morning—yesterday morning. Shepherd stepped out of it and stood holding the door open.

"What the hell is this?" I said.

"Your company car, sir. Mr. Woods thought, you being rather young, that you'd want something sporty. If it doesn't suit you, we'll exchange it."

This was really overload now.

All I wanted was to get out of here.

"Take the road to the gate," Shepherd was saying. "About three miles. Then turn left on the highway. That will take you to Interstate-10." Concern crossed his face. "Are you tired, sir? Perhaps I should drive you. I'd be happy to drive you back home."

"I'm fine," I said.

I got into the car.

I closed the door and tried to make sense of the dials. The air conditioner blew its sweet breath on me. Reba McEntire's sweetly rough voice caressed me from the CD player.

What the hell was I doing here?

I buttoned down the window. I wanted to feel good about somebody, and I said, "Thanks," to Shepherd and added, "Tell Esmeralda thanks, too."

Then I drove away.

Halfway to the gate, I stopped and figured out the controls for the top and put it down. The night air was hot and sticky, but with the car moving, it felt good, and seemed to help my headache.

A while after I passed through the W-Bar gate and

turned left onto the highway, I pulled over onto the shoulder and stopped and felt in my breast pocket and pulled out a check.

It was on Jason Woods' personal account. His writing looked as if he had stabbed, rather than formed, the letters and words.

The check was made out to me.

The amount was $25,200.93.

$25,200.93!

After I stared at the numbers for a while, I noticed something written in the corner. The writing was so compressed that I had to fumble for the map light and squint to make it out:

M. Hawks $7,000

StkpVid 8,200.93

Signing Bonus 10,000

I should have been flabbergasted, but it was all too much to think about.

Sticking the check back into my pocket, I headed my new red Chrysler convertible home to Houston.

TWENTY-THREE

Maggie Gets to Travel, after All

I fell into bed at a little after three a.m., figuring I'd sleep for about a week.

At barely eight o'clock, a trash truck's belching engine outside my window, and the banging of the Dumpster as it was lifted and rattled empty broke me wide awake.

I was irritated all to hell, but even more irritated that Spooky, who could hear a can-opener a mile away, kept on sleeping like he was dead.

I waited out the commotion and, when the damned trash truck finally chugged away, started to crap out again.

But suddenly, I bolted up and out of bed. Grabbing a pair of jeans and doing enough with them to get reasonably decent, I ran outside and around to the parking area.

The day was already hot. Bright sunlight glared everywhere. I had to dance to keep my bare feet from burning on the faded old asphalt. At the same time, I was shivering as gooseflesh ran over my shoulders and down my back.

There it was. In my parking spot.

A brand-new red Chrysler convertible.

I stared at that shiny new car. What I was thinking about was Maggie Hawk. And Grandpa. He had a saying that would fit right in, of course: "You can always tell what kind of person somebody is by the size of the payoff it takes."

Back in the apartment, I found the blazer I wore to dinner and star-gazing last night. Jason Woods' check was still in its pocket. It was still made out for more than twenty-five thousand dollars. To me!

I showed it to Spooky. He yawned.

I went to the kitchen and got his attention by running the can-opener and tabbing open another can of Fancy Feast. Then I drank a couple of cups of instant coffee and took a shower and looked at the check again.

It looked just like it had before.

Hanley Moss. Suddenly, I had an attack of conscience for having forgotten about his call.

He was home. "Mr. Moss," I said. "Sorry to have taken so long to return your call."

"No problem. Listen, I checked around a little. Don't worry—I didn't mention your name. Found out a thing or two, and just wanted to tell you I was wrong about Joe Newhouse."

I was sure that didn't have anything to do with anything, but I listened.

"You know when he got in trouble for shooting that kid?"

"Yes."

"Well, turns out he really was in the clear."

"He was?" I said, to be sociable.

"Right. That kid he shot did have a gun, after all. The other kid did run off with it. Just like Newhouse said he did."

"I see."

"The man that owned that company Newhouse moonlighted for saw it all, turns out. But he was out of town on business when all the trouble for Joe came up. The minute he got back, he went to the grand jury and cleared it all up."

"That's good for Newhouse. Listen, Mr. Moss. Hope you have a great cruise. Let's have that lunch when you get back."

"You know who that witness was? Boy, you couldn't have a more reliable one."

Suddenly, I was getting gooseflesh. "Who was the witness, Mr. Moss?"

"Why, it was Mr. Jason Woods, that's who. A man can't have a much better witness than him, can he?"

"You wouldn't think so, would you?"

"Anyway, I came down kind of hard on Joe Newhouse when you were asking about him, and I just wanted to clear that up."

I thanked him, and wished him a good trip again. Then I sat and stared at the wall for a while.

Jason Woods had cleared Vegas Joe Newhouse of a murder charge. A little later, Newhouse happened onto, and investigated, the suicide that made Woods half a billion dollars.

The wall didn't tell me a damned thing.

Finally, I got dressed and drove over to see Maggie.

But first, I sat down and wrote a check of my own. It was made out to Maggie Hawk. The amount was seven thousand dollars. The explanation I wrote at the bottom was "Refund of fee."

Parking down the block from her townhouse—for a different reason now—not to hide an embarrassingly old heap, but to hide an incriminatingly new one—I walked back. These were nice places. With a job paying sixty thousand a year, I could practically afford a place like this, myself. But not here. In some other location. Where I wouldn't be running into Maggie every time I turned around.

I rang her bell.

Rang it again before it was answered.

She was in a total swivet, talking excitedly on a cordless telephone, motioning me inside by waving a handful of papers that included a Federal Express envelope.

I stood in the entryway with her while she talked on. "Yes. Of course, I have a birth certificate. Yes. Yes. It's an original. Yes, of course, it has the notary stamp on it. All right. Yes, I'll hold on."

Finally, she had time for me. "My God!" she said, eyes wide, face totally excited. "I have to get a passport. You won't believe it. I don't believe it!" She waved the papers at me and seemed about to explain, but had to jump back into the telephone conversation. "Yes. I have to leave tomorrow. At two-ten. I do so plan ahead. But I didn't plan this. They said there was some kind of computer glitch, or something. I didn't find out about it until five minutes ago when the Federal Express lady came."

More Hold.

I reached into my pocket for her refund check.

Ignoring everything, she shoved her handful of papers at me. "Look at that, Tony. Tell me I'm not dreaming. Isn't it the most fantastic thing you've ever seen?" An expression of panic came onto her face. "I called them. They apologized. But they can't change the dates."

She was right. It was pretty fantastic. If you call an around-the-world trip fantastic. Airline tickets. Luxury liner tickets. Hotel reservations. All first-class. London. Paris. Rome. Madrid. Cairo. Sydney. Singapore. Hong Kong. Tokyo. Honolulu. San Francisco.

I had rung the bell feeling like a complete traitor, but I forgot that now because Maggie's excitement was so contagious.

Holding her hand over the mouthpiece of the telephone,

she half whispered, "Can you believe it? Look at the total—one hundred eleven thousand, three hundred eleven dollars!" She shuffled the fingers of one hand into the mess of papers I held and pulled out a cashier's check. "Plus twenty-five thousand dollars spending money. What the letter says—it's part of the sweepstakes. Because I stuck the Vacation Stamp in the right square. But their computer messed up and everything got lost until now."

I leafed through the tickets and brochures and found the itinerary. Departure date: August 20. Return date: November 8. The letterhead top of it was for something called Promotional Tours, Inc., in Dallas.

It was wonderful. It was pretty exciting stuff for an ex-barmaid from Houston, Texas, who always dreamed of traveling, and hadn't been able to fit it into her budget this year.

She did a huge sigh into the telephone. "All right. Yes. Of course, I can get there right now. Yes. Immediately. Thank you. Goodbye."

She dropped the telephone onto the mail table and pulled the papers out of my hands. "I've got to run, Tony. There's some kind of expedited passport they can do, but I've got to get going right now."

I said, "Maggie, I've got to . . ."

She pushed me toward the doorway. "We'll talk later. All right? Later."

I shoved my check back into my pocket and backed out into the steamy morning air. Grandpa had a saying about things like this, too: "Never put off until tomorrow what you can put off until the day after."

TWENTY-FOUR

It Seemed To Be Everybody's Lucky Day

Mead Bell Rockwell & Associates Advertising & Public Relations, Inc., had its offices in the Phoenix Tower.

There was no Rockwell and there were no Associates. Mead was Rita Lou and Bell was Al. When things were going well, they flaunted their long-standing affair and redecorated lavishly and threw bonuses around and hired anybody who walked in breathing. When things were bad, they barely spoke to each other and fired practically everybody, and checked the wastebaskets to find out which of their disloyal employees was trying to bankrupt them by throwing out used paper clips and rubber bands. The best way to be, if you worked for them, was dedicatedly manic-depressive.

Sarah was in her office, sitting at her desk, studying something.

I walked in and said, "Hi."

She looked up at me and smiled dazzlingly.

No. Not dazzlingly. Dazedly would be more correct.

What was going on here? I dropped by because I needed somebody normal this morning.

But I was about to find out I was in the wrong place for that.

What she had been staring at was a shiny advertising

brochure, which she now shoved across the desk toward me. "Which one? The teal blue or the bottle-green?"

I was looking at glossy photos of BMW's.

"What are you talking about?"

That dazzling, dazed smile again. "I can't decide on the color."

"Sarah, are you all right?"

"Bottle-green. I think bottle-green is perfect. To go with my eyes. That's it. That's the one."

"Make sense, Sarah."

She gave me a dazed, glazed look. "Do you know who you're looking at?" she asked me with total seriousness.

"A crazy woman."

With no faze at all, she announced, "The new Director of Advertising for Millercom, Inc."

Now, I stared at her. Millercom was big-time. One of the major local success stories. It was started fifteen-or-so years ago by a man and his wife making computer cables by hand in their spare bedroom, and had grown into a *Fortune* 500 Company by jumping early into the answering machine and fax booms. They also manufactured computers and telephones and security equipment. About four thousand of the eighty-two hundred bucks the Video King was suing me for had gone for Millercom stuff.

Sarah pulled back the brochure and stared lovingly at the picture of the bottle-green BMW. "They called an hour ago. I said yes. What else could I do? I never dreamed something like that could happen to me."

There was no point in being a jerk. I congratulated her.

I went around behind her desk and pulled her up and hugged her. I promised her celebration with champagne. I demanded the premiere ride in her new car. I told her the bottle-green one would match her eyes perfectly. I congratulated her some more.

Then she proved that her good fortune hadn't blocked out her mothering instinct. "This is exactly the kind of thing I've told you about again and again, Tony. You've got to do something with yourself. Be ambitious. Roll with the punches. Get into a real job, no matter what it is. And then network. Get noticed. It'll definitely pay off in the long run. You're never going to get anywhere at all as long as you're content to sit back and play Hardy Boys."

I stared at her.

She wasn't through. "Unless you always want to be a loser, that is. I guess that's what I'm trying to tell you—it's time you decide whether you're happy being a loser, or not. If you're not, it's high time you were doing something about it."

I kept on staring.

She leaned toward me, with that high school counselor I-can-be-as-intense-as-you-can look, doing everything but shaking her finger at me. "To be successful, you've got to think success. If you think success, well, one day, you'll pick up the phone just like I did, and find out you've been noticed."

I remembered now why we got divorced—both times—a guy can handle only one mother in a lifetime. "I guess I'd better go wait by the telephone then," I said, and got the hell out of there.

I drove my new red company car downtown and went to the city library.

The Business section.

There was lots on Millercom because it was a big local success story. There were copies of its annual reports since it had started issuing them.

The first one, 1985, was about three pages long and looked as if it had been typed in somebody's kitchen. 1987's was semi-glossy and ten or twelve pages. 1990 was when the company started really going big. There was lots of investment. The company went from over-the-counter to the New York Stock Exchange.

One sentence in the magazine-thick, extremely glossy 1996 annual report told me everything I needed to know:

In July, a controlling interest in The Company was purchased by another dynamic Houston-based corporation, Jason Woods Industries.

Moving on to Maggie—the letterhead under which her itinerary was printed belonged to something called Promotional Tours, Inc.

The circumstances surrounding Maggie's trip around the world had seemed just a tad odd to me. I'd had precious little experience in handing out millions of dollars in sweepstakes prizes, but I thought that if I was into that sort of thing, I wouldn't be too apt to let one of the flashier auxiliary prizes get lost in the computer.

Promotional Tours, Inc., was a little harder to track down because it was a Dallas company, and Houston institutions historically haven't given Dallas much shelf space. But in a cross-reference, I found that the *Houston Business Journal* had run an article on the company a couple of years ago.

The article was rather readable. It told how Promotional Tours, Inc., had become the leader in putting together incentive travel packages for companies to use in rewarding their more productive employees. And it outlined the history of the company. It had started as a small Dallas travel agency which had progressed to specializing in cruise packages. After a couple of successful years, the now large agency was bought by the America Lines Corporation, which owned and operated several large cruise ships in the Caribbean and along the California and Mexico coasts.

Interesting.

I tried a combination shortcut and hunch and walked down the shelf and pulled out last year's fat annual report issued by Jason Woods Industries.

Toward the back, there was a listing of affiliated and subsidiary companies. Right up there toward the top of the affiliated list was "America Lines Corporation."

I walked out of the library and headed for my shiny red convertible.

There was one thing I could say for sure about Jason Woods: when he did payoffs, he damned well didn't fool around.

Jeez! I should demand a cut from Maggie and Sarah, both.

But why bother?

I was getting a better than moderate payoff of my own.

TWENTY-FIVE

Miss Houston Waterbeds Goes Big-time

Creative time-killing.

This was definitely the morning for it.

I could go bomb trash trucks. I could go look for a new and suitably upscale place to live. I could go to the bank and deposit Jason Woods' check and play Scrooge McDuck with the money. I could drive around in my new red Chrysler convertible company car and give attitude to poor slobs in old Oldsmobiles. I could probably even run over to River Oaks and help Rhea redecorate her entryway or whatever. God forbid, I could go have a drink with Marlene Dietrich and help paint something.

Or I could sneak back to Maggie's while she was gone, and write her a thank-you-but-no-thank-you note and stick it under her door along with my refund check.

Yeah. But first, I headed for Sarah's apartment complex.

It was getting even muggier than usual. There were dark clouds in the west, and when I went under Southwest Freeway, I noticed that some of the cars coming off it were wet and still had their windshield wipers going.

At the first red light, I put up the top. Good. I didn't feel quite so guilty that way.

A couple of blocks later, about the time I turned into

Sarah's parking area, I started hearing thunder, but the rain still hadn't reached us.

Poor old Hizzie sat there in Sarah's guest parking spot looking like last year's bag lady.

Damn. We'd been through a lot together.

Funny how down I felt. Yesterday, at this time, I'd have imagined myself dancing on her warped hood, rubbing her scaly nose in my new car—if I could have imagined myself getting one.

"Get over yourself," I told myself. And got out and went over and unlocked her, and got my camera out of the glove compartment. Then I sat there in the midst of her shabbiness, trying to think if there was anything else I needed to retrieve.

No.

Except maybe some self-respect.

"Sixty thousand a year, you silly son-of-a-bitch!" I told myself, and got out and slammed the door and went back to my new red car.

As I stuck the camera into my new glove compartment, it started to rain. The first scattered drops that struck the hood of the convertible balled and went skidding across the glassy red finish. The ones that hit Hizzie's ancient and powdery faded blue-green paint splatted and flattened like hot bird shit.

Poor baby.

I left her sitting there and drove off.

I wandered around in the rain for a while. It was nice—raindrops drumming against the nylon top and something that I think was "The Pines of Rome" thrusting stereophonically from the radio.

This was great. I wished I was enjoying it more.

I thought again about sneaking over to Maggie's and leaving that note and that check.

Suddenly, then, I thought of Larry Milburn.

I wondered what kind of reward had just landed in good old Larry Milburn's lap. Probably a telephone call from some wheel at Big-Stuff Oil Company, a wholly-owned subsidiary of Huge-Stuff Petroleum, a wholly-owned subsidiary of Jason Woods Industries, telling him that he had just been selected for the Job-of-the-Century in some nicely Middle Eastern, but conflict-proof place, and he'd have to be there by tomorrow morning.

I headed over to his neighborhood just to satisfy my curiosity.

I drove Beechnut, past the Chrysler dealership.

Just like yesterday.

Except that the gorgeous candy-apple-red convertible wasn't sitting there in the showroom anymore. I was driving it.

I was driving it.

Yes, I was.

Oh, yes! Suddenly, a bunch of things came together in my mind.

Funny how Jason Woods happened to pick out this particular car *because I was young and would probably want something sporty.*

Happened, my rear end!

Polly . . .

There was that tossed-off comment Woods made last night while we were roaming around on his rooftop sharing astronomy: "*. . . taking time out to visit your girlfriend.*" At the time, it had jangled around in my head somewhat, but hadn't meant much to me. As far as I was concerned, I hadn't visited any girlfriend. Standing there watching a billionaire search for comets, I hadn't thought much more about it.

The intersection of Beechnut and Barlow came up. The place where, not two seconds after I passed through on an amber light yesterday, the blue-haired lady and the bald-headed gentleman had banged their cars into each other, totally blocking traffic.

Very interesting. *Totally blocking traffic.* Totally blocking anybody driving along behind me—following me.

Some private eye I was. On TV, they always know when they're being followed. But then, I wasn't on TV.

Yesterday, I had driven another couple of blocks, and then made the left turn that took me to Larry Milburn's house, which coincidentally, was practically across the street from Polly's apartment complex. From habit I had acquired since starting to drive the least attractive car in Harris County, I had parked on the street by Polly's complex and had walked over to Larry's.

I had left my car on the street by Polly's apartment complex, and walked over to Larry Milburn's house.

Son-of-a-bitch!

Some great detective I was, whether I was on TV or off.

I should have known it immediately last night when Woods mentioned my girlfriend and didn't mention Larry Milburn.

What had happened was that, after Hilda Guttman reported me for trying to fool her into talking about things she shouldn't, somebody had told somebody to start keeping track of me. Maybe my handy new subordinate, Joe Bob. He had probably been doing a pretty good job of it—I certainly hadn't had an inkling. And then he had gotten blocked by the accident.

He had lost me, but after a little assiduous scouting around, he had found my car.

Finding it, he had made an incorrect but very understandable assumption.

I made an assumption of my own. Correct, as it turned out, if a little late. Reaching into my jacket, I pulled out my wallet and thumbed through it, dropping gasoline credit cards and my driver's license and my P.I. ID and three or four extra Aapt Investigations business cards on the butterscotch leather of the passenger seat. Then I shuffled one-handed through the cards.

Sure enough.

Day before yesterday afternoon, when I talked with Maggie that first time, I wrote her name and her telephone number and address on the back of one of my business cards and stuck it into my wallet.

That card was gone. I hadn't thought about it until now. When I called my answering machine yesterday afternoon and got Maggie's message, I hadn't needed to check in my wallet for her number to call her back because she left it on the machine.

That card was gone.

Hilda Guttman.

I could see it all now. Thirty seconds after she ran me off her property, she had gotten on the telephone, able not only to report—like a good, loyal, and well-rewarded soldier—that a P.I. named Aapt had been nosing around asking questions about Jason Woods, but also to say in her cracked and gleeful voice that I was carrying Maggie Hawk's name around in my wallet.

Bells would have gone off because somebody was snooping around about Jason Woods. They'd have gotten lots louder when Maggie's name was mentioned.

Then somebody pulled up all the information available about Tony Aapt. Included in it would have been his recent rather visible association with Miss Houston Waterbeds.

Undoubtedly, as soon as I left Dr. Potter's office, he had also reacted like a loyal soldier and reported my visit. By the time I got through at the Rice library and headed for Larry Milburn's, I would have had a tail.

Then there was the accident, and the tail lost me. He probably wasn't at all happy about that. He probably was very tickled that he found my car so quickly, parked by the apartment complex where that rather visible recent girlfriend lived. The last thing the tail wanted to do was admit that he had lost me. So his story would have been that he followed me to my girlfriend's apartment. When I detoured through the complex past the swimming pool on the way back to my car, his assumption would apparently have been confirmed.

Amazing how much you can learn about the private eye business by hindsight. Grandpa would not have been thrilled with me.

It was about twenty-four hours too late for such precautions, but today, I didn't take the left turn toward Larry Milburn's/Polly's. I drove on. I couldn't pick out anybody who seemed to be following me, but I didn't take any chances. After five or six blocks, I doubled back and went toward downtown, moving over toward Richmond when I got close, getting myself as snarled as possible in the construction traffic.

At a convenience store, I stopped and used the pay telephone. The rain had long passed and, at any minute, the sun was going to come blasting out, turning Houston into what it does best—steam. Watching the cars that went by, I stuck in my quarter and dialed.

She answered on the fifth ring, sounding out of breath. Sounding sexy as hell. Damn, if only that girl had a personality that matched her voice . . .

"Hi, Polly," I said.

"Well. Of all people."

"Yeah. That's me."

"I'm in a horrible rush, Tony," she said. But the tone of her voice told me that she wasn't in so much of a rush that she'd hang up on me. Not in so much of a rush that she couldn't take five for some gloating.

I played along. "Sorry to bother you, Polly. Never mind."

Now, she really was in a rush—to keep me on the line. "You call after a month, and you're going to hang up, just like that?"

"Okay. I guess not. How are you doing?"

With practically hysterical breathlessness, she said, "Wonderful! You can't imagine how wonderful. Fabulous! Out of this world!"

I watched for a car that would stop up the block or down the block and stay there for as long as I was standing here talking on the telephone. I didn't see one. There probably wasn't one. They probably thought there wasn't much point in following me today, post-payoff.

When Polly ran down, I said, "What's so wonderful and fabulous and out of this world?"

She took a deep breath, cut the hysteria, and got sexy again. "I'm packing. I have to be on the plane to L.A. this afternoon at five-forty."

"Well, that's nice."

Just a touch of hysteria. "Nice?" More hysteria. "Nice doesn't even begin." Full-blown space-out now. "I'm *in,* Tony!"

"*In* what?"

She calmed herself down and replaced the hysteria with

edge. She was realizing that this was her chance to get in some cuts. "Some people saw some of my work. And they liked it. You might not think my work is important, but they do. My agent called this morning." She paused for drama. When she continued, the hysteria was back. "They liked it a lot." More drama. And then, The Announcement: "You just happen to be talking to the woman who's flying out to L.A. to make the new Get It! Jeans commercial! With an option for six more."

"That's great," I said. And it undoubtedly was. A Get It! Jeans commercial put my old girlfriend, Polly, right up there with Marla What's-her-name, for one, and Anna-Nicole Smith for another, and if that's somewhere you want to be, it's at least wonderful and fabulous and out of this world.

Except that I knew one thing that Polly didn't know. I didn't have to drive back to the library in my new red sporty company car to know that Get It! Jeans was definitely owned by some company that was owned or controlled by Jason Woods Industries.

Polly's voice got very cutting. "I really have to rush now, Tony. But sometime soon, maybe I'll give you a call. When I'm so famous and successful that I have to have a bodyguard. To see if there's somebody you'd recommend."

Dead line.

I stood there for a moment, debating whether to continue checking by calling Rhea and Carl. Jason probably hadn't had to pay them off—they were family, of sorts—and besides, a lady who's partial to the hired help, and a guy who wears dead mink and blue sequins could probably be quieted down without much of a payoff. I was pretty sure they'd both react to me today as if I was trying to give them free dance lessons. But I didn't verify it. I didn't want them reporting back to Uncle Jason that his new Manager of Security was still snooping.

I went back to the car.

I drove on to the end of the block and turned and stopped about a hundred feet along. No other cars turned or even hesitated. After five minutes, I drove on.

And started feeling guilty.

If I hadn't happened to beat that bald-headed gentleman and that blue-haired lady and their driving skills to that intersection yesterday, Larry Milburn would be the one who was happily packing. I couldn't exactly see him in major boobs and a pair of Get It! Jeans, but Jason would surely have figured out something nice for him.

I still didn't have anything else to do but go stick a check under Maggie's door, so I decided to go by Larry's, anyway, just to make sure.

TWENTY-SIX

I Bought My Own Damned Lawnmower

Larry was still a human cauliflower in 1960s Bermuda shorts. He wasn't packing. He wasn't hysterically elated over something wonderful and sudden.

It was kind of nice to run into somebody who gave me just a regular, ordinary "Hello" and invited me in for a cup of coffee, or a beer if I wanted one.

Sounded good to me.

Inside, I discovered that my talking with him yesterday about George Hawk had gotten him started on something besides watching baseball.

"You talking about George kind of got me off my ass," he said.

The TV set was turned off. That bedouin chest was open. Those fabulous fabrics and souvenirs were piled on the sofa. Larry led me into the kitchen where he poured mugs of coffee and pointed at a stack of empty packing boxes beside the back door. "Since I got back home, I hadn't even unpacked, except about enough stuff to fix up a TV dinner with."

I liked Larry enough that guilt came creeping up on me and I said, "Listen, I've got to tell you something."

He sat down on a spindly kitchen chair that must have been a lot stronger than it looked. "Sure. What?"

"I told you I was doing some research. Well, that's not actually true. Actually, I'm a private detective."

"Hey!" he said. "That's terrific. A private eye? Really?"

With my recent history, I said, "Really," with no more conviction than absolutely necessary.

He was fascinated. He must have missed a lot of TV while he was working in the Middle East.

I didn't want to get into any details about Maggie Hawk or George. I didn't have to. What Larry wanted was action. "Hey, tell me about private-eyeing."

I told him a couple of Grandpa's favorite war stories.

He loved them.

Pretty soon, he poured some more coffee for us, and must have felt that it was his turn to tell his own version of war stories because he picked up his mug and motioned me into what I guess was originally the family room of the house, but which for him was a workroom. It was cluttered with packing boxes, too. Some still sealed with heavy tape, but many emptied.

There was a professional-looking drafting table set up against the back wall. "I had 'em bring back my stuff out of storage when I got back," Larry said. "But I hadn't even started to unpack it."

He kicked a couple of empty cartons out of the way and pulled a folding chair over for me and perched himself beside the drafting table on a stool that looked alarmingly fragile. He was wearing a blue T-shirt that somehow stretched to cover his belly. It had writing on it in Arabic. I didn't ask for a translation. Maybe it said, "Let the infidels freeze in the dark."

He picked up a sheaf of papers and waved them for a moment. "You talking about George got me thinking how I was just layin' around, turning to shit. So I started getting busy." He put the papers down and motioned toward the drafting table. That old miniature electric fan that George Hawk had converted into a pencil sharpener had a shiny new cord and was clamped to the edge. "Still works just like new," he said, beaming.

Picking up the sheaf of papers again, and hesitating as if he was about to show his first poem to somebody, he finally pushed them toward me. "This is some of my old stuff."

The papers were engineering drawings. Some of them very old. So old that the paper was yellowed and brittle. But the drawings were terrific. At least, they seemed so to this communications major. Some of them were of very mundane things. There were about six pages of detailed, large-scale drawings of a nut and bolt and lock washer, shown from every possible angle. All of the drawings were good, but some were fantastic: spaceships that Stephen Spielberg would die for; automobiles that would make Japanese car-making robots drip oil with envy.

"These are wonderful," I said, meaning it.

Larry looked almost pathetically happy that I was being nice about them. "Old stuff," he said. And added, at just about the time I was noticing the dates in the margins, "They were class assignments." He went on resentfully, "Dr. Potter kept the good ones."

That got my attention.

He chuckled. "I told you we called him Dr. Potty, didn't I? Yeah. I told you that. Anyway, I dug this stuff out and started to get my ass in gear." He motioned toward the drawing-in-progress on the table. "Just messing around. Getting my hand in again. Then I'm going to work on some stuff I've wanted to do for years, and haven't taken the time."

I said, "Potter kept some of your drawings?"

"Oh, yeah. Some of the others did, too. But Dr. Potty always acted like they were his in the first place. Burned my ass."

"Did he keep some of George's drawings, too?"

"Sure. He kept anybody's, if he liked 'em." Larry went shyly proud now. For a moment, I could recognize, peeking out through the fat and the years, that good-looking, open-faced kid who had been in love with Maggie Hawk, and went to meetings of the Slide Rule Club with his roommate and buddy, George Hawk.

I recognized something else, too. I had been looking for payoffs in too literal a sense. I'd been lowballing to guess that Dr. Potter's payoff had been an expensively relined mouth; it had been something much more important *to* him, although it was not *for* him. His payoff over the years had been Jason Woods' money for Rice University, the thing he loved above all else.

It had undoubtedly started just after Jason Woods came out with the GRASSBUSTER. Dr. Potter had advised his old student, Jason, that he had George's original drawings for the lawnmower blade that was rebuilding his fortune, and suggested that he start paying off the school. After all, the alternative was to turn the GRASSBUSTER and its money over to Maggie. And Dr. Potter wouldn't do that—she had come between him and his favorite student.

Larry was rummaging in one of the open cartons. "Let's see. Yeah. Here they are." He handed me five or six old drawings. "These are George's. Don't know how they happened to get mixed up with my stuff. Must have been when he was moving out."

I said, "You mean, moving out after he and Maggie got married."

The air in the room suddenly seemed to get very still.

His hand clenching hard on the edge of the drafting table, Larry said, "Yeah. Then. I didn't find them until after he was dead. I should have given them to Maggie, I guess. But I couldn't stand facing her, much as I wanted to."

George's drawings didn't look much different from Larry's to me. One was of some kind of valve. The others were of a pair of pliers.

Hipping himself back up onto the stool, Larry said, with an obvious note of pride in his voice, "That was one thing I was better at than George—drafting. I helped him out some, even. I loved it—still do. But George just looked at it like work. That's the difference, you know."

Suddenly sheepish, he said, "I know everybody uses those computer drafting machines now. But I like the old way—more fun."

I stood up and went over to the table and looked at his new drawing. It was of a screwdriver. That's all. Just a screwdriver. But for the first time in my life, looking at that clear, perfect, pencil drawing, I actually *understood* screwdrivers. It sounds stupid, but it was one of those great moments that you don't get very often.

Larry was embarrassed. "No big thing." He reached down beside the table and picked up the screwdriver that had obviously been the model for his drawing and twirled it nervously in his hand. "I just like doing the drawing. I started out with something simple. That's all."

"It's wonderful," I said.

Reaching over, I took the screwdriver out of his hand and looked at it, and then looked at his drawing—really looked at it.

Then I said, "Tell you what—I'll be back in about fifteen minutes."

I went out and bought myself a lawnmower.

TWENTY-SEVEN

Hot Afternoon at the No-tell Motel

It was about one o'clock and hot as hell. Hotter than that. Any possible benefits of this morning's minor rainfall had been used up long ago.

After Larry got tired of my hovering over him asking stupid questions, and kicked me out, I drove by Maggie's. She wasn't home yet, or again—whatever.

More time to kill. Grandpa was very fond of twisting words around and coming up with new and exciting statements about watched pots, for example, but I didn't really want to remember any of them just now.

I decided that about the best thing I could do about this figurative pot in which I had gotten myself involved, on this day when I'd had about three-and-a-half hours sleep, was to go home and rest up.

Driving along on the Southwest Freeway access road, a few minutes later, minding my own business, I only halfway noticed the gold Corvette driving along in front of me.

Noticed it. At first, that was all. Yesterday, I would have lusted after it. Today, I just more or less noticed that it was there.

Then I realized it looked familiar.

Damn! Of course, it did!

It was fortunate that I wasn't driving Hizzie because the

main thing I wanted to do was run the damned thing over, and Hizzie was solid enough and old and beat-up enough to do that without even stuttering.

The right turn signal on the Corvette started blinking, and it slowed.

I started to swing over and pass.

But suddenly, it occurred to me that the Corvette was turning into the Ramada Inn, and that it was a little after one o'clock in the afternoon.

"Wait a minute, Tony!" I said to myself. "Wait just a damned minute!"

I slowed and let the Corvette turn, and then turned in behind it, and parked close to the access road.

The Corvette drove farther into the parking area and pulled into a parking slot in front of a row of rooms.

And sat there, waiting.

I waited, too. But first, I reached into the glove box and got out my camera. Then I really waited.

In about five minutes, a guy in a moderately flashy business suit came out of the motel office and walked out into the room area. He spotted the Corvette. He grinned big-time and lifted his hand and waved a room key.

I started snapshooting.

She got out of the Corvette, glanced around, didn't see anybody, and did some very serious strutting over to the man. When she got to him, he grabbed her. Correction—they grabbed each other. Big kiss. They were perfectly framed between the corners of two of the building sections with a relatively dark walkway directly behind them.

They kissed major big-time. Then the man nuzzled down her throat, all the way into her cleavage. She liked it, so she acted as if she was outraged and pushed him away and then laughed and grabbed his crotch—but most definitely not seriously enough to do any damage.

Laughing, the man pulled her around, and they started looking for room numbers. They found the one that matched his key. Doing a big burlesque of astonishment, she watched him thrust the key into the lock, and twitched her butt and probably squealed cutely when it went all the way home and he twisted it to open the door.

Then, with the door standing partially open and the nice dark background of the unlighted room interior behind them, they did another extremely serious clinch, which he finally broke up by kicking the door the rest of the way open and dragging her inside—with no sign of protest from her at all.

It was a big relief to me when the door slammed shut.

I wiped sweat off my face and checked the camera—nineteen shots left. I told myself that nothing could go wrong—that not more than one in a million rolls of film is defective. I told myself that glove compartments, surprisingly enough—like car trunks—don't get nearly as hot as the interior of a car because they don't have windows for the sun to beat through, so sitting around in Hizzie's glove compartment shouldn't have hurt the film. Just in case, though, I went ahead and snapped off the rest of the roll and pulled it out and kissed it for luck and opened another roll and kissed that one for luck, too, and reloaded the camera.

Then I got out of the car and went to the rack of vending machines near the motel office and bought two copies of today's *Houston Chronicle.* Dumping everything but the front sections, I walked over by the door of the temporary nooner-love nest, and wedged one of them into the decorative metal scrollwork of the walkway post, spreading it out enough so that part of the headline showed.

Back in my car, I checked the scene in the camera's viewfinder. Perfect.

Then I waited.

In old Hizzie, I would have waited and baked—antique gas-guzzlers with arterial problems and Freon seep don't cool efficiently when sitting still. But this was not my Grandpa's Oldsmobile, and every few minutes, I cranked it up and cooled off.

I would have sat there and stir-fried, though, if need be, I was so excited.

Damn!

Fifty-nine minutes.

The door of the room finally opened. Her hair was a mess and her makeup was rubbed off and he was combing his hair and trying to get his tie re-tied. But they took time off from grooming to do a nice goodbye clinch, standing in the open doorway, posed perfectly, with that *Chronicle* showing just over the man's left shoulder.

Finally, she pushed him away and grinned at him big and closed the door. He looked around with a mixture of embarrassment and smugness while he finished his tie and checked his hair and smoothed down the front of his shirt. Then, looking very self-satisfied, he went swaggering to a nearly new Lincoln TownCar and slid in and drove away.

I clicked off shots of them in the doorway. I got him going to his car. I got his car driving out with its license plate brightly showing.

About ten minutes later, looking perfect again, she came out of the room and went to the Corvette and got in and drove out.

I waited until she was out of sight. Then I yelled my brains out for a while, and finally started the convertible and pulled out, myself.

TWENTY-EIGHT

Let Me Tell You a Little Something about Revenge

At about three o'clock, I went breezing into the Stockpile Video building, moving fast enough that nobody stopped me.

The executive floor had changed somewhat. There was a new secretary sitting in front of the VK's office. She was about a hundred fifty years old—obviously hand-picked by Angela—and in her best days had never been anything more spectacular than pleasantly plain. The door of what used to be a conference room next to the president's office stood partially open, showing that the space had been converted into an office filled with lots of expensive pale-blue-lacquered furniture. Big gold letters on the door said

ANGELA MILLS
VICE PRESIDENT

The elderly secretary looked up in surprise as I barged past her. She wasn't very fast, and I was busting through the VK's doorway before she could do anything more than squeak a protest.

He was working at his desk. He was basically a nice guy, but you could see the mid-life big-bang working all over him—too little hair, too much gut, too many birthdays to his way of thinking—your painfully typical medium-sophisticated gracelessly-aging American boy.

He looked up, shot his eyes wide, and yelped, "Tony Aapt! What are you doing here?"

The secretary timidly poked her head through the doorway. "Do you want me to call the police, sir?"

I tossed a file folder down on the VK's desk. "Sure, *sir.* Call the cops. Call Accounts Receivable. Call everybody. Give 'em all a show."

He looked puzzled. He looked at the file folder. He looked at me.

I leaned over his desk and flipped the folder open and said, "Just thought you might like to have some nice photos of the former mother-to-be."

That pissed him off for just a second. Then he looked down. Immediately, he raised his head and barked, "Close that door!" at his secretary.

And looked at the photograph some more. It was eight-by-ten color. It was of the woman getting out of the Corvette at the Ramada Inn.

He stared at it. Then he looked up at me, his mouth going tight and angry.

I reached down and flipped the top photograph over, showing the second one, which was of the woman doing her strut toward the guy with the key.

The VK said, "What the hell is this?"

"What the hell do you think it is?" I said back. And flipped to the next shot—the cleavage-nuzzling. "It's your new vice president doing lunch."

He stared at the photograph.

Then he went to the next one.

And the next.

Etcetera.

Poor son-of-a-bitch. I hate it when aging boys want to cry, but think they have too much pride.

He finally got to the one I took afterward, when they opened the motel room door again.

I said, "See that newspaper in the photo?" and slapped its twin down on the desk beside the photographs. "Just to establish today's date."

His face was chalky-white by now. His eyes were getting pinkish.

I said, "On top of everything, you know who the man is, don't you?"

"Goddamn it! Of course, I know who he is."

I didn't feel as if I owed him any slack-cutting at all. "Yeah. It's Hank Schroeder—Video Barn. Actually, now that I think of it, I probably should have taken these pictures to him, instead of you. He's not suing me."

The VK gave me a dirty look. Then he reached out and jabbed at a button on his telephone set. A moment later, a woman's sweet and sexy voice said, "Yes?"

"Come in here!"

The door to the ex-conference room swung open and Angela looked in. Her smile dropped off when she saw me. "Tony Aapt! What are you doing here?"

She hurried to the VK and took up a stand protectively at his shoulder. "What's he trying to do to us now?"

The VK shook off her hand. He picked up the stack of photographs and handed them to her.

I sat and watched her look at them.

Revenge is sweet.

It's even sweeter than that.

TWENTY-NINE

I'm Not Going To Get on That Plane Looking like the Old Rugged Cross

A girl who looked as if she couldn't be a day over sixteen opened Maggie's front door. In one hand, she held a clipboard. In the other was a pair of scissors and a bunch of tags hanging from gold strings. She looked more than semi-bewildered.

I must have looked bewildered, too.

She smiled. "Hi. I'm Bobbie, from Timeless Temps. Mrs. Hawk hired me for today to help her get ready for her trip." She smiled dazzlingly. "May I help you?"

"I'm Tony Aapt. Is Maggie here?"

"Oh. Aapt. With two A's." She checked her clipboard. "You're right here on my list—'Aapt, Tony—make sure I have a chat with him before I leave.' "

"Is she here? I could have that chat with her right now, and you could get me off your list."

"That's right. I could, couldn't I?"

I followed her into the living room. It seemed to be about half full of luggage right out of the carton. I don't know if it was Louis Vuitton or what, but it looked like great stuff.

Bobbie waved the scissors and the tags. "Right now, when the doorbell and the phone aren't ringing, I'm getting all her new suitcases and things ready." She planted her feet and gave me that dazzling Professional Receptionist smile again. "If you'll just wait here, Mr. Aapt, I'll see if Mrs. Hawk is in."

She hurried off toward the kitchen.

The lawnmower still sat over there in the corner. It had gotten about half buried by the empty cartons the luggage came in, and it looked even older and more lost.

Maggie's gravelly voice came traveling into the living room. "Tony! Where have you been? Come in here."

Bobbie came scurrying back, clutching her clipboard. "She's in."

I left her with the luggage and went into the kitchen.

It was a scene out of hell. It made me look around for Federico Fellini.

Maggie was having her hair done. She was having her face done. And her hands. And her feet. All at once. The rest of her was covered with pink plastic. "I'm not getting on that plane looking like the Old Rugged Cross," she said through the mess of greenish gunk that covered all of her face except for her eyes and nostrils and mouth.

She was tilted back in some kind of high-tech chair that the makeover crew must have brought along. There was a huge blobby woman working on her bare feet. A tiny, wispish girl with a green stripe through her stringy platinumized hair was buffing Maggie's fingernails. A third woman, whose build suggested that she might play center with the Broncos in-season, but whose skin looked purer and pinker and softer than a baby's, was apparently in charge of face, because she leaned against the counter standing guard over a case containing jars of evil-looking chemicals and a timer that I supposed was marking off the minutes until the mask on Maggie's face either congealed or exploded. Hair was the province of a tall, thin, moderately youngish man wearing some major diamonds on his fingers, and a long pigtail and a baseball cap turned backward on his head. At the moment, he was working on strands of Maggie's hair that stuck out through holes in a piece of plastic fitted over her head. The strands looked like little bundles of corroding copper wire, but surely that would get better.

I recognized him from way too many mornings I'd spent staring at the TV while I waited for the telephone to ring and bring me a suspicious spouse who'd help pay the rent for a while. He kept turning up on those too-precious local talk shows in which he'd hint at the latest secrets of beautiful hair. The reason for his fame was that, not only did he do only the most famous and richest hair in town, but he did the famous visiting hair, also. When royalty stopped by on a tour of the Colonies, he got summoned to do emergency maintenance on their royal tresses. But obviously, he was democratic about all this: if the price was right, he'd refurbish ex-barmaids, too. Idly, I wondered if he did Rhea Chatham's hair. Probably not. She had given me every indication of preferring her workmen to be just a tad less fragile.

"I'm getting my passport," Maggie announced. "Expedited service when you have an emergency. They'll have it ready tomorrow morning."

The doorbell rang.

I said, "That's great," trying to sound enthusiastic. My eyes were starting to water; my nose was clogging. This place smelled like a toxic waste dump. I heard they outlawed smoking in beauty parlors a while back to protect the customers' lungs. Hmmm.

Bobbie came running in. "Mrs. Hawk, they're delivering your new dresses."

"Oh, good!" Maggie said. Then she realized she was a prisoner. "Oh, God."

"They'll wait," Hair-guy said. He swivelled his canary nose toward Bobbie in a gesture so abrupt it sent his pigtail flopping. "Tell them she's busy with Jules."

Maggie's eyes looked like a pair of marbles floating in a dish of mint mousse, but she managed to get an expression of total admiration into them.

"Okay," Bobbie said, looking not only bewildered now, but unsure. Turning, she squared her shoulders and popped back out of the kitchen.

"Isn't he wonderful?" Maggie said to me.

"Stop jerking your head around," Jules commanded.

"I'm sorry," she said abjectly.

I was beginning to wonder about all this. I had always wanted to be rich. Now, I wondered if it was worth all the trouble.

Bobbie was back. "They'll wait, Mrs. Hawk." She looked at Jules with admiration that matched Maggie's. "Hermie says to tell you Hi."

Jules huffed and rolled his eyes.

The doorbell rang again.

"Listen, Maggie," I said. "You're busy. I'll come back later."

The timer pinged. The large face-lady got an orgasmic expression and headed for the mask.

"Come back later, and we'll have a drink," Maggie said.

"Yeah," I said, and got the hell out of there.

Air again! Hermie was sitting on the edge of the sofa with dress boxes on his knees and more on the floor nearby. He was the size of a piece of farm machinery.

Bobbie was in the entryway with a woman who looked as if she had been carved out by an ax. She was embracing a stack of pastel-colored boxes, which I guessed must contain some kind of designer unmentionables. Firmly, Bobbie told her, "You'll have to wait. She's with Jules."

"With Jules? Oh, of course."

I waved at Bobbie and squeezed past and got outside.

I wondered why everybody else liked their payoffs so much more than I did.

THIRTY

Pop Quiz

I went home.

No calls on the answering machine.

The cat was busy with his catnip mouse again.

I still had Jason Woods' check in my pocket. I took it out and looked at it and put it away again.

Four o'clock.

I called Larry Milburn.

He told me not to bother him, that he was busy.

I drank a beer.

I drank another one.

I put on a pair of swimming trunks and opened another beer and went out to the pool. The water was hot. The air was hot. I lay down on a recliner and drank beer and thought about skin cancer.

When the beer was gone, I got up and went back inside and ran myself through the shower to cool off, and finally got my nap.

The exciting life of a P.I. Where was my borrowed Maserati and my abusive English buddy and all those gorgeous female guest stars? Oh, well. I had Spooky. Yippee!

I woke up at about six o'clock and took another shower and went over to see Sarah.

The car parked in her parking space was her old Accord.

I asked her where her new bottle-green BMW was.

"I decided to wait. At least a week. Wouldn't it be sort of ostentatious for me to show up with a new car on my first day in my new position?"

"I guess," I said.

"How's Jason?" she said.

"He's fine."

"What's the matter with you, Tony? You act depressed."

"Nothing. I'm not depressed."

"Good. With my new salary, you may have the idea that I won't care if you flake off about paying me back my money. But don't think that for a minute. I'm going to be on you every second. You have to be responsible. You have to take charge of your life."

"Is this Career-day at the Post-Marriage Counselor's Academy?" I asked.

"Whatever you say. I'm just tired of seeing you waste your life. I'm going to stop putting up with it."

I reached into my pocket and pulled out a couple of dollar bills and dropped them in her lap.

"What's this?" she said.

"For a beer," I said, and went into the kitchen. She may have decided to put off being ostentatious in the car department for a while, but she had stopped by the liquor store and done a few Yup things there. There was about three hundred dollars worth of champagne and scotch and wine sitting on the counter. The half-full bottle of Gallo we bought last night was in the wastebasket. The bottom shelf of the refrigerator was full of some kind of German imported beer.

There was one last, lonely can of Miller Lite. I chose it, and went back to the living room.

Sarah said, "I stopped off on the way home and looked

at those new apartments over on Buffalo Speedway. They're beautiful, Tony. And so spacious." She frowned around her living room. "I'll have to have all new furniture, of course. I wouldn't dare let anybody over there see this stuff."

I leaned on the back of a chair—something she hated for me to do—but she was getting ready to dump it, anyway. Waiting for a moment to get her full attention, I said, "I've got an ethical question for you:

"A . . . a decision that would be dishonest, but would make some people happy.

"B . . . a decision that would be honest, but would make some people unhappy.

"Choose one of the above."

"What kind of question is that?"

"Multiple choice. Single answer."

"Well, B, of course. Honesty is always best. You know that, Tony. Just what are you up to?"

"I don't know," I said, and headed toward the front door.

"Where are you going? I thought maybe you'd like to stay for dinner. I picked up a few things from Cafe Thoreau on the way home. I was going to call you."

"Don't call me," I said. "And don't worry. You'll get your money."

"Tony . . ."

"Sarah," I said, and closed the door behind me.

THIRTY-ONE

I Was Born the Day Those Sweepstakes People Showed up and I Fainted

Things had calmed down at Maggie's. She was alone. Most of the mess had been cleared out of the living room. Her new luggage was lined up near the entryway, ready to go.

She looked wonderful. The female coal miner was gone for good. Her skin glowed. Her nails were pink and perfect. Her hair was loose and soft and shiny. Jules certainly wasn't somebody I'd pick for my baseball team, but he seemed to be a pro at appearance.

Maggie tapped the toe of a new, shiny low-heeled pump on one of the suitcases. "Empty. Most of them are. I'll fill them up on the way. Isn't it wonderful?"

I had to agree that it was. Her enthusiasm was almost childlike, and certainly contagious.

She stood back and looked at me. "Now, I have to decide what I'm going to do with you."

I hadn't thought of it in those terms. Now that I did, I liked the idea. Let somebody who was about to vanish for a couple of months tell me what to do. Maybe everybody's big decisions should be made that way. "Okay. Decide."

She laughed and hugged me. Then she went over to the bar and did scotch.

While she was clinking ice, I glanced around. Travel brochures and her itinerary were spread over the coffee table. Several legs of her trip were on the Concorde. She was staying at hotels like Claridge's and The Ritz. On November fifth, she would fly back to San Francisco from Honolulu for some unwinding in a suite at the St. Anthony's before coming back home to Houston on the eighth.

As she sat down across from me, I noticed that the lawnmower was gone from the corner.

"I had that nice young fellow, Hermie, carry it out to the garage," she said, handing my drink to me. "Who wants an old lawnmower sitting in the living room?"

Lifting her glass in a toast, she said, "Here's to luck."

"No kidding," I said, and drank with her.

She said, "Speaking of luck, how's yours?"

"It has its moments."

She smiled into her glass. "I've been thinking about something all day. While I was running around trying to figure out how I could possibly get ready to leave so soon, I kept thinking about what I was doing—about George."

I waited.

She continued, saying, "What I've been doing is silly: saddling you with my old sorrows and my old resentments. Keeping myself in turmoil over them when I ought to be thinking about all the exciting things that are coming along. All that's just ancient history. That's what you've been thinking, too, isn't it? But you were too nice to say it."

"Well, no. Not really."

"If you weren't, you should have been. What we'll do: if you find out anything, we'll worry about it when I get back in November. We'll worry about things then. I'm not going to think about anything now but getting on that plane tomorrow afternoon. George has been dead for a long time.

It's about time I let him rest. Don't you think so?"

"Maggie . . ."

"I don't want to think about it. I want to think about how seasick I'm going to get when I get on one of those luxury liners. Whether I'm going to be so klutzy I'm going to knock over my champagne glass at Maxim's, or if I'm going to spill nail polish on the bedspread at The Ritz. I'm going to be a silly old woman having fun and worrying about silly things."

"I need to . . ."

"I mean it, Tony Aapt. When I get back, I'm going to tie you down and make you sit through all my photographs. But right now, you know what?"

"What?"

"As far as I'm concerned, I was born the day those sweepstakes people showed up and I fainted. I'm not going to think about anything that happened before that. You just tell me to have a fine trip. Tell me not to get tiddly and flirt with any cute waiters that aren't at least half my age. Tell me not to embarrass myself unless I'm really having fun."

I guess that, right about then, I definitely fell in love with good old Maggie. I stood up and said, "Have a fine trip. Don't do anything I wouldn't do." I hugged her.

She pushed me toward the entryway.

I went.

But at about the time I got the front door opened, I changed my mind. There was too much hanging. Too much left open and unresolved.

I pushed the door shut again and started to go back into the living room.

Stopped short.

Because Maggie was standing by the coffee table. She had that torn-out yearbook page in her hand, and she was staring at that photograph of her and Larry Milburn. Even from here, I could see that her eyes were shiny.

I hurried back to the door. Opened it softly, closed it very softly behind me. Had some damned shine in my eyes, too.

THIRTY-TWO

Brasso, Maple Syrup, and a Little White Vinegar

Larry had done a terrific job.

The drawings were great. They were even better than that.

The only problem was that they looked too new.

I worked on a sample. I put it on the floor and walked on it.

"It looks like you put it on the floor and walked on it," Larry said. "About two minutes ago."

I snarled at him.

Then I looked over into the corner and laughed. My new lawnmower sat there, all shiny and new-looking, even if it was somewhat dismantled. Maybe I ought to give Nathan a call and let him in on this—a new rage for the urban living space: lawn equipment art.

Larry and I went into the kitchen then, and drank some beer and talked things over. He said, "You're supposed to be a private eye. Didn't any of the big forgers you tracked down tell you how they aged stuff?"

I told him, "No. Big forgers are notoriously close-mouthed, you son-of-a-bitch."

He laughed at me. We liked each other. But I knew one thing—one look at his gut had convinced me that I wasn't ever going to let him cook for me.

We experimented.

He went into the living room and got a big pan out of the bedouin trunk. It was copper, and he said that the bedouins used pans like this to make camel's milk cheese in. We poured beer in it and dipped a sample sheet of paper in it, and then zapped the paper in the microwave a few times until it was dry.

"Naw," Larry said.

We added some brown vinegar to the mess, and some powdered sugar.

"No," I said.

We poured in maple syrup. The paper came out of the microwave a nice aged-yellow-brown, but it felt like peanut brittle.

We kept drinking beer, and we tried lots of stuff. The EPA and Meryl Streep would have been very interested in some of the concoctions we poured down the drain. Jules and the face-lady could probably have made great use of some of them.

Somewhere along the way, Larry said, "Okay. Are we drunk enough yet so you can tell me just what the hell we're doing?"

I said, "Let's talk about sports, Larry. We're lucky in one thing, you know. It's a good thing Houston has lots of nice, mild, spring-like weather and beautiful scenery and lots of public monuments and cheap electricity and great streets because we sure as hell don't have any professional sports worth a damn in this place. Except for the Rockets, and I think we dreamed them that time. Have you got any Brasso? Let's dump in some Brasso and see what happens."

"Shit," he said. "Let me look around for some."

Finally, we came up with something that made the paper come out looking pretty good after it was cooked. By that time, we didn't even know exactly what it was. We just used it.

We drank beer and we dipped drawings and we zapped them.

I was pretty well zapped, myself, by then.

I pulled the last drawing out of the microwave and felt of it and looked at it and smelled it. It looked old. It felt old. The smell was a little iffy, but close overnight proximity to the collection of damp bath towels in the corner of my bathroom should take care of that.

Ah! The end of a productive day.

THIRTY-THREE

Start Counting Your Heartbeats

Once in a great while, cats actually give. Or at least they're so good at faking it that it makes no difference whether it's real or not.

It was another heavy Houston summer morning. Blinding sunlight. Steamy air. TV weather-people with too much hair spray on their heads clucking mournfully about the temperature, but tickled to death that there were three—count 'em, three!—tropical depressions in the Atlantic and Caribbean, one or two of which, with any luck at all, might develop into a ratings-buster hurricane.

I fed Spooky and then rescued Larry's antiqued drawings from under the pile of mildewing bath towels and gave them a quick final zap in my microwave. They came out fine, appearing yellowed and old and smelling nicely musty.

Suddenly, then, I felt way too old and musty, myself. I went into the living room and sat down with a cup of coffee and wished the whole day would go away.

Here came Spooky, on his way to the bedroom for his first morning nap. Except he didn't go there. He stopped for a moment and looked at me, head cocked, eyes wide. Then he came over and rubbed against my leg and hopped up to sit beside me, sitting close, for once in his life not demanding attention or the absence of it. Just sitting there warm against my hip. Just being there.

It was nice. Maybe it was phony as hell. But it seemed nice. I needed it.

Finally, though, I had to say, "I've got to get going," and I did.

I shaved and showered.

Pretty soon, I got myself together and drove that terrific new red convertible over to the Galleria.

The place was the dream of anybody who was into malls. A medium-sized city, with upscale department stores and upscale shops and upscale hotels and upscale office buildings and movie theaters and lots of restaurants and even an ice-skating rink and a health club. If you had enough money or credit cards, you could live your whole life there.

Jason Woods Industries' executive offices occupied a gleaming thirty-story office building that nestled expensively against the side of the Galleria, accompanied by the most upscale shops. Its main marble- and highly-polished-brass-faced entrance was on the third level. I waited for Jason Woods on the walkway in front of it.

Leaning against the railing, looking down into the lower levels, I watched children skating on the ice rink, and people breakfasting at the "open air" café at the other end of the rink. A few early shoppers sauntered around, checking out jewelry and furs and high-tech electronics and semi-designer clothing in air-conditioned comfort. Stalking among them were the constant denizens of this place: teenagers sporting clothing combinations that looked as if they were put together by MTV; gaunt old men and women with too much jewelry and eyes like fish.

Practically right behind me, next door to the Jason Woods Industries grand entrance, was Tiffany's. Across the open space and below on the second level, was a designer linen shop whose windows displayed four-hundred-dollar pillow slips and three-thousand-dollar bedspreads.

Just above it, facing Tiffany's across the open space, was the Galleria Stockpile Video, the VK's big flagship store. Like all the others in the chain, its wide windows were decorated with cardboard cutouts of this summer's big movie stars, and bordered all the way around by TV screens playing tantalizing snatches of this week's big renters. In honor of the grand location, of course, these TV screens were the big-time thirty-two-inch models.

Above me was the ramp on which joggers belonging to the health club did their running, and above that were glass panes showing the clear blue summer sky.

I waited. While I did, to keep myself focused, I repeated such things as "Sixty thousand bucks a year," and "Payoffs," and less civilized things like "Shit!" and "Son-of-a-bitch!"

I was on about my eighteenth "Shit!" when, just like I'd seen him do on the TV news, Jason Woods rose grandly up the escalator to the Jason Woods Industries entrance level. Joe Bob and Shepherd tagged along, but not exactly. While Woods ascended, they took the stairway, timing their progress so as to achieve the third level about five steps behind the boss.

As Woods stepped off the escalator and paused for what I assumed was a long, proud look at the grand entrance to his empire, I waved at him.

After a beat to let me know that he wasn't used to such familiarity, but would put up with it just this once, he walked over to me.

Shepherd and Joe Bob hesitated, but Woods gave a quick nod toward the marble and brass entrance and they marched through it and out of sight. As he disappeared, Joe

Bob gave me a cute little wave of one of his gargantuan hands.

"Well, Tony," Woods said. "I expected to find you inside, ready to go to work."

Taking a deep breath, but trying not to let it show, I said, "I thought I'd wait for you out here, Mr. Woods."

He looked over my blazer and T-shirt and jeans. "Rather more casual than we're accustomed to."

I leaned against the railing and looked him over, too; it was my first chance to do so in anything like normal light. Thin lips. Gray, bottomless eyes. Expensive suit. An air of being completely in control of everything.

I said, "I hate to negotiate with a tie around my neck."

"Negotiate. I see." Without seeming at all perturbed, he moved a step or two and leaned against the railing, also. "I was under the impression that we had already reached our agreement."

"I thought it might be fun to talk it over again, in more or less neutral territory."

"In neutral territory. I see. Very well. In neutral territory, I'll state that you are a minor irritant, Tony. That's all. Aren't you afraid of overestimating your value as a minor irritant?"

"That all depends on what your top dollar is for minor irritants."

He chuckled dryly. "All right. Another ten thousand. Seventy thousand a year. Now, does that make you happy?"

"No."

He smiled. Very thinly and briefly. Then he said, "Seventy-five thousand. That's it. Take it, or leave it."

"For a man who's thinking of running for governor, you're being rather abrupt and dictatorial with me."

"A man who's *going to be governor* is able to discern those few people with whom he shouldn't be abrupt and dictatorial, and the vast multitude who don't count at all. You, my young friend, are very definitely not one of the former."

"I see."

He looked at his watch. "I'm quickly becoming bored."

"I wouldn't have you bored for anything," I said, and reached inside my jacket. Letting him see that it was only one of several, I pulled out one of Larry Milburn's antiqued drawings and handed it to him.

Deciding to humor me, he unfolded it, glanced at it, gave me a look of disdain. Glanced back. Stared at the paper and the drawing on it. Really stared.

I said, "Do you recognize it? It's one of George Hawk's original drawings of the lawnmower cutter-blade he invented that you later patented under your name as the GRASSBUSTER."

He crumpled it into a ball. "Don't be ridiculous. This is a joke."

"Is it? Look closer. In the margin, it says, 'George Hawk. Dr. Melvin Potter, Instructor, Engineering 203.' There are some of Potter's notes on it, too."

Woods unballed the drawing and smoothed it out enough to check. Then he said, "It's a fake. What kind of idiot do you take me for?"

"Not enough of an idiot to piss me off. If I were pissed-off, I might turn the drawings—I've got a whole stack of them—I just brought a small sample along—over to Maggie Hawk and drive her to a lawyer's office. All I'd get then would be my five hundred dollars a day, and she'd get all those bundles of money that you've cheated her out of. Plus plenty of punitive damages. She'd clean you out. It'd be Maggie Hawk walking in here to Jason Woods Industries when she felt like it, and calling the shots. Hell, it might well turn out that it'd be Maggie Hawk running for governor, too, after it came out what you've put her through. But assuming that you wouldn't be so stupid as to piss me off, I thought I'd give you a chance to make me an offer. A real offer. Not just peanuts."

Woods stared at me for a long moment. Then he said, "Take off that jacket."

I did, and he grabbed it out of my hands, felt of it, pulled the other two folded drawings out of the inside pocket, and felt of the jacket again before throwing it across the walkway where it fell crumpled under one of Tiffany's expensive windows.

"Lift your arms and turn around," he said.

I did, and let him look over my T-shirt and jeans, until I was facing him again. "No, I'm not wired."

He shook the drawings, wanting to rip them up, I think. His voice now was slow and calculating. "All right. Assuming these things are genuine, any of George's original cutter-blade drawings you happened to have in your possession would be worth a great deal to me. I'm not unreasonable. I buy materials and ideas. I buy the people who put them to work for me. What's your price?"

"You did kill George Hawk, didn't you?"

Woods grimaced and leaned more heavily against the railing and stared down at the children skating on the captive indoor ice. "George wouldn't be reasonable. His idea for a safe rotary lawnmower blade was stupendous. Simple, but absolutely stupendous. I offered to buy it from him, but he insisted on trying to have it all, himself." He snorted. "Imagine! That farm boy trying to control something as profitable as I knew that blade would be."

Raising his head, he looked at me with as much coldness as I had ever seen. "He was unreasonable. That should be an object lesson for you. I arranged for my friend, Clinton, to invite him to a meeting about his cutter-blade and, at the last minute, offered to ride along. I had George's gun that he kept hidden in the garage. And I had found some silly note he had written to his wife. It made a marvelous suicide note when I trimmed it just a bit."

After a pause for maximum drama, Woods said, with even more coldness, "Yes. I killed George Hawk." He raised his icy eyes to me and said, "That's the kind of thing that happens to unreasonable people. I think you should take warning from it. I'm trying my best to be reasonable with you. If you won't permit me to do so, you'll be dead, too. It's as simple as that."

The expression on his face was enough to send goose-flesh scraping over my back. I had a hard time keeping my voice solid and even. "Killing people's a problem though, isn't it? You prefer paying them off. Mrs. Guttman knew about George's invention, so you paid her off with a house in West University and a nice, cushy job running your executive dining room. You paid off Clinton McKenna by giving him stock and position. You paid off your buddy, John Scott—for whom George demonstrated that first cobbled-together blade of his—by making him a wheel in Jason Woods Industries. You and Vegas Joe Newhouse paid each other off: you got him out of a murder charge; he got himself in place to find George's body and so got to investigate his death; then you gave him the money he said he won in Las Vegas, and he became the barbecue king while you mowed the world's grass with George's invention.

"When you killed George, you thought you took all the drawings of his cutter-blade and the prototype he had made.

"It turned out, though, that Dr. Potter had George's assignment papers, some of which were the original drawings of the blade. After Potter saw the GRASSBUSTER come on the market, he knew exactly what had happened.

"Rather than turn those drawings over to Maggie, whom he hated because she had distracted his favorite student, Potter got in touch with you. His payoff for keeping quiet was buildings for the university he loved.

"You even tried to pay off Maggie just after you killed George, with a governess job that included lots of the travel that she dreamed of, but she wouldn't cooperate. She wasn't any trouble, though. Who listens to a suicide's wife? Particularly when she's poor.

"Eventually, though, she had some luck and then got me involved. I started shaking the trees a little, and you thought it was easier to offer me a job I couldn't refuse than to let me hassle you."

Breaking the coldness a little—only a little—with a glimmering of admiration, Woods said, "Yes. You have it figured out quite accurately. You're quite right about it all. That's something I learned early-on: it's easier and cheaper to buy people than to beat them—or kill them. Simple Profit-and-Loss. Do you have any idea of the cost of a competent trial attorney? I can buy any number of people for less than it would cost me for legal fees to get through just one messy trial. I end up with some very talented and extraordinarily loyal employees as a bonus.

"Now, Tony, tell me just how much it's going to cost me to buy you—assuming, of course, that these drawings you have are really the originals of George's cutter-blade drawings."

I stared at him for a few moments. Thinking rich. Thinking rich-like-Maggie. Even richer than that. It was all puffery, of course. The drawings were fake as hell, and Woods would soon find that out.

I said, "Not a dime. No deal. No chance of a deal. You know what, *Jason?* When you find that comet of yours, don't name it Comet Woods. Give it a true name. Call it Comet Scumbag."

He stared at me. Somewhere in his head he was making the cost-driven decision that, yeah, I was most definitely worth the price of a good trial lawyer.

"You are dead," he said, in a voice so knifelike that it made my belly hurt. "I gave you your chance to better yourself, but you turned it down. Now, you're as dead as George Hawk. I killed him quickly and easily. He never knew what was happening. He was brilliant, in his way, and deserved that. But you, I am going to kill slowly and with much pleasure."

"You don't sound so reasonable now."

"Start counting your heartbeats," Woods said. "Cherish each one you have left." He pushed away from the railing.

I said, "Hold on. You're forgetting something." I tossed him the keys to that shiny, brand-new, red convertible.

My quick motion startled him. But in reflex, he grabbed the keys out of the air and held them as if they were red hot.

I said, "And your check."

He snatched it out of my hand.

"By the way," I told him, "those drawings are phony as hell."

"Of course, they are. I destroyed all the originals years ago, after I copied George's design. Except for the ones that prissy little professor has hidden away. But I'm still going to kill you."

He started away, toward the entrance to Jason Woods Industries.

"Wait a minute," I said. "We're not quite through."

He whirled, came back, with his face looking like a bad-dream skull. "We're through. You're finished. I promise you that. You're dead."

I stared at him for a moment. Then I pulled out my handkerchief and wiped my face.

He liked that. Paying off people deprived him of the joy of watching them sweat. He was getting back some of that now.

I let him eat it up for a moment.

Then I stuffed the handkerchief back into my pocket and turned and motioned across the open space.

The television sets bordering the big plate glass windows of Stockpile Video were all showing nothing but jagged Rewind lines now.

Then the lines cleared.

Turned into pictures. Dozens of them. All alike.

Clear pictures in living color.

Of me standing at the railing, from a viewpoint that was right under Julia Roberts' fetching left armpit.

Coming onto all those television screens was Jason Woods.

The sound came up at just the right time. It was a tad tinny from this far away, but it was quite clear.

"Well, Tony," Jason Woods' multiple-multiple TV faces said to the Galleria. "I expected to find you inside, ready to go to work."

"I thought I'd wait for you out here," my TV faces said to his.

People were stopping in front of Stockpile Video to watch the TV sets. Some of them recognized the scenery and turned to look across the open space at Woods and me.

I felt like a regular movie star.

My old buddy, Art, moved out from behind the Julia Roberts cutout, brandishing his video camera and his

Sharper Image sound pickup, grinning as if he thought he'd just turned into Alfred Hitchcock.

I waved my handkerchief at him.

Woods was clutching the railing. His face was white.

"Oh," I said. "I almost forgot to tell you. It's show-time, you scumbag son-of-a-bitch."

THIRTY-FOUR

One Happy Ending

Good old Hizzie made it all the way out to Intercontinental Airport.

Maggie was waiting for boarding in Continental's VIP lounge, and she looked like twenty million dollars. I'd have had to pinch myself hard to make myself believe she used to sell beer for a living.

I handed her the roses I brought her and said, "You didn't think I was going to let you get away without a bon voyage, did you?"

"They're about to call my flight, Tony."

"I guess I made it just right. I hate long goodbyes."

She hugged me.

"Bon voyage," I said.

Then I reached into my pocket and pulled out an envelope and handed it to her.

"What's this?"

"A Federal Express receipt. On your way home, when you get to San Francisco and check into the St. Anthony, show 'em this. They'll have a package addressed to you, 'Hold for Arrival.' "

"What is it?"

"Don't ask. It's a surprise."

"What kind of surprise?"

"A Welcome Home surprise. Kind of an underground video, actually. About the search for Judge Crater and Bigfoot and Elvis Presley. Watch it. You'll love it."

She was totally bewildered. But she tucked the envelope into her purse.

I said, "There's something I've got to tell you."

She grinned. "I thought you hated long goodbyes."

My stomach was hurting too much for me to smile back. I said, "I'm a phony, Maggie. I didn't do all that detective work I used to blow off to you about in the bar. That was all my grandfather's stuff. Aapt Investigations is nothing. It never was, really. Because Grandpa was such a lousy businessman. And . . ."

She cut me off by waving the roses in my face. "Oh, hush."

I stared at her.

"I know all that."

I stared at her some more.

"Somebody called me the day before yesterday. He told me all about you. About the way your grandfather did business. Told me you were a phony, and I was wasting my money on you."

My stomach was hurting even more.

She said, "I told him to go to hell." Suddenly, she hugged me again. "I like you. We'll laugh about it when I get back. I told him to take his snotty attitude and his lisp and go to hell."

She took a couple of steps away and daubed at her eyes. Then she came back. "You reminded me so much of Larry when you came in the bar and talked to me that I couldn't stand it. You still do. Just get out of here now, and let me get on my plane. I told you we'll worry about things when I get back."

A passenger service agent who looked a whole lot less like Brooke Shields than she thought she did started trying to get Maggie moving.

I said, "Get moving, Maggie," and I hugged her.

She was crying.

"I hate goodbyes," I said. "Bon voyage. Remember. Check out that videotape when you get back to San Francisco. After London and Paris and the Alps and Sydney and Hong Kong and all those places."

"London!" she said. "Paris! Oh, my God! Am I really finally going?" And she ran off to get on her plane.

THIRTY-FIVE

The Other Happy Ending

Hizzie made it all the way back into town.

I was going to miss her. Retiring her in favor of some kind of semi-vanilla car suitable for Stockpile Video's new heavily contract-protected Corporate Security Consultant was going to be kind of sad.

Larry Milburn was back in front of his TV, watching the Cubs play glorious old-time afternoon losing baseball at Wrigley Field. He was drinking beer and eating chocolate chip cookies. He looked like a big, live, shopworn cauliflower.

"You backslid," I said. "How come you're not drawing?"

He said, "Why the hell can't the goddamned Cubs ever get any pitching?" Then he said, "What's in the sack?"

I set it down on that nice bedouin chest. "Yogurt. Celery. Broccoli. Tofu. And other assorted diet food." I went over and turned off the television set. Then I picked up the chocolate chip cookie bag and closed it up.

"What'd you do that for?"

"Get your butt out of that chair. We're going to start out by walking."

"Walking?"

"Hell yes. Walking's damned good exercise, I hear. We'll start out with that."

"In this goddamned heat?"

"It's a hell of a lot hotter than this in the Middle East these days, I hear. At least, walking around here, you probably won't get your ass shot off. Although that might help."

I checked my watch. Just about now, in Los Angeles, I figured, somebody would be telling Polly's agent to rip those jeans off her, and run her off the set. Probably, she'd be back on TV here in Houston selling waterbeds before long.

About now, somebody would be calling Sarah to tell her, sorry, but the Millercom job offer was a big mistake. She'd raise hell. But in a couple of days, I'd drop it on her that there was an advertising and P.R. spot—newly downsized from Vice President to Manager—open at Stockpile Video, just waiting for somebody who'd promise to stop giving spot character lectures to the new Corporate Security Consultant. She'd hate that, but she'd adjust to the bucks.

Maggie, though, was going to have a great trip; confirmed travel tickets and already-cashed cashier's checks are much harder to cancel than jobs.

An unbelieving look on his face, Larry tipped the grocery bag toward himself, and said, "Damn. You weren't kidding. Broccoli. Yogurt. Shit!" He reached into the bag. "What the hell is this?" He peered at it. "A catnip koala bear?"

"Oh, forgot that was in there," I said. "It's for another buddy of mine. Come on. Let's go."

"Walking?" Larry said. "You're crazy, aren't you?"

"I'm not crazy. I'm a romantic. Let's go. You've got until the eighth of November."

"Until the eighth of November, for what?"

"I'll tell you on the seventh." I rummaged deep in the grocery bag and pulled out a videocassette and went over and set it on top of the VCR.

"What's that?" Larry asked.

"You can look at it after your walk. Then you can see it again on the Six O'clock News."

"Doesn't seem like much of a payoff," he said. But he heaved himself up out of his chair.

"Don't talk payoffs to me," I said. "Let's go."

About the Author

Rex Anderson grew up on a farm near Ponca City, Oklahoma, and graduated from Oklahoma University. His other mystery novels are *Cover Her with Roses*, *Night Calls* and *My Dead Brother*. Since 1976, he has lived in Houston, which he finds to be a perfect setting for mysteries.